DOG RUN MOON

DOG RUN MOON

STORIES

CALLAN WINK

THE DIAL PRESS
NEW YORK

Published in the United States by The Dial Press, an imprint of Random House, a division of Penguin Random House LLC, New York.

THE DIAL PRESS and the HOUSE colophon are registered trademarks of Penguin Random House LLC.

The following stories have been previously published: "Off the Track" in *Ecotone;* "One More Last Stand" and "Exotics" in *Granta;* "Crow Country Moses" in *The Montana Quarterly;* "Dog Run Moon" and "Breatharians" in *The New Yorker;* "In Hindsight" on newyorker.com.

LIBRARY OF CONGRESS CATALOGING-IN-PUBLICATION DATA
Wink, Callan.
[Short stories. Selections]
Dog run moon: stories / Callan Wink.
pages cm
ISBN 978-0-8129-9377-6
ebook ISBN 978-0-8129-9378-3
I. Title.
PS3623.I6626A6 2016
813'.6—dc23
2015025025

Printed in the United States of America on acid-free paper

randomhousebooks.com

2 4 6 8 9 7 5 3 1

FIRST EDITION

Book design by Elizabeth A. D. Eno

FOR JIM WINK

CONTENTS

DOG RUN MOON   3

RUNOFF   21

ONE MORE LAST STAND   47

BREATHARIANS   69

EXOTICS   93

SUN DANCE   120

OFF THE TRACK   145

CROW COUNTRY MOSES   173

IN HINDSIGHT   186

DOG RUN MOON

DOG RUN MOON

Sid was a nude sleeper. Had been ever since he was a little kid. To him, wearing clothes to bed seemed strangely redundant, like wearing underwear inside your underwear or something. Sid had slept in the nude every night of his adult life and that was why, now, he was running barefoot and bare-assed across the sharp sandstone rimrock far above the lights of town. It was after two in the morning, a clear, cool, early June night with the wobbly gibbous moon up high and bright so he could see the train yard below—the crisscrossing rails, a huge haphazard pile of old ties, the incinerator stack. He was sweating but he knew once he could run no more the cold would start to find its way in. After that he didn't know what would happen.

The dog was padding along tirelessly, sometimes at Sid's side, sometimes ranging out and quartering back sharply, his nose up to the wind trying to cut bird scent. Not for the first time in his life Sid found himself envying a dog. Its fur. Its thick foot pads. A simple untroubled existence of sleeping, eating, running, fucking occasionally if you still had the parts, not worrying about it if you didn't. Even in his current predicament Sid couldn't help but admire the dog. A magnificent bird dog for broken country such as this, no two ways about it. Sid kept going, hobbling, feeling the sharp rimrock make raw hamburger out of the soles of his feet. When he turned he could see smears of his blood on the flat rock shining black under the moon. And then, the shafts of headlights stabbing the jutting sandstone outcroppings. He could hear the shouts of Montana Bob and Charlie Chaplin as they piloted their ATV over the rough ground.

Sid hadn't stolen the dog. He'd liberated the dog. He firmly believed this and this belief was the fundamental basis for the disagreement between himself and Montana Bob. Montana Bob thought ownership meant simple possession. Sid thought otherwise. He'd been in town for two months and his path to and from work took him twice daily through the alley. The dog would follow his passing through the chain-link and Sid would whistle and the dog would raise its ears without getting up.

Sid worked at a sawmill that processed logs brought down from the mountains. The logs came in massive and rough, smelling like moss and the dark places where snow lingers into July. They entered one end of a screeching hot pole building, met the saw, and came out the other side, flat and white and bleeding pitch into the red-dirt lumberyard. The men that worked the logs and the saw were Mexicans mostly, wide, sweating men who worked in dirty white tank tops, their inner arms scabbed and raw from wrestling rough-barked logs. They spoke their language to each other and Sid did not know them. He kept to himself and did his work. He was a scrap man. All day he took cast-off pieces of aspen and pine, and cut and stapled them into pallets that were eventually piled with boards to be shipped out. All day he measured and sawed and stapled. His hands were pitch-stained and splintered. All day his mind ran laps, and after work he walked back through the alley, whistled at the dog on his way by, and drank three glasses of water in quick succession, standing at the kitchen sink in the empty trailer he rented by the month and hadn't bothered to furnish. Even with the windows open the trailer smelled like a hot closet full of unwashed clothing, and Sid couldn't stand being there unless he was asleep.

In the evenings he drove. Sometimes over to the next town, sometimes for hours until he ended up in the river valley at the base of the mountains where it was always ten degrees cooler. She lived there now and he knew her house but he never drove by. He couldn't bear the thought of her looking out from her kitchen window to see his truck moving slowly down the street. He could imagine how his face would look to her. Sun-dark. Gaunt. Too sharp down the middle like it was creased. Sometimes he got a milkshake at the diner and nursed it for the drive. No matter where he drove, he took the same way back, the route that took him around front of the house with the dog. The house where the east-facing windows were covered with tinfoil and Sid had never seen anyone outside.

At the mill one afternoon a full pallet of eight-inch-by-twelve-foot boards broke free of the loader and crushed the legs of one of the Mexicans who had been standing by the truck, waiting to tighten the straps. Sid, eating his lunch, saw the whole thing, heard the man's hoarse screams over the shriek of the saw until the saw was silenced, and then it was just the man, pinned to the ground and writhing, his eyes bulging, with sawdust coating the sweat on his bare arms.

That evening, Sid drove straight to her house, still in his work clothes. When he got there her car was in the driveway and there was a pickup truck parked behind it. Sid pulled in sharply and got out, not bothering to shut his door behind him. He was striding fast, halfway up to her porch, before he noticed the dried smears of blood on his pant legs and boots. At the mill, he and everyone else had rushed to the man, frantically teaming up to move the heavy boards from his legs. There had been blood everywhere, making the sawdust dark, making the boards slick and red and hard to hold. Now, standing in her front lawn, he looked down at his hands. He tried to clean out the rust-colored crescents under his fingernails, tried to rub the pine pitch mixed with dried blood from the creases in his palms. He was rubbing his hands frantically on his stained jeans, when he saw movement in the curtains over the kitchen window. And then he ran, sliding into the open door of his truck, spinning gravel up onto vehicles in front of him as he backed out at full speed.

Sid's route home took him past the house with the dog, and, as usual, there was no sign of life outside. The truck that was often parked in front of the house was gone. Sid passed slowly and then turned around. He thought about it for a minute and then pulled over and let his truck idle. He went around back where the dog was lying on a pile of dirty straw, chained to a sagging picnic table. The dog didn't bark, didn't even get up, just watched Sid with its muzzle resting on its front paws. Sid unhooked the chain from the dog's collar, and when he turned to leave, the dog followed him to his truck, jumped in, and sat on the bench seat, leaning forward with his nose smudging the windshield. Sid drove up to the flat, windswept bench above town and let the dog run. In the hour before it got dark they put up three coveys of Huns and two sharp-tails, the dog moving through clumps of sagebrush and cheatgrass, working against the wind like some beautifully engineered piece of machinery performing perfectly the one, the only, task to which it was suited.

Sid was afraid of Montana Bob. As he ran he could feel the fear lodged somewhere up under his sternum, a sharp little stab of something like pain with each inhaled breath. It was a healthy thing, his fear of Montana Bob. You should be afraid, Sid, he thought. You should be afraid of Montana Bob like you should be afraid of a grizzly bear, a loose dog foaming at the mouth, anything nearsighted and sick and unpredictable. Sid stopped behind the wind-twisted limbs of a piñon pine and listened. He could hear the low growl of the ATV coming behind him and then the different, softer sound of the engine idling, stopped, no doubt, so that Montana Bob and Charlie Chaplin could branch out on foot to look for his sign. Sid was above them and he could see the shapes of their shadows, tall and angular, moving across the headlights, cloaked in swirling motes of red dust.

"I know who you are, Sid. I know it's you out there. We're still out here, too."

Montana Bob's voice came up to him, reverberating off the rock.

"You got the dog and I think that is a damn stupid reason to go through all this trouble. I got Charlie Chaplin here with me. He too thinks this is a lot of stupidness just for a damn dog. Also, he has a big goddamn pistol. I bet your feet hurt something fierce. You're bleeding like a stuck hog all over this lizard rock and me an' Charlie Chaplin are going to drive right up on you before long. We will. Also, you were a big damn fool to run out the back door like that. Charlie saw your naked ass. We were just

coming for the dog. You can't argue my right to it. You have that
what belongs to me. You catch up that dog and bring it down to
me. Also, hell. You know what? We'll even give you a ride back
down into town. We will."

Sid started out again, moving up and away from the voices
and lights. He found a long piece of slickrock that stretched out
farther than he could see into the darkness and he ran. He could
hear the rough whisper of the dog's pads on the rock, the click of
its nails. The dog's coat shone in the moonlight; what was black
in sunlight became purple-blue, what was normally white now
glowed like mother-of-pearl.

Would Montana Bob do as he said? Let Sid go if he came
down with the dog? Sid was unsure but he thought not. The small
oblong little organ of fear under Sid's sternum pulsed each time
his feet slapped the rock. He kept going. The moon overhead was
a lopsided and misshapen orb that at any moment might lose its
tenuous position and break upon the rocks. That might be a good
thing. A landscape of blackness into which he could melt.

The dog had been his for a week when Montana Bob found him
out. Sid was in the Mint having a happy-hour beer before heading home, and he'd left the dog in the truck. He had his back to
the door and as soon as the two men came in he had a bad feeling. The bar was pretty much empty but they sat right next to
him, one on each side. Plenty of stools all up and down the bar
but they came and crowded in on him. The big one wore a sweat-
stained summer Stetson with a ragged rooster pheasant tail
feather sticking out of the hatband. His hair was shaggy and
flared out from the hat brim. He wore a leather vest with nothing
underneath it save a mangy pelt of thick blue-black hair. His

companion was considerably smaller and extremely fair skinned, nearly bald except for a few blond strands grown long on one side and then combed over. He wore a button-up Oxford shirt and corduroy pants. Sperry Top-Siders. On his belt he had a large knife in a sheath, its handle made of a pale-yellow plastic that was supposed to look like bone. They ordered beers, and when the beers arrived the big man in the hat drank deeply, and then leaned toward Sid, a pale scum of suds covering his upper lip.

"I don't believe in beating the bush."

Sid picked at a loose corner on the label of his bottle of beer. He thought about bolting, just getting up like he was going to make his way to the bathroom and then sliding right out the back.

"I don't beat the bush so I'm going to get right down to the tacks. I believe I recognize a familiar dog in that blue Chevy out front and also since you're about the only one in here I figure that's your vehicle so I figure that I'll need to ask you where you happened to come across that dog."

The man pushed his hat back on his head and swiveled on his stool to face Sid. He smiled.

"Also, I'm Montana Bob." He extended his hand—which Sid shook, not knowing what else to do—and nodded toward his companion seated on Sid's other side.

"And that's Charlie Chaplin. Shake his hand."

Sid turned and shook Charlie Chaplin's pale proffered hand.

"I'm a local businessman and Charlie Chaplin is my accountant. Also, he provides counsel to me in matters of legal concern."

Sid considered Charlie Chaplin and when their eyes met he felt something skittering and cold move down his spine. Montana Bob was the bigger man, menacing even, with large bare arms and small pieces of pointed silver at the tips of his boots, but it was this one, small and waxen and pale, who made Sid shift uncomfortably.

Sid found himself speaking, too quickly, his voice high.

"I picked up that dog at the shelter. Bought and paid for. Got him his shots, rabies, distemper, all that. I got the paperwork in the truck. They said at the shelter that he was a canine of misfortunate past. Meaning his old owner used to stomp him. Kind of a mutt but he seems loyal. Likes to fetch the tennis ball. My kids are crazy about him."

Montana Bob nodded as Sid spoke. Charlie Chaplin nodded too. Montana Bob motioned the bartender down to them and ordered another beer for himself and Charlie Chaplin.

"Two more. Also, a large pitcher of ice water. No ice."

The bartender went away and Montana Bob spoke to Sid's reflection in the mirrored bar back.

"Likes to fetch the tennis ball does he? Well, I'll be. Did you know that that dog was given to me by a Frenchman? The dog is a French Brittany spaniel and he comes from France. Born in France of royal French Brittany stock. Also, that dog was a gift from a French count. Guy St. Vrain made me a present of that dog when it was just a pup in payment for services rendered by yours truly. You don't know Guy St. Vrain but that doesn't matter. That's how he likes it. He's in the movie business. Also, he's in the dog business."

The bartender came with the pitcher of water, and Montana Bob took off his hat and set it on the bar top. He poured half the pitcher into the hat and then replaced it on his head, the water streaming down his face and neck, matting the thick shiny hair on his chest.

"You stole my fucking dog." He was still looking at Sid

through his reflection in the bar mirror. "Also, I had a hot and dusty day out on the trail and I come here for a drink only to find my possession in someone else's egg basket."

In the mirror Sid saw his hands go up, saw his shoulders shrug.

"The shelter. I don't know anything about any of this."

He slid from the stool and caught the bartender's eye.

"I'll take one more. Be right back. Gotta take a leak."

In the bathroom he ran the water and splashed some on his face. He had his keys in his hand when he hit the door and then he was out in the last evening rays of sun, firing the truck, the dog standing anxiously with its front paws on the dash. Sid drove without looking back. He drove all the way down the river road and let the dog out. He walked a path through the thickets of tamarisk and Russian olive and when he stopped, the dog perched delicately at the water's edge, standing on a rock, lapping up the muddy red water. Before Sid had burst through the bar doors to start his truck he'd glimpsed the bar room—Montana Bob sitting astride his stool like a swayback steed. Charlie Chaplin up standing in front of the jukebox. He was flipping the discs as if looking for a particular track, a song whose name he couldn't remember or one whose tune existed solely in his head.

Sid had no clear idea where he was heading. It was a strange mode of navigation, more like divination, taking the smoothest path through a shattered nightscape of jumbled rock—watching for the wicked gleam of prickly pear and jagged cones from the piñon pines. If he turned he could still see the shafts of light from his pursuer's ATV, and he thought about circling around back toward town. The problem was the dog. Sid would have to cut a wide path around to keep the dog from straying close to the lights and if the dog was captured then what was the point? Another thought, might the dog return to its former owner willingly? Sid was unsure. He kept running. The dog spooked a small herd of mule deer out of a dry creek bed and they bounded past him, covering great lengths of ground in each leap, their forms backlit against the sky now lightening in the east. Sid had never seen the desert deer move this close before. At the apex of each jump they seemed to hang, suspended, vaguely avian, a group of prehistoric nearbirds not quite suited to life on land, not quite comfortable with their wings' ability to keep them aloft. Just then he had the thought that if he could keep going until the sun came up he might be okay.

After the encounter at the Mint, Sid had broken down and called her. She hadn't answered and he'd left a message in which he hated the sound of his voice. Tinny with the fear he'd wanted her to feel. *I'm not calling to try and get you to come back and be mine again I'm just calling to tell you that if no one ever sees me around anymore it's because I ran afoul of some bad people in a matter concerning a dog. And I never meant for you to grow against me like you did. That's it.* Sid hung up in self-loathing. He folded an old blanket on the floor at the end of his bed for the dog and when the knock on the door came—at two in the morning, three days after Montana Bob had called him out in the Mint—Sid couldn't say exactly that he hadn't been expecting it. He felt briefly the relief of the fugitive who finally feels the handcuffs encircle his wrists.

Montana Bob spoke to him on the other side of the door, his words just barely whiskey-softened around the edges.

"You, sir, are in possession of my royal French canine. Charlie Chaplin and myself come to you as missionaries. Also, as pilgrims and crusaders."

When Montana Bob kicked in the flimsy trailer door Sid had already slammed out the back, catching Charlie Chaplin off guard. The accountant was standing on the trailer's rickety back porch and the door handle hit him in the midsection, doubling him over. Sid ran down the sloping trailer court drive and across his neighbors' weed-choked lawns, down the alley across the dead main street and through the train yard, his bare toes curling around the cold iron track as he gathered himself to hurdle over the crushed-granite railbed. It wasn't until he reached the barren lots at the base of the rimrock's upslope that he realized the dog was running beside him, occasionally stopping to lift his leg on a rock or clump of sagebrush. Back toward the road Sid could see the lights of an ATV coming fast. He waited until he could see the shape of Montana Bob's hat and the pale, bare arms of Charlie Chaplin wrapped around his midsection—and then he started scrabbling his way up the slope, the dog flowing effortlessly through the rock above him.

She was a small woman, pale, so much so that the desert hurt her in ways that Sid would never fully understand. Like Sid, she was a nude sleeper. When he found this out it became one of those happy little intersections of shared personality, the slow accumulation of which is love. With her it was years of nights spent bare back to bare chest. Sometimes, when it was hot, they woke up and had to peel themselves apart, their tangled limbs stuck together like the fleshy segments of some strange misshapen fruit.

They were alike in other ways as well, and at one time these things had seemed natural and unaffected, important even. They both liked the river. Sid got inner tubes from the tire store and when the heat got unbearable they would float, keeping their beer cool in a mesh bag trailing in the river behind them. And, if she never fully came to love the desert, Sid was pretty sure she came to understand why he did. Once, Sid took her up to see the hoodoos in Goblin Valley. It was midnight on a full moon and they were half-drunk and a little high. They played tag and hide-and-seek around the hulking sandstone formations, laughing, hooting and shrieking, the sounds careening, giving voice to the rocks themselves. For a while after this if one of them initiated an impromptu game of tag, the other would have to follow suit, no matter the location—the grocery store, the front lawn, the movie theater, at a neighborhood barbecue with half the town watching, everyone laughing and shaking their heads. Things were good this way for a long time and then one night he woke to the sound of her crying in the bathroom. And the next night she came to bed in one of his T-shirts and boxer shorts. And the next night Sid slept alone.

As he ran Sid could clearly see her, laid out on their bed, a night-blooming moonflower, her white limbs like petals unfolding finally in the absence of light. He remembered the first house they'd ever lived in, the way the door latch was broken and how the wind would blow the door open if they didn't remember to throw the bolt. They'd be sitting in that little dining room, eating dinner, a table full of mismatched cups and plates and silverware, and all of a sudden the door would swing open like someone pushed it in. She'd always flinch like someone was breaking in on them, uninvited. Sid used to tease her about it but now he found himself wondering who exactly it was she thought was coming unannounced into their home. Who was the man with his hand on the doorknob ready to push his way into their kitchen like the wind?

Sid ran and the rocks cut him; the piñon pines clutched and tore at him. Dried sweat crusted his bare torso and thighs and any moment of rest brought cramps, the muscles of his legs twitching and popping of their own accord. He found himself moving his cracked lips, making strange utterances with each painful footfall, the desert a silent observer, an expressionless juror to whom he tried to make his plea. *I ran afoul of some bad people in a matter concerning a dog. Irana foul. Iranafoul. I ran, a foul?*

It sounded melodramatic and desperate, a wild call for attention. Best to leave the dog out of it. Get right to the point.

Since we dissolved I've been a specter running blind and naked in the desert. Is that melodramatic? Well, that's what is happening to me now.

He imagined driving to their old house and stepping up onto the porch. She'd be alone and come out to meet him in one of the sundresses she always wore in the hot months, the fabric like gauze, like a soft bandage laid over healing flesh. She'd offer him a cool drink and they'd sit in the shade and the words, all the right ones, would flow from him, an upwelling, an eruption of cleansing language.

Remember when we went way up north that winter and rented the cabin and there was a hot spring not too far away? We'd go out at night and shiver down the path to the water and slip in the warmth like pulling a hot sheet around us. My feet in the sulfur-smelling mud of the pool, your legs twined around mine like white, earth-seeking roots. Remember that? The way the deer would come down when it got really cold just to stand in the steam rising up from the water? And then, the day we left for home? How cold it was? We went outside and our eyes started to freeze up at the corners and you, southern girl, had never seen anything like it and took a picture of me standing next to a thermometer that was bottomed out at forty below. In that picture I'm standing on the cabin porch and behind me there's the river frozen solid, or so it seemed.

Here Sid imagined moving in a little closer, putting his work-rough hand on her smooth one.

I've been thinking about that picture and that river on the coldest day of the year. Underneath that ice, the river was still moving. Forty below, but even then the water closest to the riverbed will be moving, cold but unfrozen. It's like a river exists in defiance, or has a secret life. Everything above is frozen and stiff but down below it moves along, liquid over the rocks, like nothing happening on the surface matters. On a day like this you could walk across the river like crossing the street. But you can't forget that just below that shell there is current. That is my love for you.

And that would be it. She'd come with him, push up next to him on the bench seat of his pickup, and he'd drive with the windows down, her hair tossing into his face and mouth and eyes. Dust and the scent of her shampoo in his nose. They'd pick up right where they'd left off.

He was moving up a dry creek bed, shuffling through the soft red sand deposited by spring floods in years past, when he had had the feeling that the creek wasn't dry after all, that he was splashing through the ankle-deep current of muddy red water. He was thirsty. Christ was he thirsty, but when he scooped a great double handful of water up to his cracked lips it turned back to sand and flowed through his fingers. This seemed like a particularly cruel joke and he had thoughts of finding a dark place to curl up inside, a rock for a pillow and a soft blanket of sand. But there was the matter of the dog, the matter of Charlie Chaplin's vacuous eyes

and pistol, which in Sid's mind, had achieved magnificent pro-
portions. Charlie Chaplin rode it like an evil old mare with
cracked hoofs and faded brand. It was the gun itself in pursuit,
half horse, half instrument of percussion and death. A spavined
nag whose blued flanks were singed and smoking.

At first, running on the sand was deliriously comfortable,
the soft ground like an answered prayer for the raw soles of Sid's
feet. But then, the farther he went the harder it became, the sand
shifting and giving way under his feet so that each stride required
more effort from his already screaming calves.

When the twisting and turning of the creek bed became
unbearable Sid clambered out onto the exposed rock. From this
vantage point he watched the now greatly diminished moon drift
down toward the far black horizon like a pale phosphorus match
head broken off in the striking. If Montana Bob and Charlie
Chaplin were still in pursuit he had no evidence. In fact, some
small, dislodged part of him was unsure that they had ever existed. Sid couldn't see the dog most of the time. Sometimes he
forgot about it all together. It ran ahead silent and unperturbed
as the earth itself.

It was a loud dawn. Sid had never seen or heard anything quite
like it, the sun breaking the horizon line with a sound like a dull
knife ripping a sheet. He was walking stiffly now, moving his arms
in great circles, slapping his thighs and torso to fend off the cold.
He looked down and for the first time could see himself clearly,
the angry red whip welts on his calves from branches, the purple
cracked toenails and raised blue lines of engorged veins and capil-
laries, over everything a grimy patina of sweat crust and desert
dust and leaking blood.

He crested a small hill where, on the backside of the slope, there was a rusted stock tank fed by a leaning windmill that rose out of a clump of acacia. He didn't believe in the stock tank. It was like a river of muddy water, a thing that would dry up and slip through his fingers. He sat on a flat rock and looked. The windmill was missing some slats and he knew there was no water in the tank. This was a definite truth and Sid felt it like gravity. After a while the dog emerged from a tangle of sagebrush and with no fanfare proceeded to lap from the tank, its tail fanning slightly in a breeze that did not reach Sid.

Down the slope in jerks, his muscles and ligaments tightened like catgut tennis racket cord. Sid submerged his entire head, eyes wide open, into the water, metallic-tasting, gelid with the flavor of the past night. The bottom of the tank was lined with a slick layer of electric green algae over which a single orange carp hovered blimplike. Sid wanted to get in, to live with this carp alone in this desert within a desert. But the water was cold and he knew the carp did not want him. He drank for so long that points of black began to form at the edges of his vision, small, black-legged forms like water striders skating the clear pool of his periphery. He broke for air and collapsed with his back against the tank, the rivets pressing his flesh. From this position he could see into the twisted inner workings of the windmill, the busted-sprung parts, the pieces held together by coils of baling wire. The dog was moving around the base of the acacia trees, its snout plowing last year's dead grass, the fur ends around its paws just slightly reddened by the touch of the desert rock. Above the dog, in the twisting acacia branches, Sid could make out two sparrows, dead and skewered on thorns.

When Sid woke he found Charlie Chaplin squatting next to him, his Oxford shirt stained desert red, his corduroys dusty. His pale cheeks were streaked with twin rivulets of what looked like tears and his eyes were leaking and red. He had his knife out and was poking Sid's bare thigh, raising bright little beads of blood, a ragged collection of blood drops like pissants gathering on his skin. From the number of them it looked like he'd been at it awhile. Seeing that Sid was awake, Charlie Chaplin swiped at his cheeks with his sleeve. He gave Sid one more poke and then sheathed his knife and went to stand beside Montana Bob, who held a length of chain he'd hooked to the dog's collar. The dog lay at Montana Bob's boots with its muzzle resting on its paws.

"What the hell. Why?" Montana Bob tilted his hat brim down against the sun.

Sid considered this for a moment and then put up his hands and shrugged his shoulders.

"I've always liked running." Realizing as he said it that it was true.

"You look like something from another planet. More dead than alive. Also, Charlie Chaplin isn't happy with you. He wears contact lenses and, seeing how you kept us out here all night in the dust, his eyes are in poor shape. He wants you to know that that's why he's tearing up. He's not actually crying. He suffers from the dust. Also, he lost his pistol. Fell out of his waistband on the ride. I know he feels badly about that."

Sid found himself nodding in agreement with Montana Bob. It was a nearly involuntary movement and he had to force himself to stop.

"You dumb bastard. I don't even know what to do to you. But, also, I guess you done it plenty to yourself. What do you think, Charlie Chaplin?"

Sid looked up into the pale, dirt-and-tear-streaked face of the accountant. He tried to read what was there but came up blank. Charlie Chaplin knelt creakily and untied his Top-Siders.

He kicked them off his feet toward Sid and then turned to climb on the ATV, his socks startlingly white from the ankle down. Silently, Montana Bob took his seat in front of Charlie Chaplin and drove away, his accountant clinging to his waist from behind, his dog padding along at the end of the chain.

It was a long time before Sid could get to his feet and walk, slowly retracing his bloody tracks. It was even longer before the pain made him slip the Top-Siders over his ruined soles, feeling when he did, at once something like balm and betrayal. With the shoes he was somehow more naked than before, and he faced the reality of shuffling back to town, no longer unfettered, just exposed. He thought then about going for it, turning east and just continuing on till he either evaporated or made it, collapsing in a heap on her porch. Begging her to wash his feet.

RUNOFF

It was June 21, the longest day of the year, and the snow on Beartooth pass was still eight feet high on either side of the road. Dale drove Jeannette and her two boys up there. It was seventy degrees when they left town, at least twenty degrees cooler when they got to the top. They glissaded down the soft edges of the glacier and had a snowball fight. The sun at that altitude was close and they all got a little burned. Later that evening, back at her house, Dale grilled hamburgers, and they ate on the porch. The creek that normally trickled through her backyard was on the rise, noisy, the color of watery chocolate milk.

After dinner Jeannette rubbed aloe on the boys' red cheeks and put them, complaining, to bed. "Its not even dark yet," he heard the oldest one say. "I can't go to sleep when it's light."

"You've had a big day," Jeannette said. "You just don't know you're tired yet."

She came back out on the porch with a beer for him and a glass of wine for herself. She had the bottle of aloe too and she sat on his lap. She rubbed in the lotion, working it into the skin on his neck, his ear lobes, his cheekbones. Jeannette had small hands, strong fingers, blunt nails. Before she'd met her husband she'd been a massage therapist. She told Dale that when they got married her husband hadn't *quite* demanded that she stop working. "He was always good at that, making demands seem like something less. I was a good massage therapist. And I enjoyed it. He said it was too sensual. He didn't like me doing that with other men."

"Too sensual?" Dale said.

"It wasn't like I was giving happy endings. I'm thinking about getting back into it. It's been ten years but I've still got my table and everything. I could use the money."

"I volunteer to be your practice dummy. Maybe you could reconsider that happy ending policy."

She laughed and swatted at him.

The aloe was tingling on his cheeks. Jeannette had her head back on his shoulder. He could feel her heat through the thin material of her sundress. She was a small woman. Small breasts, small waist, delicate feet, good thick heavy dark hair. She had an aversion to undergarments that he found attractive. This year she'd lost her father to cancer, turned forty-three, and watched as her husband was led away in handcuffs.

She sat on Dale's lap, wriggling a little, as if she was just trying to get comfortable. She sighed. "What a great day," she said. "That was the best day I can remember having in quite some time. The boys had fun. They really like you. They tell me that, I'm not just assuming."

"I always kind of wished I had younger brothers," Dale said, realizing immediately that it was probably not the right thing. Jeannette gave a soft laugh and sipped her wine. "How old would your mother have been?" she said.

"Much older than you."

"How much?"

"It doesn't matter. You're beautiful."

"I guess I'm not quite a hag yet."

Dale had recently turned twenty-five. He hadn't managed to finish college. He was almost done with his EMT certification but for the past few months he'd been living in his father's basement. He considered meeting Jeannette to be the single best stroke of luck that had ever befallen him. Before Jeannette, he'd been dating a girl for almost a year. A bank teller. She called him every day for a week before she gave up.

Occasionally, he thought about Jeannette's husband, but only occasionally. The last thing she had told Dale about him was that he was in a halfway house in Billings. The boys wanted to see him but she hadn't decided yet. She thought maybe it was too soon. For the most part she didn't talk about him, and Dale didn't ask.

They sat on the porch in the slow solstice twilight. The lilacs had opened and the air was musky with them. Dale was rubbing the back of her neck with his thumb, listening to the sound of the creek, hearing in its dull murmur something like a gathering crowd, just beginning to voice its displeasure.

Dale ran in the mornings. It was a habit he'd picked up recently, part of some more general desire to straighten himself out. He'd tried meditating. That had never really worked. Running, though, was good. He laced up his shoes in the dark of his childhood bedroom, took the stairs two at a time, and did a five-mile loop. Across the tracks that bisected town, the gravel of the railway crunching under his shoes, down the hill to the river.

His dad would have considered all of it—meditation,

breathing exercises, even running—nothing but hippie bullshit. Dale would have agreed, not too long ago. But then he went on his first ride-along with the Park County EMT crew and he'd seen a girl, a few years younger than himself, bleed out on the side of the highway while her drunk boyfriend got handcuffed and pushed into the police car. The boyfriend's pickup was upside down in the barrow pit, the headlights still on, shooting off into the trees at a crazy angle. The girl was coughing, blood coming up. She'd been thrown from the truck and impaled on a jagged limb of a fallen pine tree.

He asked the other EMTs how they did it, coped with the constant trauma. Margie suggested meditating. That hadn't worked. Tim said that he ran every day, no matter what. Dale tried this, and was surprised that it seemed to settle him in some way. Everyone said you became numb to it, or if not numb then just more able to break it down into a series of responses you needed to make to perform your job. Every situation, no matter how horrific, had a starting point, a place you could insert yourself to go to work.

He had to do something. He knew that. He'd floundered for three years at the university in Missoula, changed majors four times, finally just decided to not return for what should have been his senior year.

He'd been in the bar, drinking with some friends, half-watching a football game, when an old guy a few stools down keeled over and hit the floor, his back in a reverse arc, the cords of his neck straining, lips going blue. Dale stood up, looking around. Someone had his phone out, making the call. A guy that had been sitting at a table with a woman—maybe they were on a date, they were both kind of dressed up—came hustling over. He got down next to the old man, turned him on his side. He'd taken his jacket off and rolled it up under the old man's head. He was holding his arm, saying things to him that Dale couldn't hear. Aaron Edgerly, one of Dale's friends, walked over, started saying something about jamming his wallet in the old guy's mouth so he wouldn't choke on his tongue, but the man waved him off.

"Just stand back," he said. "If you want to do something, clear these barstools away. They're going to need to get in here with a stretcher."

Aaron grumbled a little. But he put his wallet away, started moving stools. There was something in the man's voice, ex-military probably. He was calm when everyone else was freaked out. Eventually the ambulance showed up. The paramedics carted the old guy off and the man went back to his date and Dale had spent the whole night thinking about how it would feel to be the guy who knew what to do in a situation like that, the one who people listened to when things got heavy.

Dale signed up for the EMT course the next day. He hadn't told his dad. He wanted to wait until he had something, a certificate or diploma or whatever you got when you passed the exam.

Not long after he'd quit school and moved back home he'd overheard his dad talking to his uncle Jerry. They were sitting out on the porch listening to a baseball game on the radio. The kitchen window was open, and Dale was pouring himself a glass of milk.

"He's a good kid," his dad was saying.

"He is," Jerry said. "A great kid, always was."

"He's just kind of a beta dog. You don't like to say that about your only son but it's true. He's willing to be led, is what I'm saying. I love him to death."

"Of course you do."

"There's alphas and betas. It's how it has to be, but you just want the most for your kid. You know?"

"He's young. I bet he gets it together."

"I'd started my own business by the time I was his age. Bought a house."

"Everyone's different, man. He's a good kid."

"I know. That's what everyone says."

Dale went back down to his room at this point.

Though Dale's first ride-along was forever burned into his memory—months later and the sight of the girl run through with a pine stob was still freshly horrible—his second was oddly pleasant, fortuitous even. It was a quiet evening in town, they'd only had a couple calls. One older guy who thought he might be having a heart attack but was just suffering from indigestion. A minor fender bender, a passenger complaining of whiplash. And then, a call from a residential neighborhood not too far from Dale's father's house, a child with a possibly broken arm. They got to the scene, and there were bikes on the sidewalk. A boy of about ten writhing on the grass, a woman kneeling next to him, trying to keep him still, smoothing his hair. Dale helped the EMT on duty check the boy over and apply a splint. He stole glances at the mother, cutoff shorts and a tank top, hands dirty like she'd been working in the garden.

In the ambulance the boy's wailing slowed, and the woman caught Dale looking at her. She smiled.

Later that week he went for a walk and passed her house. She was out in the front yard carting a wheelbarrow load of mulch to spread under the rhododendrons that lined her driveway. The boys were playing basketball, the one in the cast making awkward one-handed shots. Dale was just going to walk by, but then she saw him and waved him over.

He played a game of H-O-R-S-E with the boys and then he fell out and sat there on the lawn with her, watching them play until it started to get dark.

"Well, I've got to get these hooligans to bed," she said, nodding to the boys. "But, if you're not in a huge hurry, you could finish spreading this mulch for me. I could probably dig up a beer for you." She laughed as if she were mostly joking but Dale—who had very little experience with these things—could tell fairly easily that this was a woman at some sort of departure point in her life.

Dale stayed. He spread the mulch. It was pitch-dark when she had returned. He was sitting on the front step, and she sat close enough to him that their legs touched. She had beers for each of them and she told him that she was very impressed with people that devoted their lives to helping others in their most dire time of need.

"I agree," he said. "It's not for everyone. Very rewarding, though. Or, at least I think it will be." He was going to say something else but she had her hand on his leg now.

"You could stay," she said. "Here, tonight, I mean, with me. If you don't have anything else to do." She was talking fast now, like now that she'd started, her words were gaining momentum, coming downhill out of control. "I'm not going to sleep with you, I mean, I want to sleep with you but that's it. I mean, I want to do more than sleep with you but tonight I just want to sleep with you. Maybe this is weird. I don't know. Never mind."

"Okay."

"Okay?"

"Sure."

"Really? I'm forty-three years old and I'm still married, technically."

Dale shrugged. "I just dropped out of college, and live in my dad's basement."

Jeannette laughed like this was the funniest thing ever. "God, that sounds perfect," she said. "If we could all be so lucky. You want to take a shower?"

"Okay."

"Okay, again? You're pretty agreeable aren't you?"

"I guess."

"My husband, ex-husband, whatever, once called me a bossy bitch."

"You seem nice to me."

She stood, reaching to pull him up too. "My shower's not real big," she said. "But, I bet we can both still fit. It might just be a little tight." She said this last bit right in his ear. Dale figured that sometimes when a woman wants you to sleep with her but not *sleep* with her she actually means it. This turned out to not be one of those cases.

Later, in bed, her hair still wet, she pulled his arms around her and sighed. "This is what I wanted most," she said. "I wanted all that other stuff we just did too, but this is it. I miss this so bad sometimes." Eventually her breathing slowed and Dale thought she was asleep but then she gave a little kick as if startled. "Shit," she said. "You've got to leave in the morning before the boys get up. It would just confuse them."

I'm kind of confused myself, Dale thought.

———

Five years ago, her husband had been in a motorcycle accident. He'd been left with horrible back pain and had developed an addiction to OxyContin. He was unable to work. He got caught with three different prescriptions from three different doctors. That had scared him straight for a while.

"I thought he was better," Jeannette said. "It was a hard thing. I never blamed him. I still don't, really. He was trying. He still seemed out of it, though, like he was when he was on the pills, but he swore he wasn't taking them anymore and I believed him. I had gotten another job at this point. I was still working days at the nursery and then nights at the Bistro when my mom could watch the boys. Anyway, I'm not complaining, but that's why I did it. I was fed up. I was tired all the time and I just snapped."

"What do you mean?" Jeannette had made him dinner. They were doing the dishes when she was telling him this. Standing side by side at the sink, Dale scrubbing a pan, Jeannette drying plates.

"I had him arrested," she said. "Maybe it wasn't the right thing to do. I came back from my second job and the boys were home from their grandmother's, watching TV, and I looked all over for him and I eventually found him in the bathroom, sitting on the toilet. He was—it was—*heroin*." She said the word so quietly he could barely hear it over the running water. "He played baseball in college. He was a regional sales rep for outdoor gear. I still can't really believe it. I called the cops on him. He tried to drive off and they got him before he'd made it five blocks. He did a year in Deer Lodge. He's in a halfway house in Billings now." With this, Jeannette finished drying the last plate. She snapped him on the rear with her towel. "Enough of that sob story."

That night she didn't tell him that he needed to leave, and

the next morning she made him breakfast, the boys looking at him, solemn eyed, across the table.

"Our dad can throw a ninety-mile-per-hour fastball," the one with the cast said. "How fast can you throw it?"

"Football was always more my sport," Dale said.

The boy eyed him skeptically. "How tall are you?"

"Five-ten."

"Where did you play?"

"Right here at Park High."

"I meant after that."

"That was it. There was no after that."

The boy nodded as if this had confirmed some more general suspicion he'd been harboring. "My dad played in college."

"Okay," Jeannette said. "Boys, go brush your teeth. Dale, would you like more coffee?"

Dale had never been good at taking tests. He could know the material front to back, inside and out, but as soon as he was confronted with that sheet of empty, lettered bubbles—the knowledge that the whole enterprise was timed, the feeling of all the other test-takers silently massed around him, the smell of the freshly sharpened number-two pencils—his eyes would blur over, he'd second-guess himself, he'd sweat through his shirt. The EMT exam was a brutal gauntlet of 120 questions laced with words like: hypovolemia, necrosis, eschar, maceration, and diabetic ketoacidosis.

After running every morning, Dale sat at the kitchen table with a glass of orange juice and took practice tests. He put his watch on the table so he could time himself. Sometimes his dad would interrupt him, coming in to get some water, or making toast, or firing up the lawnmower right under the window, but Dale didn't mind. He could have done his studying in his room, but he liked to do it out in the kitchen where his dad might see. So far, his dad hadn't asked him what he was up to, but Dale knew he was curious. He'd caught him drinking his morning coffee, thumbing through one of the study manuals, his eyebrows raised.

Dale was taking a practice test, in the middle of trying to decipher a particularly dense question, when Jeannette called. He let it ring. He was fairly certain that the correct answer was C. But, it was one of those questions where there could be multiple right answers, just one was *more* right than the others. He was pretty sure it was C, but it might have been A as well. These things confused him. He knew it was C. But then it might be A as well in which case it would be D because answer D was both C and A. Fuck. After a moment's silence, his phone was ringing again. He answered this time and her voice was panicky.

"The creek," she was saying. "It's overflowing and it's going to come in the house and I don't even know if I have flood insurance and everything is going to be ruined and then mold sets in and maybe the foundation is already getting undermined and then when that happens you might as well just bulldoze the house. And—"

"Okay," Dale said. "Hang on. Don't worry about all that. No bulldozing. I'm coming over."

When Dale got there, Jeannette was standing on the back porch, her hands wrestling themselves. The boys were on the couch watching a movie, and she shut the door so they couldn't hear.

"I put a stick in the ground to mark where it was last night. That was completely dry yesterday. Now look. It's come up a foot."

The creek was huge, out of its banks, sluicing through the willows. The low spot in the yard where Jeannette had her rhubarb was completely underwater. There was a small rise and then the ground sloped back to the house. From what Dale could tell, if the water was to come up another foot it would top the rise and come pouring down the back side; there'd be no way to keep it out of the house at that point.

"Shit," Dale said. "Okay. Well." She was looking at him. Waiting for something. Dale imagined he could see it in her face, her want of husband writ large. He didn't know what to do. "All right," he said. "We'll figure it out."

He went down to the creek, slogged over the saturated ground, cold water rising above his boot tops. He could feel the trembling in the soil, the bushes rollicking in the flow, their roots trying to maintain their hold. A basketball came bobbing down the flat, turgid center of the creek—obscenely orange against the gray current—it caught for a moment against a branch, and then was gone. The creek that normally meandered sleepily through the backyards on this side of town had come awake, answering the call of the main river, bringing with it for tithe anything it could catch up.

"Don't get too close," she said, shouting so he could hear over the roar of water. "It's dangerous."

He slogged around some more, looking at the small rise that was the last defense against the rising creek, the stick she had pounded into the ground, trying to calculate how much time they had. It didn't look good. He went back to stand next to her on the porch. He tried to put his arm around her, but she was too nervous. Pacing up and back on the porch.

"Shit, shit, shit. What else?" she said. "What in god's name can be next?"

Dale didn't know what to do. He called his dad.

Dale hadn't told his father about Jeannette. But the town was small, and it hadn't taken him long to find out. He'd been driving through the park, and spotted them sitting on a blanket, the boys playing in a sandbox, Dale's head in Jeannette's lap.

That night Dale's father had insisted on making dinner. "I'm going to grill some elk steaks," he said. "You make a little salad or something. We haven't sat down together in a while."

Dale was at the kitchen table reading about how to spot the signs of diabetic ketoacidosis. He looked at his father warily. "Why?"

"What do you mean, why? We always run off and do our own thing. I haven't seen you in a week. You too busy to eat a steak with your old man?"

"No. I guess not."

"Okay, then." He went out to get the grill going, and Dale washed some lettuce. They ate on the porch, the elk meat leaking red onto their paper plates, the salad mostly untouched, as if it were existing for memorial's sake, a small gesture of remembrance for the woman who had been gone from their lives for a long time now.

His father had finished eating, his feet kicked up on the porch railing. He took a drink of his beer and belched. "I saw you got a girlfriend now, eh?"

"What do you mean?"

"Saw you in the park. Now, that was a domestic scene. Got yourself a little ready-made family going there."

"It's not like that."

"I recognize that one. That whole thing was in the paper. He used to be a T-ball coach. A drug addict T-ball coach. Hard to imagine. He was embezzling too."

"He doesn't really factor into our equation."

Dale's father laughed. "Oh, son. Wetting the wick is one thing. Picnics with the kiddies is a whole different story."

"Don't worry about it."

"Who said I'm worrying? Trying to impart some advice upon you is all. Pretty soon, you're going to have fucked the interesting out of her and then you're going to be in a world of hurt."

"Save it."

"I'll not. You live in my house and you'll hear me out. All I'm saying is this—women are already a little bit ahead of men, age-wise. So, you start taking up with one who's got a few years on you, and you're putting yourself at a big disadvantage. She's got a head start on you and there's no way you're going to catch up, she'll be lapping you before long and you won't even know it. There's damage there. Trust me. When a baby comes out, part of her rational mind comes out with it, caught up in that stuff they throw away."

"Jesus, Dad." Dale carried their plates into the kitchen and then retreated to his room. Like his father had some great wealth of knowledge from which to draw his theories about women. As far as Dale knew, there had only been his mother, and god knows that hadn't worked out too well.

Dale went around to the front of the house to make the call where the sound of the rising water wasn't so loud. When his father picked up the phone Dale could hear voices in the background, phlegmy laughter.

Once a week Dale's father and a number of his cronies met at the Albertsons for fifty-cent coffee and day-old donuts. It was an hour-long bullshit session. Topics veered, but usually returned and settled comfortably on: the current administration's latest outrage against common sense, the weather, the elk herd numbers in relation to the burgeoning wolf population, what was hatching on the river, and why it was that the trout were all smaller than they used to be.

Dale filled him in on the situation, and in a few moments he was at the house in his pickup, donut crumbs in his beard. Jeannette was in the driveway, a worried half-smile on her face. Dale's father brushed off Dale's attempt at introductions.

"Forget all that," he said. "No time to spare here. Fairgrounds. They got the Boy Scouts down there filling sandbags. Let's go."

At the fairgrounds, the Boy Scouts had a small mountain of sandbags. They were working in pairs, one boy fitting an empty bag over an orange traffic cone with the end cut off, the other boy shoveling sand in the funnel. Trucks were coming in and out, people tossing bags, classic rock turned up loud. It was Dale's father's type of scene. He immediately recruited a couple of loitering Boy Scouts and they hoisted the bags up to the truck bed where Dale stacked them. Dale's father was circulating, shouting good-natured insults and encouragement. He'd found a Styrofoam cup of coffee somewhere and Dale heard him talking to the Scout leader. "Nah," he was saying, "our house is on a hill. It would have to get biblical for it to touch us. This is for Dale's little girlfriend. She's about to get washed away."

They stacked sandbags all afternoon. Dale and his father standing up to their knees in the icy water, Jeannette right there with them, ducking down to balance bags on her shoulder, walking from truck to stack to truck, a slight woman, but surprisingly capable of bearing weight. She dropped a bag with a grunt and went back for another. Dale watched his father watching her. He was a man who valued work above all else. He'd told Dale a long time ago that he wanted the inscription on his gravestone to read: HE GOT HIS WORK DONE.

The three of them stacked feverishly until their wall was built, a three-foot high barrier spanning the low spot in Jeannette's lawn. When Dale looked up he could see the boys inside, their faces pressed to the sliding glass doors. His dad occasionally made an exaggerated scowl at them, and they ran back into the kitchen.

It took them two loads of sandbags until they had something that seemed capable of holding back the water. The rain had slackened, and they sat on the back porch, exhausted. Jeannette had gotten them beers and they drank watching the water rush by, still rising.

Eventually Jeannette stood and gathered their empties. "I want you both to go home and get cleaned up," she said. "And then I want you both to come right back over for dinner. I've got lasagna that I made last week and froze. I can heat it up and make a salad and some garlic bread." Dale's father was starting to say something to protest but she held up her hand to cut him off. "I insist," she said. "Dinner in forty-five minutes. Hit the showers. I make a damn good lasagna."

"Yes, ma'am."

After dinner, Dale's father thanked Jeannette, and she hugged him, kissed his cheek, his face going red. Dale walked him out to the porch.

"I guess you'll not be needing a ride home?"

Dale shook his head. "Guess not."

"Can't say that I blame you there."

"Yep."

"That was good lasagna."

"Not bad."

"Well." He was looking down, scratching at his beard. He cleared his throat and spit. "Good work, son." He stomped down the steps and Dale could hear him belching as he swung into the cab of his truck.

Dale went back inside and helped Jeannette with the dishes. They went to the porch with a blanket wrapped around them, listening, trying to gauge the depth of the water in the dim broadcast of the moon, not talking much. Eventually she fell asleep with her head on his chest, her arms and legs twitching occasionally.

Dale woke, sun just peeking up over the lilac bushes in the backyard. One of the boys was crying, he could hear it coming through the upstairs window. Jeannette was still sleeping, curled, knees to chest with her back to him. He waited for a moment for her to wake up, but the boy continued to wail, and she showed no sign of movement. He nudged her and she groaned and rolled over, her face still under the blanket.

"One of the boys is up," he said.

She said something, mostly unintelligible, that might have been, "It's your turn."

Dale lay there listening to the boy wail for a few more moments. He slipped from under the blanket and squelched across the soggy, cold lawn in his bare feet. There was a brown scum line on the sandbags marking the high point the creek had reached. Their wall had held. The creek was still rushing but it had settled back within its banks, running straight and hard and tea colored. He walked back to the porch, and the lump under the blanket that was Jeannette had not stirred. It was silent, and then another sob from upstairs. Dale deliberated for a moment.

He went inside. They're just kids, he was thinking, why are you nervous? He opened the door to the boys' room and immediately, the crying stopped. They looked at him expectantly, red faced.

"Mom?" one of them said, trying to look around Dale to see if she was back there.

"She's still sleeping," Dale said. "Let's let her sleep." They were staring at him. The younger one was looking like he was going to start crying again. "Do you guys like coffee?"

Silence. The older one shook his head.

"I bet your mom doesn't let you have coffee, does she? No? Well, she's asleep so we can do whatever we want. Let's go. We're going to have to hurry before she wakes up and shuts us down." Dale headed downstairs, not sure if they were going to follow. He was filling the carafe with water when they came into the kitchen, blinking, hair standing on end.

"It's very important to do this correctly," he said. "Come here and watch this. You've got to put five scoops of grounds in the filter. Okay? Five. Your mom makes coffee and she puts in four, on a good day. We're men. Right? We want strong coffee. Five scoops. Got it?"

Serious nods.

"Okay. We need mugs. Lots of Cream. Lots of Sugar. When you get older you'll drink it black. But this is how you start. It's how my dad used to make mine. You don't want to go right to the hard stuff." They sat at the kitchen island. Each with a mug in front of him.

"Now what?" one of them asked.

"We drink our coffee. We talk about the weather."

"It stopped raining," one of them said, looking out the window.

"Yep," Dale said. "I think it's going to be a nice day."

"It's been raining a lot."

"I like snow better than rain."

"I like it when it's sunny."

"You guys are naturals at this," Dale said.

Jeannette came in the back door. She had the blanket wrapped around her shoulders and her eyes were puffy. She stopped when she saw them sitting there, Dale with her two boys. He could imagine the way it looked to her. The scene almost the way it should be, one note off. If she was jarred by it, she hid it well.

"Dale made us coffee," one of the boys said. "And we're talking about the weather."

Jeannette sat down. "Girls allowed?"

"I guess."

She reached for Dale's mug. I can't believe I slept for so long," she said. "Jesus. My back. I'm too old for sleeping on porches." She was squeezing his knee under the counter, smiling at him.

"We didn't flood," Dale said.

"I noticed. I'm going to bake your dad a pie or something. My god, this coffee is horrible. Are you boys actually drinking this?"

"It's good," one of them said.

"Because we're men," said the other.

———

The summer progressed. Dale studied for his test. He ran in the mornings when it was still cool. Sometimes there was fog coming off the river, and when this happened he found himself picking up the pace, unable to see more than an arm's length in front of his face, a headlong feeling. Less like running, more like falling.

He did a few more ride-alongs. A few minor incidents, nothing like that first night. He was there for a shooting. An accident, two kids playing with their dad's handgun. The one kid shot through the leg, a puckered purple hole, his face white. Dale helped carry the stretcher and load the kid into the ambulance. "My dad is going to be so pissed," the kid was saying. "Is this expensive? It is, isn't it? He's going to kill me."

"You're all right, man," Dale said to him. "Your dad's just going to be happy that you're going to be fine. Don't worry."

He was feeling quietly confident about the test. About things in general. He'd made flashcards and sometimes Jeannette quizzed him, lying on the couch in the evenings after she'd put the boys to bed. She'd have her bare feet in his lap so he could rub them.

"What are the two types of cerebral vascular accidents?"

"Embolic or ischemic strokes and hemorrhagic strokes."

"Correct-o. You're going to kill this."

"I don't know. We'll see."

"Nonsense. You know all these forward and backward."

"Until I sit down in that room with the clock."

"Just imagine everyone else in the room naked. Right? Isn't that what you're supposed to do?"

"That's if you're scared of public speaking."

"It might still help, though."

"I'll try it and let you know."

The morning of the test, Dale rose early. Jeannette, a soft, sleep-warmed shape next to him. He hadn't seen his own bed in weeks.

She'd recently told him that if he wanted to move his stuff in, that would be fine with her. It actually sounded like a pretty good plan. He was spending so much time there anyway, it made sense. He'd be able to help with money too, just as soon as he passed the test, and the fire department could formally hire him. They'd already given him a verbal agreement. The test would make it official, and then he'd be making a decent wage.

He laced up his shoes in the dark, the house silent. He drank a full glass of water and then closed the door behind him quietly. He hit the sidewalk, his legs nearly twitching with pent-up energy. He was going to fly through this run, and then get another quick half hour of studying in before the test time. He was going to kill the goddamn test, and then his life was going to unfold in a solid, meaningful way with Jeannette, kids and all. You never can tell, he thought. You can't predict these things.

The sun was starting to come up over the hills just outside of town. He was cruising down the river path now, breath coming easily, occasionally reaching out to brush his fingers over the deep furrows of the cottonwoods that lined the trail. Just before the 9th Street bridge, there was something—a blur on his periphery—a figure in a hooded sweatshirt holding something, coming at him in mid-swing, a stick, a bat. And then Dale was running, but his feet weren't on the ground. Fog creeping in off the river, black fog, and Dale plunging right into it.

Ken hadn't gone to coffee with the guys in a long time. He didn't know if he was up to it or not, but he had to get out of the house someway. Last night the leaves had been blasted from the trees in one brutal windstorm. He'd gone to bed and woken up to bare limbs. Clouds forecasting snow. It had been months since he'd come down to the Albertsons like this. He went to the self-serve kiosk and got his paper cupful, pushed fifty cents into the slot in the counter. He sat down at the table, and Greg Ricci, who'd been talking, barely broke stride. He nodded at Ken. "And then I told him, I says, you have to premix the damn oil and gas. I knew this kind of stuff when I was a little kid, and this is a guy with a college education. He'd never mixed up oil and gas for a lawnmower in his whole life. I don't know. It's a changing world. I'm sometimes glad I'm on my way out of it."

"Oh, hell."

"I'm serious. You go to a bar and no one's talking to each other. Everyone's looking down at their phone, or whatever. I went down to Denver to see my kid. I was in the airport. The bars in the airports have all got those damn iPods. Right in front of the stool so you can't move them. I try to order a beer with the bartender and he tells me he can't take my order. I have to punch it in on the iPod. I says, what the hell are you standing back there for then, if you can't take my order? And he says, well, someone still has to twist the top off it, and I says, well, watch your ass because they'll figure a way to get around that too." He stopped to take a sip of his coffee. "How you been, Ken?"

"Okay, considering."

"I hear you. Nice to see you." Nods all around.

"Yep. A bit blustery this morning."

"No shit. My old lady is going to be on me to start raking."

"Goddamn raking."

"Hell with it, this might be the year I pay someone to do it."

"Oh, bullshit, you're too much of a tightwad."

"We'll see. Hey, I saw the bench they put up on the river trail for your boy, Ken. Looks like they did a real nice job."

"It's just a bench."

"I know. But it's in a good spot there. A person could sit there in the shade and see the river."

"I don't even know who came up with that idea. I had nothing to do with it."

"I think it was the folks at the fire department. The other paramedics down there."

"They never asked me."

"Well, it's a real nice bench. There's a plaque and everything."

"It's just a bench."

"Looks well made, though. Comfortable."

"It's just a fucking bench. Okay? Can we all agree on that?"

"They should have asked you."

"We could go down there and tear the bastard out."

"I don't want to tear it out. It's only a bench, and it means nothing to me. Dogs will be pissing on it long after we're dead and buried." Ken took a sip of his coffee. He checked to see if his hands were shaking and they weren't. This was recent, something he'd never had to do before in his life. "You hear they're going to start issuing wolf tags?" he said. "I think we should all go get one."

"Kill one wolf, save a thousand elk."

"Shoot, shovel, and shut up, that's what I always say."

"Goddamn right."

They said that he was on his way to get her. That's what the cops said, and she had to believe they were right. She didn't truly think he would have harmed the boys. But who's to say? Obviously she didn't know him anymore and maybe she never had. She'd been saved by a traffic stop of all things. He was driving too fast through the park, and when the trooper hit his lights, Tony had sped up going the other way. He was going almost eighty, they said, when he hit the berm along the river. His car came up and over and landed in the water upside down.

Sometimes in the early morning she came awake with the feeling that a hand was on her hip, a male presence at her back. If she was still half asleep she might remember the dream she was having. Sometimes it was Dale, kind and considerate and serious, and when this was the case she woke up sad. Sometimes it was Tony, the old Tony, the one who knew her better than anyone, and on these occasions she woke up flushed and hating herself.

After it happened, weeks after the funeral, she stopped by Dale's father's house. She brought him a pan of lasagna. He stood in the doorway. Made no move to let her in.

"I'm sorry," she said. "I don't know what to say."

"There's nothing to be sorry about," he said. His eyes saying just the opposite. "I'll bring your pan back to you tomorrow," he said. "And I'd appreciate if you never did anything like this again. I'd just as soon you didn't." He shut the door carefully and Jeannette walked home. She had to sit on the front steps for a long time before she'd found a face she could present to her sons.

They'd gotten a big snow overnight and school was canceled. Their mom had stayed home from work and made them hot chocolate. His little brother had the hot chocolate, but he told her he'd rather have coffee. He made sure she did it correctly, five scoops. He put a lot of cream in it and sugar and a little hot chocolate too and that was pretty good. They sat drinking in the kitchen watching the flakes come down fat and white as the pom-poms on a Christmas hat.

"Let's get all our warm stuff on and go out to the park," his mom said. It was her cheerful voice, the one she used a little bit before but seemed to use a lot now.

He shrugged.

"We could build a snowman," his little brother said.

His mom was stirring her coffee. "That sounds like a good idea," she said. "Let's do it."

On the way to the park, someone passed them on skis, going right down the middle of the street. The trees were coated in a thick, white blanket, the pines with their branches weighted down and sagging, so that if he bumped them they'd shed their load and spring up in a shower of fine crystal.

They made a snowman, but they hadn't thought to bring a carrot for a nose or coal for eyes, so they just used sticks but it didn't look quite right. He and his brother karate-kicked its head off.

He got the idea that he might like to build a snow fort. Kind of like an igloo, but also with some sticks, like a tipi. He enlisted his brother's help. His mother helped for a while, too, but then she said she was tired and went to sit on a bench. There were some trees over there, and he could just see the river behind her. She was wearing a bright-red Livingston Fire Department hat that used to be Dale's, and he had the thought that if snowmen had blood, their insides would look like a cherry snow cone.

When he looked up again a short time later, he saw that there was a man, sitting on the bench next to his mother. They were at opposite ends, and he was too far away to see if they were talking. It didn't look like they were. It looked like the bench was too small for the two of them, like they didn't want to be on it with each other. The man was wearing a bright-orange hunting cap. Neon orange. His mom had her bright hat on, and this man had his on, and everything else was white snow or gray tree trunks or black river. He stopped working on his fort wall and started to walk over. His mom thought he was a little kid still, but he wasn't. He was ten years old now and he'd picked up a fallen cottonwood stick as big around as his wrist, and he was stomping fast through the deep snow, watching his mother the whole time.

When he got closer, he could see his mother wiping at tears, smiling. This was fairly common now too. She had her cheerful voice and then her even more cheerful wiping-away-tears voice.

"It's fine," she said. "I'm okay, honey. Say hi to Ken. We were just talking."

"Hi, Ken." He still had his stick resting on his shoulder. Ken's eyes were red rimmed, and his nose was running. He was leaning over doing something with his hands in the snow next to his leg. He threw the snowball with almost no warning. "Batter's up, kid," was all he said.

Probably Ken thought he'd miss, but his dad had taught him how to hit a long time ago, and he was ready even though it looked like he wasn't. He swung his cottonwood stick as hard as he could, and the snowball evaporated into a mist of cold white powder that slowly filtered down over all three of them. He could feel it melting on his neck under his collar. It turned to wet drops like tears under Ken's cheeks. It coated his mom's dark hair so it looked like she'd instantly gone old and gray.

"Hot damn," Ken said. "What a cut that was. You might make the big leagues yet."

ONE MORE LAST STAND

At the last rest stop before Crow Agency, Perry pulled off and donned the uniform in a stall in the men's restroom. Navy-blue wool pants and high-topped leather riding boots. A navy-blue wool tunic with gaudy chevrons and large gilt buttons. Elbow-length calfskin gloves. A broad-brimmed hat with one side pinned up rakishly. He smoothed his drooping mustache and ran his fingers through his long blond hair. When he got back into his car, he had to take off the hat. He was tall, and the crown crushed against his Camry's low ceiling.

Out over the Bighorn range the sky was going red, a red shot through with sooty black tendrils of cirrus horsetail. He came in fast, pushing the Camry up to ninety down the last hill into the Little Bighorn valley. It felt like a charge, headlong and headstrong, brash, driving hard into the final waning moments of a lurid sunset. He put the windows down to feel the rush of air. Only in this place, Perry thought, could the sky look like an expanse of infected flesh. What was the saying?

Red sky at night, sailors take fright?

Red sky at night, keep your woman in sight?

How about: red sky at night, bad men delight?

He'd gotten his usual room at the War Bonnet Motel and Casino. There was a king-sized bed and an ironing board that folded down from the wall and an unplugged mini-fridge. The first thing he did was plug in the mini-fridge. The second thing he did was take off and hang up the uniform. Then Perry stretched out on the bed in his boxer shorts and undershirt and fell asleep.

When he woke an hour later it was full dark. He drank a beer and flipped through the channels until he found the weather and was pleased to see the weekend forecast called for high eighties and almost no chance of rain. It was going to be hot and dusty out there but better that than rain. Nothing like rain to ruin a reenactment.

Perry called home. It was only nine, but Andy sounded sleepy when she answered.

"Did I wake you?"

"No. It's okay."

"It's only nine, I didn't think you'd be asleep."

"It's okay. It's just I had a feeling like I wasn't going to be able to sleep tonight so I took something, and then there was this documentary about meerkats on PBS, and I started watching that and fell asleep and was having these absolutely insane rodent dreams. You know, that's the problem with when you take something, you fall asleep and then you dream so hard it's like you have a full day or sometimes it seems like a year, and then, just as you are ready to lay down for sleep, you wake up. You know what I mean? You take something and you sleep, but you're not rested. Anyway, how was the drive?"

"Fine. Long. I got an audio book at a truck stop in Sioux Falls. It was about this guy in New York who tried for a year to follow the Bible exact. Did you know that the Bible says you shouldn't wear clothing that is made of fabric that mixes wool and linen?"

"I had no idea."

"Seriously. Also you shouldn't trim your sideburns, and the corners of your garments should have tassels."

"Tassels?"

"Yes."

"Why?"

"I'm not sure. But, according to the book, there's a store in New York City that sells nothing but tassels. Tassels Without Hassles."

"What?"

"That's what it's called. The store. Tassels Without Hassles."

"Huh. Why was this guy doing this? Trying to follow the Bible exact, I mean, what was his reason outside of trying to come up with an idea for a book?"

"To awaken his spiritual side I guess. Connect to his Old Testament ancestors."

"Is he Jewish, the author?"

"Yeah. In the book he went to a Hasidic dance in Crown Heights in New York, which, from what I gather, is like an Indian reservation but for Orthodox Jews. There weren't any women there—they didn't allow them to come to the dance. It was a life-changing experience, he said."

"Sweet, sounds fun."

"Yeah."

"I think if I were a Hasidic woman I'd have a big problem with not being allowed to dance."

"Perry, I think I'm going to go to bed now."

"Sounds like it might be a good idea. I'm tired myself from all the driving."

"Love."

"Love."

Perry drank another beer, then put on the uniform and headed down to the War Bonnet Lounge. He was surprised to see a new bartender this year, a young guy with a black goatee and a spiderweb tattooed over his elbow. "Well," the bartender said when Perry bellied up, "looks like the reenactment is in town. Either that or you're lost. In the wrong century." He laughed.

"Maybe both," said Perry. "Where's Nolan?"

"He died."

"No shit. When?"

"April."

"How?"

"He was old. And diabetic. And Indian. How do you think he died?"

"I was accustomed to seeing him here. We were kind of friends. I didn't know. How old was he anyway?"

"I have no idea, old enough to die and not have it be much of a surprise to anyone that actually knew him."

"Okay, fair enough."

"Beer?"

"PBR with a shot of Evan."

Perry shot the Evan and chased with a small sip of Pabst. He scanned the slot machines. When the bartender came around, Perry asked about Kat.

"Kat who?" the bartender said, narrowing his eyes. "Kat Realbird?"

"Yes, Kat Realbird. She been around tonight?"

The bartender leaned his elbows on the bar and spun an empty shot glass around on the bar top.

"Not tonight. Last night, though."

"How was she? I mean, how did she seem? How did she look?"

"What do you mean, how did she seem? She came in and played nickel slots with her old grandmother. She had two Coronas with lime. She looked fine. She wore pants. And a shirt. And she had black hair. And she looked Indian. I mean what the fuck do you want from me here?"

"Nothing. That's it. That's all I wanted. Thank you."

Perry finished his beer, and when he did, flagged down the bartender.

"Another?"

"No, I'm done. But a quick favor for me, if you would. When you see Kat Realbird give her a message for me. Tell her the General is back in town."

That night Perry fell asleep waiting, nursing a beer, still in full uniform on the king-sized bed. When the knock on the door came, he thrashed awake and spilled the beer down the side of his tunic.

She stood in the shadows thrown by the motel vapor lights. She was in full regalia—a turkey-bone breastplate, a fawn leather breechclout—her hair braided and adorned with a single raven's feather. Her paint was different this year, the left side of her face starting below the eye was chalk white; the right side was unpainted except for a red, quarter-sized circle on her high cheekbone.

Crossing the threshold she was on him hard, her hands

twisted in his tunic, her lips dampening his full mustache. She drove him back onto the bed and her smell—a mixture of leather, bear-grease face paint and knockoff Chanel No. 5—came over him. He breathed in where her neck met her shoulder and it was like a return home after a long journey fraught with uncertainty and peril.

"I think about you," he said. "Back home at work I sometimes put on my uniform and imagine this. I'll sometimes spend whole days downstairs in my office, in full dress. I do conference calls in my hat and gloves and cavalry pants. It makes me feel closer to you—to this."

He was still on the bed. She was in the room's small bathroom washing off the face paint and rinsing the grease from her hair. She came out toweling her hair, her face clean and bare. He could see the faint pockmarks on her cheeks.

"I have to wash that stuff off, or I break out terribly."

"Kat, did you hear me?"

"Yes."

"And? Do you think of me? During the year, in your real life?"

"I do. But it doesn't change anything, so I try not to."

She got in bed and put her body tight next to his, her face on his bare chest. She twisted a lock of his long blond hair between her fingers and then put the ends in her mouth, wetting it to a tip like a paintbrush. She traced invisible designs on his chest.

"You painted your face different this year," he said. "I almost didn't recognize you."

"Oh? You have a lot of half-naked Indian women in traditional dress coming to your hotel rooms these days?"

"Of course. But I send them all away."

"Sha, you know no one but me is crazy enough to do this with you. Just so you know, I wasn't going to do it this year, the reenactment. But when I came to the War Bonnet, and heard you were back I just couldn't not come. I gave John some half-assed excuse and came up to my cousin's. You realize that I just snuck out and walked a mile across Crow Agency in the dark in a breechclout with no panties or bra?"

"Thank you. You were beautiful. You *are* beautiful."

"Sha, yousay. General?"

"Hm?"

"I've had a bad year."

The first day of the reenactment went as well as could be expected. They did three shows each day of the weekend, and the first was always the roughest. There were always logistics to be straightened out. Horses that acted up. That was Perry's least favorite part about the whole thing. The horses. Inevitably he got stuck on some knobby nag that wanted to stop mid-battle to take a mouthful of grass or take a shit right were Perry was supposed to lie after being killed.

As had become their custom, on the first day Perry waited on Last Stand ridge until Kat had time to get there and kill him. He knew it pissed some of the guys off, the way he refused to go down until Kat came flying up the ridge and vaulted from her horse with a piercing war cry—but so what, tough shit for them. She would run at him and he would fall under her weight. As she pretended to slit his throat she always gave him a full kiss on the lips, her body shielding this from the people watching in the grandstands. He never wanted her more than right then. Pretend dead on his back in the dust and the horseshit, an erection straining the front of his blue cavalry trousers.

This year was different, but only a little. Perry staggered and gestured as if he were in agony. The field was littered with the bodies of the fallen, and he could sense their annoyance. Fucking go down already, man, one of the dead bluecoats lying in the dust near him muttered. It's hotter than hell out here. Show's over. Warriors on horseback were circling and Perry stumbled and then rose slowly to his feet. The crowd was clapping and cheering, and he was scanning the ridgeline for Kat. And then she came and it was a sight to see. She and her horse were cast from the same mold. Her brown thighs rippled and tensed, echoing, rhyming the muscled brown haunches of her mount. Everything was black streaming hair, black flowing mane. He turned to face her and when she swung one leg and sprung from the horse he caught a fast glimpse of taut inner thigh. His heart hiccupped. She rushed him and tackled him full force. He tried to get a quick feel of breast as he went down but she made a show of pinning his arms as she straddled him with her knife between her teeth. She brought the dulled blade across his throat theatrically and when she leaned in close for the kiss he thought he saw tears smearing the paint on her cheeks. It could have been sweat. But then he saw her sad smile.

There were no good restaurants in Crow Agency—actually no restaurants at all if you didn't consider fast food a viable option—so he bought steaks and they grilled them on the small fenced patio off the back of his hotel room. It didn't matter, about the lack of restaurants, because they couldn't have been seen like that anyway, out together. The reservation was small. Word would have traveled.

Perry got the beer she liked, Corona, and they drank them while he messed with the steaks. Kat painted her toenails, her knees drawn up to her chest. Over the top of the warped vinyl patio fence Perry could just make out a ragged flock of turkey vultures circling over the battlefield, searching for stray hot dogs and partially eaten Indian tacos left by the tourists.

"Do you mind if I call my wife quickly?"

"You know I don't."

"Okay, we'll eat soon."

He went into the room and left the door open behind him. He sat on the edge of the bed and called.

"Andy. Hi, it's me."

"Oh, hi, I was just loading the dishwasher, just a minute." Perry heard the phone being fumbled. He could see her fumbling it, her hands wet with soap.

"Okay, I'm back. How did it go today?"

"Pretty good. Hot and dusty. But we put on a good show. I think the people were happy. During the second act the guy that finally killed me was a little rough with the takedown. I've got some bruises."

"Geez, my poor banged-up man. What do these guys think? It's not your fault how everything worked out, you know, the scope of history and all that. They won the battle; we won the war. No need to take it out on you. Actually, I don't know how you do it. I think it would start to get to me, you know, dying every day. It's like you're a sacrifice."

"Or a martyr for the greater American conscience."

"Yeah, that's it, Jesus II. Custer dying for our sins. Three times a day."

"Whose sins exactly, do you suppose?"

"I'm not sure, everyone's, I guess. What are we even talking about?"

"I don't know either, never mind. How are you feeling today? Yesterday you seemed tired."

"Yeah, to tell you the truth I hardly remember our conversation. I was a little whacked-out. This new stuff they've got me on is potent."

There was a pause, her sharp intake of breath, and a soft laugh that couldn't mask what lay underneath.

"Jesus, I feel like shit."

"I'm sorry. Maybe I shouldn't have left."

"No, it's not your fault. It's just the thought of another round of this next month makes me want to die. I mean, seriously. I'm actually surprised that I'm saying this but maybe they should just cut that fucking thing off and be done with it. I could get a prosthetic. I could still wear bikinis."

"They make those? Prosthetic breasts?"

"Yeah. You can pretty much get a prosthetic anything these days."

Perry could tell she was crying and trying to hide it. He could smell the steaks cooking on the grill, could hear Kat humming tunelessly to herself out on the patio.

"I know it sucks now but it will all work out. You won't need a prosthetic anything."

"Promise?"

"Yes."

"Okay, I'm being depressing. Let's say good night."

"Love."

"Love."

They ate their steaks out on the patio. There was no furniture, so they sat on the bare concrete with their plates balanced on their laps, cutting their meat while a dusky swarm of moths batted around the single halogen bulb.

"We've been doing this for a long time now," he finally said.

"Yes. This is our seventh year. And?"

"And, it's funny to think that we existed, us together, before either of our marriages."

"So?"

"Doesn't that beg the question, which is the marriage, which is the affair?"

"I married John at the First Church of Christ in Hardin. We live together. Every day. That's the marriage. Don't be dumb, General."

Kat was right, of course. She had a smear of steak juice on her upper lip. Perry thought that that was unbearable.

Later, she emerged from the bathroom in a one-piece dress of white beaded deerskin, cinched at the waist with a wide, quill-stitched belt. Her face was scrubbed clean without paint, and she had used a thin plait of her own hair to tie the rest back into a ponytail. The dress was short and ended in fringe at her upper thighs. Strong thighs, horse-squeezing thighs. The dress was new. A new thing for them.

"Christ, you are beautiful."

"Sha, yousay."

And then she straddled him on the bed. Rode him like she had stolen him and god himself was in pursuit.

After another hot day on Last Stand ridge, Perry spent an hour posing for photographs with tourists. He put his arms around two rotund sixty-something women and they all smiled for the photographer.

"We are twins," one of them said. "And we're from Michigan. Did you know Custer was from Michigan himself?" Perry smiled behind his mustache and made a show of examining the women. He thought they only looked like twins the way all fat older women looked like twins. He wanted a beer, he wanted a steak, and he wanted Kat's head in his lap. "We love Custer trivia," one of the twins said. "Did you know he graduated from West Point at the top of his class and would probably have been made president one day had his career continued on its natural path?"

"I did know that. In fact I have a PhD in Custer studies, and my dissertation was a theoretical projection of the scope of American politics had Custer survived the battle and gone on to be elected president." Perry thought this to be sufficiently lofty to discourage further conversation.

"Oh, how interesting! Did you know that Custer had size-twelve feet and was married to Elizabeth Bacon?"

Perry was developing a headache. There was a shimmer of heat out over Last Stand ridge, and he could feel hot rivulets of sweat roll from his underarms.

"I did know that," he said, "now I have one for you ladies. Did you know that when a reinforcement cavalry regiment finally arrived on the scene of the battle, they found Custer had received over thirty-two assorted stab wounds, arrow punctures, and rifle shots, was scalped, and had his penis and scrotum cut off and stuffed in his mouth?"

That night after dinner, they walked together on a path along the bank of the Little Bighorn River. They slapped mosquitoes off each other's necks, and Perry threw pebbles in the air to make the bats dive to the ground in pursuit.

"It's because they can't see," he said, "that's why they chase a pebble. They emit noises too high for the human ear to hear and it's like sonar. The sound bounces back to the bat, and that's why they think any small thing flying in the air is probably a bug."

"Bats have eyes don't they?"

"I think so."

"Well, they must be able to see a little then. I'm nearsighted too; I know what that's like. It's not the same as blind. General?"

"Yeah?"

"Do you think you could catch a bat that way, if you wanted to? Like have a net ready and when one swooped down for the pebble you could snag it?"

"Maybe. But, I guess this begs the question, what would you do with a bat after you caught it?"

"I don't know, keep it for a pet. Let it hang upside down from a hanger in my closet. Nice and dark in there. They are kind of cute, especially when they are babies."

"Bats? Cute? I don't see it."

"Pretty much anything that is a baby is cute. I read somewhere that's Mother Nature's way of helping something defenseless survive. Like, when I was a kid and we had cats that lived out in the barn. My dad always hated those cats, and bitched at the way they kept producing litters left and right up in the haymow. But, I remember one time I came out to the barn to get him for supper. He was sitting on a hay bale playing with a little calico kitten that was barely half the size of one of his boots. The rest of the litter mewled and rolled over each other in a pile of hay, and my dad had a gunnysack and a piece of twine in one hand and that little calico licking the other. I was young, maybe seven or eight, but even then I knew what he was going to do. He looked at me standing there in my barn boots, I was probably crying, I don't remember. Anyway, he didn't say anything, just pitched the calico back in the pile with its brothers and sisters. He threw the gunnysack and twine in the trash on the way out of the barn, and he carried me on his shoulders all the way up to the house. I don't remember him doing that very much."

They had been holding hands but Kat pulled away and walked on a few steps ahead.

"Let's head back. These bats suck at what they do. The damn mosquitoes are eating me alive."

In Perry's room at the War Bonnet, she stopped him when he went to put on the uniform.

"Let's just do it like normal people tonight. If you don't mind."

"Normal people? I thought you liked what we do."

"General, you know I do. It's just tonight, I don't want to be your Indian tonight. How about we do something different. How about you pretend I'm your wife. How about we do it like that?"

"I don't know."

"Please, what does she wear to bed? How does she like it?"

"I don't know, Kat. It feels like a wrong thing. Dishonest."

"Just once, General. Then we can go back to the old way until you leave. You said yourself that you were unsure what was the affair, what was the marriage."

She had her arms around him, and was rubbing her fingers in tight circles down his back. Looking down on her he could see where she had missed some white face paint behind her ear.

"Okay. Fine. She wears one of my T-shirts and a pair of my boxer shorts. I usually work late and she likes to read. Most of the time she's asleep with her book by the time I get to bed."

"Sometimes do you wake her up?"

"Sometimes."

"Sha, I bet you do. Okay. Go into the bathroom and come out in five minutes."

Perry went into the bathroom and sat on the toilet seat. It was a small bathroom and his bent knees hit the shower door. He realized he had forgotten to call Andy. He waited as long as he could, and when he emerged, the lights were off in the room except for the small bedside lamp. Kat had let her hair down. She was on her back on top of the comforter and her black hair spilled across the pillow. She had the hotel Bible split open facedown on her stomach. She was wearing one of his white T-shirts, a pair of his white-and-red-striped boxer shorts. Her skin was very dark against the white cotton, her nipples erect and visible through the thin material. She had her eyes closed and her arms lay out by her sides.

"Oh, hi," she said drowsily, "I was asleep. I must have just nodded off while reading."

On the final day of the reenactment, clouds came down across the Bighorn Mountains and the sky opened up. It was a mud bath. Between acts everyone stood under the pavilion at the visitor's center. The warriors' painted faces streaked. Their feathers soddened. Soldiers drank coffee, miserable in wet wool tunics and pants. During a short break in the rain, Perry found Kat retouching her paint, using the side mirror of a Winnebago in the overflow parking lot.

"Can you believe this," he said. "I checked the weather and there was no mention of rain."

"Imagine that, the weatherman being wrong." She was

using two fingers to rub the white paint over her cheek and the side of her jaw.

"In the last show I got killed in a puddle and had to lay there for fifteen minutes while the crowd cleared the grandstands."

"Poor General." She flashed him a quick smile.

"Kat?"

"Yeah?"

"My wife has breast cancer."

She turned to him slowly. She put her arms around him and her painted face left a dull smear on the rough wool of his tunic.

"But it's going to be okay. I think we're going to be all right."

After the last show everyone went down to the War Bonnet Lounge and got drunk. It was an annual tradition on the final day of the reenactment. All the reenactors piled into the dim bar, most still in full dress. The place was hazy with cigarette smoke and the stink of slow-drying wool. A gray-haired man in a full eagle-feather headdress played the jukebox. Grimy cavalry soldiers played pool with shirtless warriors. Perry ordered a beer and when the bartender—the same goateed guy from the other night—extended the bottle, he didn't release his grip when Perry tried to take it from his hand.

"Don't think people don't know about you, man."

"What?" Perry said, unsure he'd heard correctly in the noisy bar.

"Don't *what* me, man. You come to get you some red pussy? Is that your deal? John Realbird is my cousin, man. You think you can come here and do whatever the fuck you want?"

Perry felt the blood coming to his face. He looked to see if anyone else was hearing the conversation. "I don't know what you're talking about, pal. I'm just here for the reenactment like everyone else. They pay me to come. I've been coming here for years." Perry backed away from the bar and the bartender said something but Perry couldn't hear over the jukebox and raised voices. Someone clapped Perry on the shoulder and pressed a drink in his hand. When Kat came in he nodded at her and left out the back door. After a while she followed.

They were both a little drunk, and in the room they got drunker. Kat perched precariously on the shaky foldout ironing board and Perry sat on the end of the bed. They passed a pint of J&B.

"My paint is different this year," she said.

"I know. I asked before, what does it mean?"

"I've been wanting to tell you. I just didn't know how."

She touched her cheek, the red circle. "This is a part of me, a piece of my heart that is gone forever." She touched the other cheek, the chalky white paint. "This is my soul, blank as a field of snow, white like a ghost wandering the world." Perry nodded solemnly. Kat gave a snort and shook her head. "You white people are suckers for that Indian shit. Hand me that bottle." She drank deeply and laughed like none of it was true.

He nearly forgot to call Andy, and when he remembered, it was late. Kat was slid up against him on the bed, maybe asleep, maybe just being quiet. He dialed with one hand to not disturb her.

"Hello?" Andy's voice was groggy with sleep.

"Hi, it's me. Sorry it's late."

"Jesus, it's late."

"I know, I just got caught up with everything here and forgot to call you yesterday and I just wanted to see how you were doing and so I'm sorry but I called you anyway."

"You sound kind of drunk."

"I am kind of drunk. End-of-reenactment party. Drinking firewater with the locals. That kind of thing."

"Sounds fun. I'm kind of jealous. Tonight I tried to make a tofu stir-fry. I'm not sure what happened but the tofu ended up scorched and the vegetables were still raw."

"Tofu can be tricky."

"Apparently. You know what else I did?"

"Hm?"

"I bought a pack of cigarettes and smoked almost half of them."

"Really?"

"Yes."

"What kind?"

"Don't laugh."

"What kind?"

"Virginia Slims. Long skinny girly ones."

"I've never seen you smoke before. I'm having a hard time picturing it."

"I'm new to it, so I'm not very good at it yet, but maybe I'll do it for you when you get back."

"Wearing something sexy, holding a glass of wine?"

"If you'd like."

Kat had reached one arm across Perry's chest and pushed her face down against his neck. The raven feather in her hair brushed his cheek. Her hand found his, the one that wasn't holding the phone.

"Okay. I look forward to it. Have you tried blowing smoke rings yet?"

"No."

"Well, practice."

"I will. I was going to leave it as a surprise. You know, you come home from your reenactment and all of a sudden you have a smoking wife. A wife that smokes. That is something you'd probably never expect."

"Well, it's still a surprise, this way. I almost don't believe it."

"Yeah, you know why I started?"

"It is a question I had considered asking. Why?"

"Because what's the point of not smoking? I've been not smoking for thirty-three years. Look at where it has gotten me. Now I'm going to be smoking. Make sense?"

"Perfectly."

"Okay, I'm going to let you go, very tired."

"Okay."

"Love."

"Love."

"Love."

Kat's lips brushed his ear in her whisper. He hung up the phone. He was a scalped and bloody mess.

Before dawn Perry woke to find Kat's side of the bed empty. He turned and saw her standing over him in the dark, fully clothed in jeans and T-shirt. She brought her fingers to his face and smoothed his mustache. When she moved her head down to him her hair folded like black wings around them.

———

In the morning Perry crammed the uniform, now smelly and stained, into his suitcase and gave a final look around the room to make sure he hadn't forgotten anything. He put the empty bottle of J&B in the trash can. When he went out to the parking lot, he found a fluorescent orange aluminum arrow shaft protruding from the rear passenger tire of his Camry. Perry considered the arrow for a moment and then pulled it, with some difficulty, from the tire. The fletches were glued-on pieces of hot pink vinyl. The shaft had the word WHACKMASTER printed down the sides, and black squiggly lines, which, coupled with the orange, were supposed to give the appearance of tiger stripes. The edges of the broadhead were chipped and rusty. Perry got the donut tire from the trunk and switched out the flat. He put the arrow in the backseat and left the War Bonnet driving slowly on the small spare.

The only repair shop in Crow Agency was Robidoux's Fix-it, a lean-to built off the back of a double-wide trailer. Perry pulled in and Ted Robidoux came down the trailer steps in his bathrobe running his hand through his short black hair. Ted occasionally rode in the reenactment. Three years ago he had taken care of a clogged fuel line in Perry's car.

"Morning, Ted. It's Perry. Remember me, the General?"

"Hey, Perry. Of course. I didn't make the reenactment this year. How did it go?"

"Well, it was a spectacle, as always."

"Good. Good. Looks like you got a bum wheel there. This country's hard on tires."

"And other things."

"Ha, well, I should be able to handle the tire at least. Let me go put my pants on."

He went into the trailer and reemerged clothed, with a mug of coffee that he handed to Perry. "Take a seat," he said. "This could take a few."

Perry sat on the porch and sipped at the hot coffee. It was still early and cool and the land seemed refreshed from yesterday's rain. There was a stack of freshly cut lodgepoles leaning up against the trailer wall, and after he had finished his coffee, Perry went over to take a closer look. He was running his hand over their smooth, peeled surfaces when Ted came from the lean-to.

"Hey," he said, "you like my new poles? I just finished peeling those yesterday. Last time we went to the mountains and put up the good ol' lodge I had two poles break in the middle of the night. You should have seen how pissed my old lady was when the whole thing came down on us and we had to sleep in the cab of the truck."

"Well, you did a good job with these," Perry said. "They're smooth. I can't imagine doing it myself. I can't even peel a potato."

"The secret's a sharp drawknife. And a light hand. And practice." Ted patted one of the lodgepoles and laughed. "Ah yes," he said. "The good ol' tipi." Then he patted the side of his trailer and laughed again. "And here's the new tipi. I got a leaky roof. Fuck me. Well, anyway, we got her patched—the tire. A good-sized hole."

"Thanks. It was the damnedest thing. I had an arrow sticking out of it this morning."

"An arrow? Like a good ol' Indian arrow?"

"Not exactly."

Perry got the arrow and handed it to Ted, who held it between two fingers as if it were something particularly distasteful.

"Whackmaster?" he said.

"I have no idea."

"Well, you know what we need to do, Perry?"

"What?"

"Back in the old days, if a warrior got hit by an arrow he had to break the shaft to make sure the guy who shot him didn't still have power over him. So his wound would heal." Ted handed the arrow back to Perry.

"Really?"

"Sure. I'm an Indian. I know what I'm talking about when it comes to situations like this."

"Okay. How should I do it? Is there, like, a certain way it should be done?"

"I think just over the knee, like a piece of kindling for the fire."

Perry brought the shaft down over his knee. The aluminum didn't break, but bent sharply. He looked up at Ted, who shrugged. Perry bent it back and forth a few times and eventually the shaft broke cleanly, like a paper clip.

"There," said Ted. "Now you keep that forever."

BREATHARIANS

There were cats in the barn. Litters begetting litters begetting litters—some thin and misshapen with the afflictions of blood too many times remixed.

"Get rid of the damn things," August's father said. "The haymow smells like piss. Take a tire iron or a shovel or whatever tool suits you. You've been after me for school money? I'll give you a dollar a tail. You have your jackknife? You have it sharp? You take their tails and pound them to a board and then after a few days, we'll have a settling up. Small tails worth as much as large tails, it's all the same."

The cats—calicos, tabbies, dirty white, gray, jet black, and tawny sat among the hay bales scratching and yawning like indolent apes inhabiting the remains of a ruined temple. August had never actually killed a cat before, but—like most farm boys—he had engaged in plenty of casual acts of torture. Cats, as a species, retained a feral edge, and as a result were not subject to the same rules of husbandry as those that governed man's rela-

tion with horses or cows or dogs. August figured that somewhere
along the line cats had struck a bargain—they knew they could
expect to feel a man's boot if they came too close, in return they
kept their freedom and nothing much was expected of them.

A dollar a tail. August thought of the severed appendages,
pressed and dried, stacking up like currency in the teller drawer of
some strange martian bank. Fifty dollars at least, maybe even
seventy-five, possibly even a hundred if he was able to track down
the newborn litters.

He went to the equipment shed to look for weapons. It was
a massive structure, large enough to fit a full-sized diesel com-
bine, made of metal posts skinned with corrugated sheet metal.
August liked to go there when it rained. He thought it was like
being a small creature deep in the bowels of a percussion instrument. The fat drops of rain would hit the thin metal skin in an
infinite drumroll punctuated by the clash of lightning cymbals
and the hollow booming of space.

In the pole barn there was a long, low workbench covered
in the tangled intestine of machinery. Looping coils of compressor hoses, hydraulic arms leaking viscous fluid, batteries squat and
heavy, baling twine like ligaments stitching the whole crazy mess
together, tongue-and-ball trailer knobs, mason jars of rusting
bolts and nuts and screws, a medieval looking welder's mask, and,
interspersed amongst the other wreckage like crumpled birds,
soiled leather gloves in varying degrees of decomposition. August
picked up a short length of rusted, heavy-linked logging chain
and swung it a few times experimentally before discarding it. He
put on a pair of too-large gloves and hefted a broadsword-sized
mower blade, slicing slow patterns in the air, before discarding it.
Then he uncovered a four-foot-long spanner wrench, a slim stain-
less steel handle that swelled at the end into a glistening and
deadly crescent head. He brought the head down into his glove

several times to hear the satisfying whack. He practiced a few horrendous death-dealing swing techniques—the sidearm full-swing golf follow-through, the overhead back-crushing axe strike, the short, quick, line-drive baseball check swing—the wrench head making ragged divots in the hard-packed dirt floor. He worked up a light sweat, and then shouldered his weapon, put the pair of gloves in his back pocket, and went to see his mother.

The old house was set back against a low, rock-plated hill. A year-round spring wept from the face of the rock, and the dampness of it filled the house with the smell of wet leaves and impending rain. The house was a single-level ranch, low slung like a dog crouching to avoid a kick. August's mother's parents had built the house with their own hands, and lived in it until they died. The old house looked up at the new house, the one August's father had finished the year after August was born. The new house was tall with a sharp-peaked roof. It had white shutters, a full wraparound porch. August's grandparents had both died before he was born and the first thing his father had done when the farm became his was sell fifty acres of fallow pasture and build the new house.

"He feels like it's his own," August's mother had said to him once, smoking in the kitchen of the new house. "His people didn't have much. Everything we got came from my side, you know. He would never admit it in a hundred years, but it bothers him." She coughed. "It's too big. That was my complaint from the get-go. It's hard to heat, too, exposed up on the hill like this, the wind gets in everywhere. My father would have never done it like that. He built a smart house for himself and my mother, but, that's the type of man he was."

August tapped the door a few times with the wrench and

went inside. The old house was built by folks interested in efficiency, not landscape, and the windows were few and small. The kitchen was dimly lit by a single shaft of light coming through the window over the sink. The room smelled like frying bacon, and the radio was on. Paul Harvey was extolling the virtues of a Select Comfort Sleep Number Bed. *At my age there are few things I appreciate more than a night of restful sleep. Get this mattress. It was dreamed up by a team of scientists. It's infinitely adjustable. Your dreams will thank you.*

"Augie, my fair son, how does the day find you?"

His mother was at the kitchen table playing solitaire. A pan of thinly sliced potatoes fried with pieces of bacon and onion sat next to her ashtray. She smoked Swisher Sweets cigarillos, and a thin layer of smoke was undulating above her head like a smooth, gray flying carpet waiting for a charge to transport.

"I made lunch and it smelled so good while it was cooking, but then found myself suddenly not hungry. I don't know, I may have finally broken through."

August pulled out a chair and sat across from his mother at the small table. "Broken through to what?" he said.

"Oh, I didn't tell you? I've been devoting myself to a new teaching." She stubbed out her cigarillo, and shook another from the pack sitting on the table. She lit it, a fine network of lines appearing around her mouth as she pursed her lips. Her nails were long and gray, her fingertips jaundiced with tobacco stain. "Yeah," she continued, "I've become an inediate."

"A what?"

"An inediate, you know, a breatharian?"

"I don't know what that is."

"Air eaters? Sky swallowers? Ether ingesters?"

"Nope."

"You can attune your mind and your body, Augie. Perfectly attune them by healthy living and meditation so that you completely lose the food requirement. I mean, not just that you're no longer hungry—that's not too hard. I'm talking about all you have to do is breathe the air, and you're satisfied. You get full and you never have to eat. And you can survive that way, happy as a clam." She took a sip of coffee, smoke dribbling from her nose as she swallowed. "That's what I've been working on."

She pushed the pan of potatoes and bacon toward him, and August ate some even though Lisa had told him she would make him a sandwich when she got up from the barn. The potatoes were greasy and good. The bacon in it was little pieces of semi-charred saltiness. The onions were soft, translucent, and sweet. August ate, and wiped his hands on his jeans, and put his wrench on the table for his mother to see.

"Dad gave me a job," he said. "For money."

"Oh, well I'm proud to hear it. Did you negotiate a contract? Set a salary review option pending exemplary performance?"

"No, I'm just killing some cats."

"I see. And this is your Excalibur?" She tinked the chrome-handled wrench with her fingernail.

"Yeah. It's a spanner wrench."

She made a low whistle and coughed softly into the back of her hand. "It's a big job, Augie. Is he paying you upon completion or piecemeal?"

"I'm taking the tails. We're going to settle up at the end of the week."

"Grisly work, son. That's the kind of work you stand a chance of bringing home with you, if you know what I mean."

"The haymow smells like piss. It's getting real bad."

"Your father. This is gruesome, even for him. Jesus." She looked down blankly at the cards in front of her. "I keep forgetting where I'm at with this." She gathered up her game, her nails scrabbling to pick the cards up off the Formica. "I can get only so far with solitaire before I get stumped. You ever win?"

"I never play."

"I suppose it's a game for old women."

"You're not old."

"If I'm not, then I don't want to feel what old is like."

"Are you ever going to come back to the new house?"

"You can tell him no, if you want. About the cats. You don't have to do it."

"She's been staying over."

"I found all Grandma's old quilts. They were in a trunk in the back closet. Beautiful things. She made them all. Some of them took her months. All of them hand stitched. I never had the patience. She used to make me sit there for hours with her learning the stitches. I'll show them to you if you want."

"Sure. I should get to work now, though."

"Next time, then."

August ate a few more potatoes and then stood up.

"I wish you Godspeed," his mother said, coaxing another cigarillo from the pack with her lips. "May your arrows fly true."

"I don't have any arrows."

"I know. It's just an old Indian saying."

She blew smoke at him. "I don't care about the cats," she said, smiling at him in such a way that her mouth didn't move and it was all in her eyes. "I look at you, and it's clear as day to me that he hasn't won."

———

The barn was empty. His dad and Lisa were out rounding up the cows for milking. August put on his gloves and wedged the wrench down under his belt. He climbed the wooden ladder up to the haymow.

Half-blind in the murk, holding his nose against the burning ammonia stench of cat piss, August crushed the skull of the first pale form that came sidling up to him. He got two more in quick succession—and then there was nothing but hissing from the rafters, green-gold eyes glowing and shifting among the hulking stacks of baled hay. August tried to give chase. He clambered over the bales, scratching his bare arms and filling his eyes and ears and nose with the dusty chaff of old hay. But the cats were always out of reach, darting and leaping from one stack to the next, climbing the joists to the rafters where they faded into the gloom. August imagined them up there, a seething furry mass, a foul clan of fanged wingless bats clinging to a cave roof. This was going to be harder than he had thought.

August inspected his kills. A full-sized calico and two skinny grays, thin and in bad shape, patches of bare skin showing through their matted fur. He pitched them down the hay chute and climbed after them. On ground level, he breathed deeply of the comparatively sweet manure-scented air, and fished his knife from his pocket. He picked up the first cat by the tail and severed it at the base, dropping the carcass on the cement with a wet thud. He dealt similarly with the other two cats, pitched them all in the conveyor trough, and went looking for a hammer. By the time he returned to the barn his father and Lisa had the cows driven in and stanchioned in their stalls. The radio was on, loud enough so Paul Harvey's disembodied voice could be heard over the muttering of the cows and the drone of the compressor. *I don't know about you all, but I have never seen a monument erected to a pessimist.*

August nailed his three tails to a long pine board, and propped it up in the corner of the barn where it wouldn't get knocked over by cows milling in and out. He could hear his father doing something in the milk room. He passed Lisa on his way out of the barn. She was leaning on a shovel and spitting sunflower seeds into the dirt. She had on blue overalls and muck boots, and her frizzy blond hair was tamed into a ponytail that burst through the hole in the rear of her Seedco cap.

"Hi, August," she said, scooping seeds out of her lower lip and thwacking them into the dirt at her feet. "You didn't come up to the house for lunch."

"Yeah. I ate at the old house with my mom."

"Oh, okay. I'm going to stick around tonight. I think I'll make some tacos for you guys for dinner. Sound good?"

August looked at her face, her round, constantly red cheeks. She called it rosacea, a skin condition. It made her seem to exist in a state of perpetual embarrassment. He wondered if she'd been teased about it at school.

She was only seven years older than him and had graduated from the high school last year. In her senior year August's father had hired her to help him with the milking, and she'd worked before school and after school and on weekends. August's father said that she worked harder than any hired man he'd ever had. Now that she was done with school she put in full days. She could drive a tractor with a harrow. She could muck out the barn. She could give the antibiotic shots to the cows—and when the calving season came she could plunge her hands in up to her wrists to help a difficult calf come bawling into the world.

"Crunchy shells or soft shells?" August said, knocking at the toes of his boots with the wrench.

"Soft?"

"I like crunchy."

"Well, I'll see what you guys have in the cupboards, but I bought some soft ones already."

"Flour or corn?"

"Flour, I think."

"I like corn." August spat at his feet, but his mouth was dry so the spit trailed out on his chin and he wiped at it with the back of his sleeve.

"I asked your dad what kind he wanted and he said it didn't matter."

"He likes the crunchy shells too. Trust me. Do you make them with beans or without?"

Lisa hesitated for a moment and tugged at the brim of her cap. "Which do you prefer?" she said.

"Well, that depends."

"I bought some black beans. I usually put some of those in. But I don't have to."

"I like beans. But, I don't eat black beans. I think they look like rabbit turds. My dad thinks that too."

"Okay, I'll leave those out, then. Sound good?" The red on Lisa's cheeks had spread. A crimson blush was leaching down her neck all the way to the collar of her barn overalls. "All right, August, see you at dinner. Your dad's probably wondering where I got off to. We have to get these cows taken care of."

Lisa headed into the barn, and August wandered out to the back pasture, swinging his wrench at stalks of burdock and thistle, stepping around the thick plots of fresh manure.

He climbed the low hill before the tree line on the property boundary and sat next to the pile of rocks that marked Skyler's

grave. There was a slightly bent sassafras stick with the bark whit-
tled off jutting up from the rocks. It had once been the vertical
member of a cross August had fashioned from two such sticks
lashed together with a piece of old shoelace. It was a gesture August had seen performed in all the old westerns he watched with
his father. Any time a gunslinger went down his buddies erected
a cross just like that. Over the course of the past year the sun had
rotted August's old shoelace so that the horizontal crosspiece had
fallen off, leaving just the vertical stick pointing up at the sky like
a crooked, accusatory finger.

Skyler had been his birth dog. His father had brought the
tiny six-week-old pup home when August had been out of the
hospital less than a week. It was something August's father had
said that his own father had done for him. He thought it good for
a boy to have a dog to grow up with. And, against August's
mother's objections, he put the soft, pug-faced shepherd mix in
the crib with August—"to get acquainted," he'd said. "A boy
with a dog is healthier, more active, less inclined to allergy and
listlessness." And, it seemed true. August had been a particularly
healthy baby, a bright, energetic boy who grew up with a tongue-
lolling, shaggy, good-natured four-legged shadow.

At twelve, Skyler had been in remarkably good shape, a little
stiff in the mornings, but by noon harassing the barn cats like a
dog half his age. And then, one day after school, August didn't
see him anywhere in the barn or yard. He went to the equipment
shed and found him, stretched out on his side with a greenish-
blue froth discoloring his grayed muzzle. He'd chewed through
a gallon jug of antifreeze that August's father had stored under
the workbench.

August and his father had carted the body up to the hill,
and they took turns with the pickax and shovel. When they fin-

ished, they stood and regarded the cairn of rocks they'd stacked over the raw earth to keep the skunks out.

"I guess twelve is as good an age as any," his father had said. At the time August thought he'd been talking about the dog. Later, he thought that maybe his father had meant that twelve was as good an age as any for a boy to lose a thing he loved for the first time.

August watched the sky in the west become washed in dusky, pink-tinged clouds. Unbidden, the turning sky made him think of Lisa, the crimson in her cheeks that spread like hot infection down her neck and shoulders and back and arms, all the way to her legs. That this was the case wasn't mere supposition. He'd seen it.

It was an early dismissal day last fall. August off the bus and out of his school clothes, eating a piece of cake from the new house. He wandered down to the barn, the air sharp with the acrid tang of the oak leaves his father had been burning in the front yard. The pile smoldered. There was no one around. Skyler slept in the shade of a stock tank. The cows were yoked up in their stanchions. The whole barn was full of the low rumble of suction, the automatic milkers chugging away.

And then, through the open doorway of the grain room, there was his father. Muck boots on, barn overalls around his legs, thrusting behind Lisa, who was bent over a hay bale, her cheek and forearms pressed down into the cut ends of the hay. Their overalls were around their legs like shed exoskeletons, like they were insects emerging, their conjoined bodies larval, soft and pale. August saw the flush of Lisa then, the creeping red that extended all the way down her back to her thick thighs to her spread calves. She had her underwear pulled down around one knee and their brilliant lacy pinkness was a glaring insult to the honest, flyspecked, gray and manure brown of the barn.

On his way out, August turned the barn radio up as loud as it would go. *Golf,* Paul Harvey was saying, *is a game, where you score a six, yell "fore," and write down a five.*

At the dinner table, Lisa and August's father each had a beer. Lisa cut a lime wedge and jammed it down the neck of her bottle and August's father said, what the hell, he might try it like that too. They smiled at each other and clinked their bottles together and drank, and August watched the lime wedges bobbing in their bottles like floats in a level held on a surface that was out of true. When they'd finished eating, August's father leaned back in his chair and belched mightily, wiping taco juice from his hands, his rough, callused fingers shredding the paper napkin.

"Best meal I've had in a while. Thanks, Lisa."

Lisa smiled and said, "You're welcome, Darwin. I'm glad you liked it."

"I got three cats today," August said to break up their stupid smiling competition. "I did it with a wrench. Right in the head. They never knew what happened." Out of the corner of his eye, he could see Lisa wrinkle her nose slightly.

His father finished his beer and piled his fork and knife and napkin on his plate. He was a large man, all his joints seemed too big, hard knobby wrists and knuckles, his hands darkened from the sun up until the point where his shirt cuffs lay. He was forty-five years old and still had all his hair, dark brown, just starting to gray at the temples. In the cold months, he liked to wear a bright silk cowboy scarf knotted up around his neck. He smiled at women often, and, August noticed, women often smiled back. His mother used to say that for a guy with manure on his boots he could be fairly charming.

"Come on now, Augie. I gave you a job and I appreciate you getting right down to it. But there's barn talk and there's house talk. I'm sure Lisa wouldn't mind a little house talk now. How about you clear the table and clean up the dishes. And why don't you thank Lisa for making that delicious meal? She worked all day, and then came up to do that for us."

"Thanks," August said and scooted his chair back loudly. He stacked the dishes into a precarious pile and carried them off to the kitchen. He ran the water until steam rose and squirted in soap until the bubbles grew in great tumorous mounds, and then he did the dishes. Clanking plate against plate, banging pots against pot, running the water unnecessarily, making as much noise as possible to cover the low murmur of Lisa and his father talking in the next room.

Through the kitchen window he could see the murky green cast of the yard light, the hulking form of the barn, and, farther out, the long, low shape of the old house, completely dark. When his father came in to get two more beers, August didn't turn around to look at him. He stood next to August at the sink and took the tops off the bottles. He nudged August with an elbow and August scrubbed at a pan, ignoring him.

"How's your mother?"

August shrugged.

"I'm not going to run her down, Augie, but she's not a woman that will ever give you her true mind. You know what I mean?"

August shrugged.

"She's been disappointed her whole life, probably came out

of the womb that way. You don't disappoint her, I know that. But everything else does, me included—always have always will. She never learned to hold herself accountable, that's the way her parents allowed her to grow up. She's very smart, and she thinks she sees things I don't see but she's wrong, I'll tell you that. I see plenty. You hear me?"

August swirled a cup in the dishwater and didn't say anything. His father slapped him on the back of the head.

"I said, You hear me?"

"Yeah. I hear you." August looked straight ahead out the window.

"Okay, then." He reached into the dishwater, came up with a handful of suds, and smeared them on August's cheek. "You're all right," he said. "When you think it's time you let me know and we'll go find you a pup."

In the morning, the smells of toast and coffee and bacon pulled August from his bed before the sun had even hit the east-facing window. He clumped down the stairs into the kitchen and sat at the table rubbing his eyes. Lisa stood at the stove making eggs. Her feet were bare and she had on the gray long underwear she wore under her barn overalls. They were made for men and were tight around her hips, and when she bent over to get the butter out of the refrigerator, August could see the faint lines of her panties curving across her full rear.

"Would you like coffee, August?" August nodded and she put a steaming mug in front of him.

"I figure you like it black, like your dad likes it?"

"Sure," he said, taking a sip, trying not to grimace. "Black and strong."

His mother mixed his coffee half and half with hot whole milk, dumping in heaping spoonfuls of sugar. She told him that's how she learned to make coffee when she lived in New Orleans, in another lifetime, before she married his father. August knew that Lisa would never go to New Orleans in a million lifetimes.

His father came from the bedroom. He had a dab of shaving foam under one earlobe. He put his hand on Lisa's waist as he got a coffee mug from the cupboard and she turned and wiped the shaving foam from his ear with her sleeve.

"How long before the eggs are done?" August asked, tapping his fingers on the tabletop.

"A few minutes. The bacon is almost ready."

August sighed, downed his coffee, and took a piece of toast from the plate on the counter. "Well," he said, "some of us can't sit around. I have to get to work."

He got his wrench from the mudroom, and slid on his boots, leaving them unlaced, and walked across the lawn with his boot tongues flapping like dogs breathing in the heat. The cows were milling in the pasture, gathered up close to the gate. They rolled their dumb baleful eyes at him and lowed, their udders straining and heavy with milk.

"Shut up, you idiots," August said. He picked up a small handful of pebbles and continued to walk, pelting any cow within reach.

The trees that lined the back pasture were big old oaks and maples and a few massive beech trees with low limbs and velvet gray bark. The ground around them was covered with the scattered spiny shells of their nuts. There was an ancient barbed-wire fence strung across the trees. It was rusted and had been mended many times, so old that it had become embedded in the trunks. August walked down the line and ran his fingers over the rough oaks and maples and the soft gray crepe of the beeches with their bark that looked like smooth hairless hide stretched over muscle. He let his fingers linger on the places where the wire cut into the trunks, and then he knelt and sighted all the way down the fence and squinted into the strengthening light and imagined he was looking at a row of gnarled old people, the soft skin of their necks—the throat cords, the veins, and esophagus—garroted by barbed wire, the twisted branches like arms raised, fingers splayed, trembling and clutching for air.

Until last year August had helped with the milking every morning before school and every evening after school, and then his mother forbade it and his father had been forced to hire Lisa full-time.

"Do you like helping your father with the milking?" his mother had asked one evening as he helped her clean up the dinner dishes. His father was on the porch listening to a baseball game, and the sound of the play-by-play came through the screen door, garbled and frantic. Someone had made a triple play. The announcer spit hoarsely, a *hard line drive, he's going, he's going, he's going.*

"I don't mind it too much," August said, wiping a plate dry. "Most of the time I like it."

"Huh, well, that's a problem," his mother said. She had a cigarette tucked into the corner of her mouth, and ash drifted into the dishwater as she spoke. "You'll be in high school soon, you know. And then there'll be girls. They're going to find you so handsome. And then there'll be college, and then there'll be any life you want after that. This is just a small piece, Augie—and if you hate it then you should know that soon you'll be making your own way."

"But I said I don't hate it, Mom."

"Jesus. I really hope you don't mean that. Getting up early, the shitty cows, the dullness?"

"What about it?"

"My god, Augie, look at me and tell me you don't hate it." She turned to him and held his chin with her soapy hand, and her cigarette trembled and August tried but couldn't tell if she was serious and about to cry, or joking and about to laugh.

"I don't hate anything. It's fine. I like everything fine."

"You're serious?"

"Yes."

"Then I'm disappointed in you," she said, exhaling smoke forcefully through her nose and turning back to the dishes. "But I suppose it's my fault, for letting it go on. I'm going to talk to your father. Your barn days are coming to an end. I'll finish up here. Go out and listen to the game with your dad."

Out on the porch, his father was on the rocker, his legs stretched out long in front of him. He nodded as August sat on the step.

We're going into extra innings. Hang on as we pause for station identification—you're not going to want to miss this. The radio crackled, and an ad for a used-car lot came on. Bats flew from the eaves, and August threw pebbles to make them dive, and then the game came back on and Cecil Fielder won it for the Tigers on a long sacrifice fly to center field. August looked at his father. He was slumped in the chair with his eyes closed and his hands clasped together over his chest.

"Night," August said, getting up to go inside.

His father yawned and stretched. "Night," he said.

Later, his parents' arguing had kept him awake, and the next morning his father hadn't rousted him for the morning milking—and soon after that Lisa was always around, and not long after that his mother had started spending time at the old house. At first, just a few nights a week, and then one morning she didn't come back to make breakfast and his father burned the toast and slammed the door on his way to the barn.

August tied his boots. He climbed up to the haymow and surprised two cats that had been intently pawing at a dead sparrow on the hay-littered floor. He broke one's back with a quick chop of the wrench, and stunned the other one with a jab to the head. The cats were indistinct as they writhed, blurred in the gloom. August silenced their yowling, each with a sharp blow from the wrench, and then gave chase to a few more slinking forms that eluded him by leaping to join their wailing, spitting clan in the rafters.

August didn't curse much. His father always said that no one took a man seriously who cursed too much, and it was better to be the type of man who, when he *did* curse, made everyone else sit up and take notice.

Now, however, in the dark barn with the hay dander swirling around his face, and the cats twitching and seething out of reach above him, he cursed.

"Motherfucker," he said. "Motherfucking, cocksucking, shitfaced, goddamn fucking cats."

It was the most curse words he'd ever strung together, and he hoped the cats were sitting up to take notice, trembling at the rain of fire that was about to be visited down upon their mangy heads.

At the old house his mother had the blinds drawn. She had cut a ragged hole in a quilt, pulled it over her head, and belted it around her waist, poncho style. Her arms stuck out, bare, and the quilt ends dragged over the floor when she got up to let him in. With the shades drawn, it was dark. She had lit an old kerosene lamp and the flame guttered, sending up tendrils of black smoke. She had been playing solitaire. There was a fried pork chop steaming in a pan on the table.

"You want some lunch?" she said after she had settled herself down in her chair, smoothing the quilt down under her and over her bare legs. "I'm finished. You can have the rest."

She slid the pork chop over to August. It hadn't been touched. He took a bite. It was seared crispy on the outside and juicy and tender on the inside, quick fried in butter and finished in the oven. That's how she always made pork chops. Lisa wouldn't know how to do this, he thought. His father would get so fed up with dried-out tough pork chops that he might send her away, and his mother might come back to the new house and he'd start helping his dad with the barn chores again.

"Are you still not eating?" He picked up the pork chop to gnaw at the bone where the best tasting meat always lived.

"Augie, that's a common misconception about us breatharians. I eat. Good lord, I eat all the time. Here, actually, let me have one more bite of that." She leaned over and wafted her hand around his pork chop, bringing the smell toward herself, and then took a quick, hiccupping little breath and smiled and leaned back in her seat. "Meat from an animal you know always has the best flavor," she said, lighting one of her little cigars. "That's something city people probably don't understand. You remember taking kitchen scraps out to that hog every night after dinner? You fed that animal and now it feeds you. That lends a certain something to the savor—I'm sure there's a word for it in another language."

She pulled her quilt tighter around her shoulders. "Did you

know that, Augie? That there are all sorts of words for things in other languages that we don't have in English? It's like your soul is tongue-tied when that happens, when you have a feeling or experience that you can't explain because there isn't a specific word for it. If you knew all the languages in the world, you could express yourself perfectly and all experiences would be understandable to you because you would have a word, a perfect word, to attach to any possible occasion. See what I mean?"

August wiped his greasy hands on his jeans. He was fairly certain his mother was naked under her quilt. He wondered if there was a word for that in another language. A word to classify the feeling you get sitting across from your mother, eating a pork chop, with your mother naked under a quilt.

"I don't know," he said. "Just because you have a word to put on something doesn't mean you understand it any better. Does it?"

"Oh, I think so. Definitely. I don't think things really exist until we can name them. Without names for every living thing, the world is populated by spooks and monsters."

"Just because you give something a name doesn't mean you change what it is. It's still the same thing."

"You couldn't be more wrong, Augie dear. How about death?"

"What about it?"

"What if instead of death everyone called it being born and looked forward to it as the great reward at the end of seventy or so years of slow rot on earth?"

"That doesn't make any sense. Why would anyone look forward to death?"

"Maybe you're too young for this conversation," she said, coughing into the back of her hand. "That's an interesting thought. I bet in some language there is a word for the state you exist in now—the state of being incapable of formulating concepts of, or discussing abstractly, death in all its various forms, due to a lack of experience. You need to have someone you love die, and then you get it. All the understanding of the world comes rushing in on you like a vacuum seal was broken somewhere. I'm not saying you'll ever understand why the world works the way it does, but you'll surely come to the conclusion that it does work, and that, as a result, it will absolutely someday come to a grinding halt, as nothing can work forever. See what I mean?"

"No."

"Huh. Well, in time you will. I'm sure."

She picked up her solitaire game and shuffled the cards, splitting the deck, riffling the ends together with a brisk splat, and then condensing the deck back together by making the cards bow and bridge and shush into one. August sat listening, enjoying the sound of her shuffling, thinking, knowing she was wrong. He *had* loved someone who had died.

"How's the job coming?"

"Not great."

"Motivational issues?"

"No. They're just fast. I've been thinking about a change of tactics."

"Oh, yeah?"

"I don't know if it will work. Can I borrow some bowls?"

Lisa stayed for dinner again. August sensed that his life was now split in two distinct pieces. There was the part when Skyler was alive, when his father and mother and he had all lived in the new house, and now, this new part, where things were foggy and indistinct. August twirled Lisa's spaghetti around on his fork and realized, for the very first time, that the whole of his life up until this very point existed in the past, which meant it didn't exist at all, not really. It might as well have been buried right there in the pasture next to Skyler.

It was dark and cool in the barn and he switched on the radio for company. August hadn't been able to sleep, and he'd risen early— before Lisa, even—and he hadn't had breakfast and his stomach rumbled as he climbed the wooden ladder up to the haymow. In the darkness he could see the faint pinpricks of stars through the knotholes and chinks of the barn planks, and then his groping fingers found the pull chain and the haymow was flooded with fluorescent light.

The floor was carpeted with twisted feline forms, tabbies, calicos, some night black, some pure white, intermingled and lumpy and irrevocably dead. They lay like pieces of dirty laundry where they'd fallen from their perches after the tainted milk had taken its hold on their guts. August coughed and spit, slightly awed, thinking about last night, and the way the antifreeze had turned the bluish white milk a sickly rotten green. He nudged a few of the still forms with his boot and looked to the rafters and found them empty except for one, where he spotted a calico, its dead claws stuck in the joist so it dangled there, like a shabby, moth-eaten piñata.

He pulled his shirt cuffs into his gloves against the fleas jumping everywhere, and began pitching the cats down the hay chute. As he worked the voice of Paul Harvey found its way up from the radio on the ground floor.

There's going to be unrest. There's always going to be unrest but things always get better. Tomorrow will always be better. Just think about it, is there any time in history in which you'd rather live than now? I'll leave you with that thought. I'm Paul Harvey, and now you know the rest of the story.

August climbed down the ladder and stepped shin deep into a pile of cats. He got out his jackknife and stropped it a few times against the side of his boot and set to work separating the cats from their tails. He pushed the cats into the conveyor trough as he worked and when he was done he flipped the wall switch to set the belt moving. August watched the cats ride the conveyor until all of them went out of sight under the back wall of the barn. Outside, they were falling from the track to the cart on the back of the manure spreader. He didn't go out to look but he imagined them piling up, covering the dirty straw and cow slop, a stack of forms as lifeless and soft as old fruit, furred with mold. Tomorrow or the next day his father would hook the cart up to the tractor and drive it to the back pasture to spread its strange load across the cow-pocked grass.

It took him a long time to nail the tails to the board and as he pounded the last one they were already stiffening. The sky was just starting to take on the milky light of predawn when August carried the board up to the new house. In the mudroom he stopped and listened. There was no sound of his father and Lisa in the kitchen but he knew they'd be up soon. He leaned his board against the coatrack, directly over his father's barn boots, and regarded his work as it was, totem and trophy, altogether alien against a backdrop of lilac-patterned wallpaper.

August tried to whistle as he walked across the lawn and down the hill to the old house. He'd never gotten the hang of whistling. The best he could muster was a spit-laced warble. On the porch he wiped at his lips with the back of his sleeve and looked in the window. His mother was at the kitchen table. She held a card in her hand, raised, as if she were deciding her next move but August could see that the cards in front of her were scattered across the table in disarray, a jumbled mess, as if they'd been thrown there.

EXOTICS

On the last day of class before summer vacation, his students—all fifteen of them, ranging in age from eight to sixteen—filed out the door saying their goodbyes. Before leaving, one of his sixth graders, Molly Hanchet, stopped at his desk. She had red hair and freckles and, in five years, would likely be Park County's Fourth of July rodeo queen. After that, she would go on to premed at Stanford. She had her thumbs hooked in the straps of her backpack and she said, "Have a good summer, Mr. Colson. I hope next year you feel better."

She left, and James was forced to ponder the implications. It had to be bad if a sixth-grade girl could see that he was fucked.

Carina lived in a small rental cabin on the river, set back in a grove of old cottonwoods. Once, in a windstorm, he'd lain awake, envisioning whole trees shearing off at rotten points in their trunks, branches punching through the roof, flattening him and Carina in the bed. He imagined them being found out that way.

Carina wasn't home and he sat on her front step. He was preparing to leave when her car pulled in behind him. She got out and groaned at the sight of him. "I've had a bad day," she said, "I don't know if I can handle you right now."

"Maybe I've come here to profess my undying love."

She snorted.

They did it with her bent over the small two-burner stove, her skirt up around her waist. In their frantic movements, one of them nudged a burner switch and soon the cabin was full of a strange odor. James thought for a moment that he was having some sort of olfactory response to imminent ejaculation. And then Carina was slapping him and swearing. A section of her hair had begun to curl and smoke.

He sat at the foot of the bed facing her. She was on her back inspecting the ends of her hair.

"God," she said, "what a day."

"She's moving her stuff out right now. That's partly why I'm here. I can't really go home for a while. I drove by the house, and she was loading boxes."

Carina didn't say anything. She wet her fingertips in her mouth and rubbed at a burnt end.

"Boxes. Moving, dying, breaking up. All life's great tragedies are marked by the appearance of those goddamn square cardboard units. Such an ominous shade of brown." He'd thought of this earlier today, and now it pleased him to say it. He wished she'd come to his side of the bed and put her hand on his leg. He didn't think that was asking too much.

"Fuck," Carina said. "I may have to get a haircut to fix this."

"Part of me didn't actually believe that she was going to leave. We had some serious work-it-out talks. We went camping up on the Stillwater last weekend. We sat side by side next to the campfire. She said the stars above were like a *million diamonds.* She said that. I almost asked her to marry me."

Carina was pressing her hands to her face. Her fingernails, as always, were immaculate, painted a brilliant red. Each nail was like a little cherry hard candy that James wanted to crush between his teeth.

"I'm serious," he said. "I was going to propose. And you know what? Why *can't* the stars above be like a million diamonds? And why, when she said that, did I want to tell you about it immediately?" James stopped. There was some sort of noise emerging from behind Carina's hands, both of which were now clamped over her mouth. Her fingernails were digging into her cheeks and her eyes were screwed shut. And then she rose from the bed and he could hear her retching in the bathroom.

When she emerged, her dark hair was in beautiful disarray. She was brushing her teeth, one arm crossed over her bare breasts.

Carina had come from San Francisco on a grant to teach creative writing to at-risk girls on the Crow Reservation. She was writing a book about her experiences. For someone who could be so sarcastic, downright caustic, it surprised James to see the level of earnestness with which she approached her job. She loved it. She loved the at-risk girls—a classification that, on the reservation, seemed synonymous with the general population. She approached each class day with happy anticipation. If he happened to entertain the idea of staying over on a school night, she would kick him out so she could prepare. She was a teacher and he was a teacher, but what she did was something completely different. He fully acknowledged that. She had a passion. He enjoyed the really nice sense of calm that came from having good health benefits.

She sometimes read him sections of stories or poems, written by her girls. James had to admit that some of the stuff was pretty remarkable. There was one he always remembered, the words themselves and the way Carina had read it, in bed, naked, on her stomach with her feet up in the air, her heels knocking together in time with the words. *I look at him, the boy that doesn't love me, and it's like a badger has climbed into my chest. The badger tramples my stomach while it chews on my heart.*

Carina got in bed. She continued to brush her teeth. She also started to cry.

"I'm sorry," James said. "I shouldn't have been talking about all that stuff. It's been tough for me lately and I'm—"

Carina was shaking her head, pointing at the kitchen. "Can you get me a glass to spit in?" she said, her voice garbled by toothpaste.

When he returned with the glass she spit, handed it to him, and then rolled in bed to face the wall.

"Today Ellen Yellowtail went to the bathroom and sawed through her wrists with an obsidian spearpoint from the early Clovis era. She asked to be excused and was gone for twenty minutes, and I had a weird feeling and I went into the bathroom and there was blood under one of the stall doors and she was in there. James, she was still kind of moving around, slowly, in a pool of her own blood. She was making, like, fish movements or something. Trying to swim through the floor. That will never go away.

I will have that forever. And then, on the way home today, I literally caught myself thinking, for a split second, *Damn you, Ellen, you little bitch. Do you have any idea what kind of thing you have just lodged in my brain?* Can you believe that? What kind of person thinks that in response to something like this?

James was still holding the glass with Carina's toothpaste spit in it. "Jesus Christ," he said. "An obsidian spearpoint? The Clovis era?"

"In science class, they were having a prehistoric unit. Apparently, there was a guest speaker from Montana State who brought visual aids. Ellen pocketed it at some point when no one was looking. Last week I asked them to write me a paragraph about some of their writing goals for the summer. She wrote that she had gotten a job at the Dairy Queen and that she was going to carry a little notebook in her waitress apron so she could just jot down observations about all the interesting people she would see. That's how she put it. She was going to observe and *jot things down*. No one who *jots things down* kills themselves."

James got in bed and put his arms around her. He'd come to tell her that he was leaving. It seemed rather impossible now—the telling, not the leaving.

In the morning, Carina still sleeping, he pointed the car south. It was green-up, the best time to be driving through the great swaths of western grassland. Crossing Wyoming was like riding a fresh swell of chlorophyll. He pushed his way into Colorado until he hit the front range traffic on I 25 and then he got a room and ate a bad meal and watched sports highlights before surrendering to the pull of stiff hotel sheets.

He was up early, an egg sandwich and coffee to go. Past

Denver, the traffic eased and the land flattened. It was still Colorado, but it could have been anywhere. Eventually he broke out and covered the skinny Oklahoma panhandle in about the time it took to listen to a full Townes Van Zandt album. And then—just as the sun cracked itself down on the vast, oil pump–studded plain that stretched around as far as he could see—James crossed over into Texas.

His brother lived in a maze of culs-de-sac and identical two-story homes with two-car garages. The streets were named after trees or Ivy League colleges. James imagined that if you lined up all the kids and golden retrievers of the neighborhood on the sidewalk, they, too, would prove indistinguishable.

Casey's wife, Linda, met him at the door. She was big and brassy and blond. James had seen her in a bikini once, and she had the Lone Star of Texas tattooed on the small of her back. She pressed a beer into his hand and led him into the study, where, predictably, Casey had deigned to remain instead of coming out to meet James. Like Don Corleone, he had always enjoyed *receiving* visitors, especially family members, as opposed to just greeting them, like a normal person.

Casey was sitting at his desk, shuffling some papers. He looked up, surprised, as if he hadn't known James was there, as if he hadn't heard him talking to his wife in the kitchen. He stood, they shook hands, and then Casey pulled him into an awkward hug, both of them leaning over the expanse of desktop between them.

They hadn't seen each other in almost a year, and they launched into all the usual topics—last year's presidential election, weather as of late, the state of the MSU men's basketball

program, their respective health, their mother's continued de-
scent into Jesus-tinctured battiness.

Linda brought them sandwiches and more beer. When she
put the plates down in front of them they each got a smile, a
"there ya go" and a personalized heartwarming southern term of
endearment. He got "honey" and Casey got "darlin'."

"Damn it, Casey," James said while Linda was still within
earshot, "why is your wife such a horrible nag?"

"Oh, you stop," she said. "Ya'll are too bad. Ya'll holler if
you need anything." And then she went back to the living room
to watch TV.

James had read somewhere that a study done of three thousand American couples found that those engaged in traditional
gender roles—male breadwinner, female homemaker—were 50
percent happier than couples who comported themselves less
conventionally. He thought about mentioning this to Casey, but
decided against it. In general his brother was not a man who
needed validation that his ways were correct.

Casey got up and closed the door to his study. He poured
two glasses of whiskey from a decanter on the sideboard and gave
one to James gravely before settling back into his chair. James
knew he was loving this. Casey leaned back and sipped his whiskey.

"Well," he said. "What's the deal? You having a bit of trouble?"

Casey was a lawyer. One of the most unsatisfying parts of his
life, as far as James could tell, was how infrequently his family
members needed legal counsel. It was endearing how ready he
was to spring into action, to roll up his sleeves and get litigious to
preserve the family honor. "Going to Billings to get a new muf-
fler put on your car, you say? Well if you get in any trouble over

there you call me, understand?" At some point, James realized he might have to get himself incarcerated, just to make Casey feel needed.

"It's not really a legal matter," he said. "Affairs of the heart and all that." Casey shrugged, disappointed. Somehow, most of his whiskey was already gone. "Hell, I don't know, Casey. I just needed a change of scenery. Do you mind if I loaf around for a little bit?"

"My *casa es tu casa*, brother, you know that."

"*Gracias, amigo*. Let's drink more of your fancy whiskey." James watched Casey pour them both more bourbon, man-sized slugs this time, and he thought that Casey seemed more at home here in his den, with his wrinkle-resistant khakis and his big-haired wife in the next room, than any man had a right to be. If it were anyone other than his brother, he might have hated him for it.

They reached across the desk and touched glasses. "Nice to see you, brother," Casey said.

"It is," James said.

Casey leaned back and kicked his feet up on the desk. He wore fleece-lined moccasins.

"Nice slippers."

"They aren't slippers. They're house shoes."

"What's the difference?"

"The sole on these is slightly more rugged, I believe. One could feasibly spend a short amount of time out of doors with them. Linda got them for me for Christmas. She's been making baby noises."

"What do those sound like?"

" 'Casey, honey, my ovaries are speaking to you right now. They're parched. They're starting to wither. Are you going to fertilize this garden or what, boy?' "

"She says that?"

"And worse. Much worse. That's the version generally fit for public consumption."

"You might as well just do it. What's there to wait for? You're rich. You could support a small tribe."

"A boy wouldn't be too bad. I'd like that, actually. But a girl, I don't know if I could take it. And this isn't something I can talk to Linda about very well."

"What's wrong with having a girl? Girls love their daddies. You wouldn't have to fight with her like you would a boy. Linda would get to have all the awkward talks."

Casey took a drink of his whiskey and swished it audibly around in his mouth. He swallowed and grimaced. "One time I was involved with a gal that liked me to put my hand around her throat and squeeze. I mean, she liked me to choke her, James. Now, can you tell me what happens to make a little girl grow up to become a woman who wants something like that?"

James laughed and then he saw that Casey was serious. "I'm not sure," he said. "But, how'd you handle that situation? I mean, did you, you know?" James made a gripping motion with his hand.

Casey shook his head. He drank the rest of his whiskey and set the glass down carefully on a coaster shaped like a bass.

"Shit, man, I did more than that. I married her."

It was mid-June, and North Texas was a smoking hot plate. In the cotton fields outside of town, farmers were doing something to raise the dust. There was nothing to see and you couldn't see it if there was.

In the late evening James sat on the back porch drinking a beer, half-reading a newspaper, sweat dampening the pages. He watched the sun turn red as it sunk through the dust. The houses and roofs and backyards of the neighborhood were cast in a blood-dusk glow. A martian suburb awash with the smell of a thousand barbecues being lit.

James finished his beer and finally, mercifully, it was dark. A few degrees cooler, maybe. There were fireflies blinking on and off in the yard. He hadn't seen a firefly in a long time. There were none in Montana as far as he knew. Maybe it was too cold. Years ago, he'd been camped next to an old hippie couple in Yellowstone and they'd told him that once, in Iowa, they'd dropped acid and went out and gathered a whole jar of fireflies and then rubbed them all over their naked bodies and then had luminescent sex in a moonlit cornfield. Their obvious happiness at relaying this story gave him a shiver. He saw in them all the couples of the world for whom the past held more promise than any potential future. Relationships based largely on reminiscence of things come and gone. Was this what it meant to be rested, content, settled in love? Or, were the old hippies, and all others like them, just wound-up machines, running on memories? Was it inevitable?

After a week of loafing at Casey's, the dust and feedlot smell of Amarillo started to wear on him. Casey worked long hours at his office. Being in the house all day with Linda—she did yoga in the living room, she constantly wanted to feed him sandwiches—was making James uncomfortable. The probing questions from Casey at the dinner table made him feel like an underachieving son, stalled out after college, living in his old bedroom.

James found himself a job. An unlikely one at that. It was a ranch-hand position at an outfit outside of Austin, in the hill country. The job description in the classifieds was spare.

WANTED:

SEASONAL RANCH LABORER.

NO EXPERIENCE NECESSARY.

BEAUTIFUL LOCATION. REMOTE. HARD WORK. FAIR PAY.

James called. He talked to a man who occasionally let out clipped groans, as if he were in pain. Their brief conversation was punctuated several times by loud birdcalls. In less than fifteen minutes, he was hired. He had two days before he was to start and he'd forgotten to ask about pay.

When James left Amarillo, Casey shook his hand and wished him luck, as if he were shipping off to basic training. Linda gave him a hairspray-scented hug. "Y'all take care now, darlin'," she said.

He pointed his car south into the fiery bowels of the Summertime Republic of Texas.

Outside of Austin, the land began to show some contour. The pure flat of the north gave way to wrinkled hills and canyons with cream-colored limestone walls. He was pleasantly surprised. He'd never known Texas to look like this. He admired the swells of oak-covered ridges, the white caliche ranch roads, glowing under the sun.

Two hours and several wrong turns later, he pulled up to a low ranch house tucked under a grove of pecan trees. There was a small pond and a windmill. A red heeler with a gray muzzle came out from under the shade of a parked truck and eyed him without approaching. Peacocks scratched in the gravel, bottle-green feathers resplendent. James stretched and looked around. His shirt was stuck to his back with sweat.

A man came out of the house. He wore a straw hat and had a cast on one of his legs—ankle to mid-thigh. The leg without a cast was jean-clad and it took James a moment to figure out that the man had apparently taken a pair of his Levis and cut one leg off three-quarters of the way up. He'd put a double-wrap of duct tape around the shortened pant leg to keep it snugged down over the cast. On the foot with the cast, the man wore a large rubber galosh. On the uninjured foot, he had a cowboy boot. Some folks with a full leg cast in Texas in late June probably just wore shorts. This man was obviously cut from a more rugged cloth.

"You James?"

"Yessir."

"That's good. I'm Karl. We've talked. Montana, eh?"

"Yes."

"I been there once. Saw Old Faithful. It could have been worse. Montana's better than a lot of places. But, you know what they say?"

James thought about telling Karl that Old Faithful was actually in Wyoming. He didn't. "What do they say?"

"In Montana, they make cowboys. In Texas, they make men." Karl laughed and wiped at the sweat on his face with his shirtsleeve. "Montana, I got a broken leg here." He pointed at the offending member. "Usually I do everything here myself but as you can imagine, this has got me limited. How's your back?"

"My back is fine."

"That's good. We're going to be working. You're going to be working mostly. I'm going to be telling you what to do. There's where you'll bunk. Everything you need should be there." Karl pointed to a low-ceilinged wing built off the side of the barn. "Stow your gear and then come on back and I'll give you a tour."

The bunkhouse was more pleasant than James had expected. There was a double bed. A small kitchenette. A table with a bouquet of dried flowers. Most important, an air conditioner. James cranked it up and tossed his single bag on the bed. The back window looked out over the pond where the heeler was standing up to its belly in the water, panting. James looked in the small fridge. There were two cans of Tecate and a jar of peanut butter. He'd had a refrigerator just like this in his dorm in college. The sight of this one made him indescribably happy.

When James emerged from his room, Karl was sitting behind the wheel of an off-road vehicle, kind of like a golf cart but with large knobby tires, a camouflaged awning, and a rifle rack on the hood. There was a cooler in the back, and as James slid into the passenger seat, Karl reached around and rummaged in the ice pulling out a beer for each of them. He drank deeply and belched.

"You said on the phone the other day that you're a teacher?"

"Yes."

"What subject do you teach?"

"Everything, pretty much."

"What, like kindergarten?"

"No, I actually teach in a one-room schoolhouse. I have around fifteen kids."

"A one-room schoolhouse? They still have those? Jesus, employment offers weren't exactly flooding your mailbox, or what?"

James laughed. "It was actually a competitive position. People *want* their kids to go to Pine Creek School. It's selective. We have to turn students down every year. It's a *unique learning environment* and we consistently get high test scores. We have brochures. That's what they say."

"I see." Karl drank and then released the parking break on

the golf cart. "It's a yuppie one-room schoolhouse, not a real one-room schoolhouse. I'm sure the pay is better. Anyway. It don't matter because your ass is mine for the rest of the summer. Let's get you acquainted with the lay of the land."

They embarked upon a rambling tour of the two-thousand-acre Echo Canyon Ranch, stopping frequently so Karl could lever himself out of the driver's seat to take a piss. Occasionally, deer bolted out in front of them. Once James saw something larger and darker moving off into the brush and then it was gone.

"What happened to your leg?" James asked.

Karl laughed. "Buffalo fell on me," he said.

Then the beer cooler ran dry. Karl, reaching and coming up empty, said, "Well, shit."

Sooner than James would have thought possible they were back in front of the house. "There you have it, Montana, what'd you think?" Karl said.

James could hear the clank of the windmill turning lazily. The red dog came and put its muzzle on Karl's broken leg. "It's great," he said.

"Likely as not you've noticed that we haven't got so much as a milk cow on the whole spread."

"I thought maybe they were in a different pasture or something."

"Nope. Closest thing we've got is a few buffalo. Nasty things. Stay clear. They'd just as soon gore you as look at you. Same with the elk. Even the females. Especially the females. They'll kick you through a barn door."

"Elk?"

"Sure. This is a hunting ranch, son. We've got all the exotics. Aoudads. Sitka deer. Feral hogs, New Zealand red deer. Elk.

A few different kinds of antelope. There's things out there that I can't even name off the top of my head. I was driving down to Bandera the other evening, and coming up out of the riverbed I saw this animal almost the size of a horse. It had corkscrew-looking horns, spots on the rear half of its body. Now what the hell was that? I have no idea. Who knows where it came from and who knows how long it's been running? All I know is that there's a dentist in Dallas who would pull his own eyeteeth to have that thing's head hanging on his wall. That's what we do here. It's what all the ranches around here do. Been that way for a long time and that's why you'll occasionally see a random like that."

"What do you mean, 'a random'?"

"Just like it sounds. Some animal that was released at one time to be hunted but that just never got killed and was forgotten about or jumped a fence, or whatever. Ranches sell all the time. Fences fall over. Inventory is hard to keep track of. The hill country's full of loose exotics. You've seen the brush. You can't get much more than a few steps off a road and it just swallows you. The African species especially seem to find it just like home."

James was slightly disappointed. He'd been under the impression that he was going to be out mending fences. Rounding up doggies and slapping hot iron to calves.

"What exactly, then, will I be doing?"

"Oh, we'll keep you occupied. At least once a week we have to go around and fill the feeders with shelled corn. That takes a full day. There's over forty of them on the property. Some fences might need shoring up. Some brush might need to be cleared out to keep the shooting lanes open. Like I said, I usually do it all myself but it's just a little bit much right now for this ol' boy."

James got his own four-wheel-drive golf cart. One of the perks of the job. He filled a gallon jug with water, and set out to explore more on his own. Karl said the pain pills he was on were making him woozy and he was going to take a nap.

James started noticing the feeders. They were metal tripods with a hopper operated by some sort of timing device. At a set time each day a measured amount of shelled corn would fall from the hopper to the ground. The feeders were placed in small clearings hacked from the brush. Twenty yards from each feeder, in a lane cut through the trees, was a blind—a small, tin-roofed camouflage-painted shack with low windows from which a rifle could be fired. James went to one of these blinds and opened the door. Inside was an office chair and a pair of ear-protecting headphones.

An *office chair*—with adjustable lumbar support and rollers and pneumatic suspension system. It was the seat every accountant in the world sat in all day. It seemed strange to think that that same accountant might get a day off and come down here to Echo Canyon Ranch to sit in that same chair some more, listening to the rhythmic clunk of the feeder hopper opening, the musical shower of corn falling to the leaf litter. Waiting with anticipation for something, anything, to present itself for killing.

All the blinds were numbered. The two-track roads were like fairways claimed from the mesquite and shin oak and cedar. James felt that he'd landed on some sort of morbid golf course, where, instead of clubs, the camouflaged hackers toted .30-06s and tallied their day's end score, factoring in missed-shot bogies, sand trap woundings, extra clip mulligans—counting pars and birdies and eagles in hides and horns and tusks.

"Fore," James shouted.

His voice was swallowed immediately by the tangle of dense

green that surrounded him. Echo Canyon was kind of a mis-
nomer.

That night his air conditioner melted down. He woke in the early
hours, his bed sheet drenched in sweat. There was the god-awful
squealing of the hogs rooting in the brush behind the barn. He
lay in the dark, thinking about a conversation he'd once had with
Carina. She had called him on his lunch break at school to tell
him that he didn't value his own profession, and this made him
unattractive to her.

"You have disdain for those who teach," she said. "And yet
you do it yourself. That must be exhausting."

"Why do you say that?"

"Because, when we first met, when you told me you were a
teacher, and I said that's great, you said, 'You know what they
say, those who *can't,* teach.' That's a bullshit philosophy. And if
you truly feel that way then you should quit teaching immediately before you infect any more students."

"You called just to tell me this?"

"Yes, I thought you should know."

James tried to imagine Molly Hanchet, his red-haired sixth-
grader, smuggling a scalpel from their dissection unit into the
bathroom and opening her veins. He imagined finding her, the
red of her blood shaming the red of her hair. He tried to imagine
returning to the classroom the next day, all the days after, and it
was here that his imagination failed completely. He didn't know
much about Carina's childhood but he knew enough to realize
that she had once been an at-risk girl. Her resilience and dedication seemed to stem from some deep-seated need to save an earlier version of herself. Could he fairly fault himself for lacking this

dimension of commitment? Did one's vocation need to be so deeply personal?

He got up and banged on the AC with his boot heel. It clanked to life slowly. Out behind the barn, there was a vicious cacophony of squealing and grunting and thrashing and then it was silent. Clearly it was going to be a long night, the mind chasing the heart in circles around the moon.

The days passed. True to his word, Karl kept James moderately busy. But, it was pleasant work, at a stately pace. Lots of golf cart driving, and standing around discussing strategy before anything was actually done. James patched a few fences. He cut and cleared some brush. He filled the feeders, hauling sacks of corn, winching the hoppers down to the ground, smelling that good midwestern smell as the golden stream poured forth from the tipped bag. On weekend evenings he and Karl would load up in the truck and head to Bandera, the nearest town, for beers and a hamburger. As far as James could tell, Bandera was not populated by a single attractive female between the ages of eighteen and forty-five. This relaxed him in a way that he, up until this point, had thought impossible.

He called Casey to update him on ranch life. After listening for a while Casey said, "Hey, while I got you on the phone, I wanted to ask you for something."

"What?"

"Your life, basically. I want your life."

"Like, you want to sacrifice me for something, or you need a heart transplant, or—?"

"I just want to take off when I want to and go live on a ranch and mend fences and screw around with strange women and drink beer."

James laughed. "Don't tempt me, brother. I'd take your place in a heartbeat. Wear your house slippers. Drink your fancy whiskey. Enjoy your bank account. Choke your wife." There was silence on the line for a moment.

Casey cleared his throat. "Please never mention that again."

"You're right. Sorry."

"Seriously, though, James. Never change. For the sake of all of us sad bastards who need to live vicariously through you, never stop what you're doing."

James knew what his brother needed. He gave it to him. He said, "I have a feeling that all this will be decidedly less thrilling when I'm fifty. You ever think of that? Because I do, all the time. I worry that I'll be doing all the same stuff, just none of it will be quite as good as it used to be. There'll still be strange women but most of the time I won't be able to get it up anyway. I'll still have my freedom but I'll be too tired to go anywhere, and I'll probably start to accumulate cats and when I finally ride the big one, sitting alone in my recliner in front of the TV, no one will find me for three weeks and the cats will have eaten most of my face. So, there. Stop your bitching. You're living the dream."

Casey didn't say anything for a few moments. James could hear the rhythmic clicking of a pen.

"You remember Linda's ovaries?"

"How could I forget?"

"Well, we've been walking the tightrope with no safety net for a while. Flying with no parachutes. Rafting with no life jackets."

"What in the hell are you talking about?"

"We agreed that Linda should go off birth control and just see what happens."

"And?"

"We're knocked up over here in Amarillo."

"Oh, man. Congratulations. Tell Linda I love her. That's great."

"I still don't know if I'm ready for it all, but I guess it's too late. We are about to go shopping for stuff to make one of the spare bedrooms a nursery. Lord help me."

James could hear the happiness in his brother's voice, and felt a small twinge. It stopped short of jealousy. But *just* short.

There was a rainy day. A small miracle. The air was thick and humid and it was still hot but the dust lay down. James and Karl pulled the golf carts into the barn and did some maintenance. James had never been mechanically minded and Karl was having a good time exposing his ignorance. "Hand me that oil filter wrench there, Montana. No, I said the oil filter wrench. No, the *oil filter wrench*."

"Karl, I don't know what that is."

"Goddamn, son, are you serious? You've never changed your own oil? The decline of a once great nation. Evidence."

Later, James drove up to the hill where he was able to get spotty cellphone reception. He had one voice message from Carina. "Call me *immediately*." This was how she always left him messages. No one else he knew did this and it always drove him to think the worst, that she had been involved in an accident of some kind or that she needed him to bail her out of jail or that she was pregnant. There was something about Carina that placed all of these things firmly in the realm of possibility. But, up until this point it had always been something benign, something like, she had just heard an NPR program about life on the Wind River reservation that she thought was horribly off base and she wanted to discuss it with him.

He wasn't sure he was ready to talk to her. He'd called her only once since leaving, and he'd kept it vague. He'd told her he was going to visit his brother, and that was it. His life at the ranch was simple, unexamined, not something she'd understand. He could picture the conversation, trying to defend himself in the face of her incredulousness. *You're filling deer feeders with corn? Are you serious?* Everything unraveling under her scrutiny. She would accuse him of trying to hide. "My god," she had said to him once. "Am I the first adult woman you've ever had to deal with?" They were parked in his car on the hill overlooking town. This was when they were still stealing moments wherever they could.

"What is that supposed to mean?"

"Just that you seem incapable of taking anything seriously. Is that how *she* likes you to be? Or, is it just a coping mechanism you've developed in order to endure swimming in a pond that shallow?"

"Shallow ponds are the best for swimming. They warm up the quickest. And you can always touch the bottom if you get tired." She looked at him for a long moment. Shook her head. Got out of his car and into hers.

He figured that she had probably never been swimming in a pond her whole life. He could see her as a child, in the summer, running wild through the concrete heat of whatever hellhole she'd grown up in, the busy city pool her only escape. After that, how could she help it if her aura was clear-blue California chlorine?

He sat for a while watching the rain dapple the truck windshield. Then, he drove back to the bunkhouse and stripped, running through the rain, to dive into the spring pond. He kicked down until his outstretched feet had felt the muck bottom, and then he turned and drifted slowly back to the surface, opening his eyes to see the raindrop-pocked roof of water above him. He floated for a while on his back trying to evaluate his level of enthusiasm for the return home. A new school year at Pine Creek. Anxious parents. Lesson plans. His classroom had two long bulletin boards that would need to be rehung with inspirational quotes and motivational posters. These bulletin boards had become nightmare fodder. In one memorable dream his posters had somehow morphed overnight, so that, on the first morning of school, the children were greeted by walls plastered with profanity-laced diatribes and pornographic pictures. He woke up soon after his firing.

He toweled off and sat at the small table in the bunkhouse. *Call me immediately.* Maybe he'd write her a letter.

Somehow, it was mid-August. There was more activity on the ranch than there had been all summer. Housekeepers came to air out the guest cabins. Men in camouflage shirts with binoculars around their necks patrolled on golf carts. Hunting season was approaching. The actual owner of the ranch came from Austin for the day. He was a big, white-toothed, red-nosed man who didn't have much to say to James but immediately fell to back slapping and exchanging barely coherent Texas good ol' boy insults with Karl. They loaded a cooler with beer and departed on a golf cart and were gone for the rest of the day. Apparently he'd made his money mostly in real estate. Probably a little oil revenue there on the top, like salad dressing.

To James, it was fairly clear that men of certain standing in Texas needed to own ranches. They needed to have a man like Karl on the payroll. It's what separated them from the citified businessmen on the coasts. During the week they might sell and trade commodities but on the weekends they were ranchers, desperately. How else to justify their existence, if not by holding themselves to a moral code developed in large part from watching John Wayne movies as boys?

James gassed up his golf cart and took one last long evening drive. The summer was all but spent. He had a six-pack on ice and he drove slowly on his favorite two-track, the brush gathering evening shadow on either side of him until he broke out on the hilltop overlooking the ranch. He was going to watch the sunset, and tomorrow he was going to leave. He was surprised to find that he would miss Echo Canyon. He really would. He hadn't been to town in a week. Hadn't bought anything. Hadn't had lust-filled thoughts toward a strange woman, hadn't had a hangover, or a fast-food meal. It was amazing how these things could accumulate in your system, like toxic heavy metals, without you realizing it.

He drank his beer and watched the deer that were coming out of the trees to the feeder near the hill's summit. He leaned back and propped his feet on the golf cart's dash. A flock of mourning doves came and settled in the grass, close enough that he could hear their chortling love warbles to one another. He noticed the deer at the feeder were looking back over their shoulders to the tree line. And then, a zebra poked its black-and-white striped head out of the brush and made its way slowly across the clearing as the sun set.

A *zebra*. It joined the deer at the feeder. The sinking sun burnished its flanks so it glowed like polished variegated copper. The deer were sad dead leaves next to its majesty.

He sat stunned, didn't want to move, but then it was dark and the mosquitos came out in full force. He turned on the golf cart's headlights and caught the zebra, its eyes like huge white marbles, before it disappeared. He drove slowly back to the bunkhouse, straining for just one more look, but it was gone.

Karl was on his porch scratching the red heeler behind the ears. James pulled up a chair and sat. "Well," he said. "I just saw a random."

"Yeah?"

"A zebra."

Karl straightened. "You're shitting me."

James shook his head. "No shit."

"Huh. I'll be damned. We got a crew of hunters coming in from Fort Worth next weekend. That would be a hell of a way to kick the season off. Those ol' boys would lose their minds over something like that."

"You'd really let them shoot it?"

"Sure, what the hell else would you do with it?"

"I don't know. Just doesn't seem right."

Karl shook his head, crushed his empty beer can in his fist. "I know what you're getting at, and you're off base. That thing you saw wasn't a zebra."

"No. It was a zebra. I'm sure of it."

"Nope. Zebras are in Africa. That's the only place. A zebra anywhere else in the world ain't a zebra. See what I mean?"

"Not really."

Karl gave an exasperated sigh. "You set these Fort Worth

boys down in Africa and let them unload on a zebra, and then maybe I can see your point. That's not something they're worthy of. But here, in Texas? A Texas man is worthy of anything in Texas. That's how I feel."

"Karl, I was thinking, what if I stayed on through the fall?"

"What about your one-room schoolhouse and all that?"

James shrugged. "They'd find a replacement for me quickly enough."

"What's that supposed to mean?"

"Haven't you ever wanted to be indispensible?"

"Shit. Indispensible don't exist. God's a junk man and he's got spare parts to replace everything he's ever made."

"What if you have a family, children? My brother's wife is pregnant. No matter what happens, that kid will never have another real father."

"All sorts of ingrates reproduce. There's nothing sacred about it."

"I guess," James said. "But, I'm serious, if I called and told them I wasn't coming back to teach, would you let me stay on through the fall?"

Karl was using a straightened metal coat hanger to scratch under his cast. "I'm supposed to get this damn thing cut off in a week," he said. "I'm tempted to go get a hacksaw and do the job myself." He stopped scratching and leaned back. "Montana, why do you think men come here? The thrill of the hunt and all that? Bullshit. In olden times, when you were sick, you went to the doctor and he vented your blood to release the bad humors. I've seen men cry. Grown men with tears on their cheeks confronting the mangy old buffalo they've just shot. Tears of joy, mind you." Karl waved his hand as if to encompass the yard, the ranch, Texas as a whole. "You're here for the same reason as those Fort Worth boys. Even if you try to hide it behind something else. And, I'm going to do you a favor here and tell you what I tell all of them when they get a little drunk on the last day of their vacation and start in about how they want to come down here and buy a little ranch and *just leave it all behind.* Do you know what they say in the bar at closing time?"

"What do they say?"

"You don't have to go home but you can't stay here."

James packed his things, and then stretched out on the bed. In a few days he would walk back into his house, his life. It would be stuffy after the summer's vacancy. Her things would be gone— gaping holes in the closets where her clothes had been, the empty place in the toothbrush holder like an unblinking vacant eye. He felt like he deserved a better homecoming. Maybe he'd go to Carina's first. They could sit outside in the grass under the cottonwoods. She would tell him about her summer school girls and he'd describe Echo Canyon Ranch in ways that made it all seem more spectacular than it really was. He wanted to tell her about the zebra. It was very important that he do it in such a way that she wouldn't dream of laughing.

It was out there, the zebra, somewhere, moving through the sticky darkness. He imagined what the land would look like if you could somehow strip away all the brush—the mesquite and the cedars and the prickly pear and the madrones—to expose the animals. All the randoms. It would be like a goddamn menagerie.

Maybe there was a lion. If there was a zebra then it seemed like anything was possible. He hoped so.

If all was right in the world, there was a lion out there right now stalking the hills, eating deer and hogs to pass the time, but really hunting the zebra. Eventually the two would cross each other in the brush. The zebra would run, gratefully, and the lion would chase, and, ultimately, under the low shade of a live oak, the lion would feast on the zebra's flesh before either one of them had to suffer one more indignity.

SUN DANCE

Rand spent whole afternoons sitting in his trailer, head in his hands, blueprints in rolls on the tables around him, the water cooler giving an occasional gurgle. Sometimes a shadow crossed the sun, flocks of starlings, coming down to perch, chattering in the trees.

It was early spring. When the ice had come off enough, he took his boat up to the Bighorn reservoir. He'd always liked fishing but now he had a hard time concentrating on it. After a while, he stopped bringing a rod. He'd pack a sandwich, a thermos of coffee, and a six-pack of beer. He'd fill an extra gas tank and run upstream against the placid flow of the river, hugging the soaring canyon walls, hearing nothing but the drone of the outboard.

When it was time for lunch, he'd nose the boat into a side canyon and tie off in the lee of a boulder to get out of the wind. After the constant noise of the motor his ears would taste the strange silence of the canyon, and Rand would feel for a moment that there had been a reprieve. He would sit perfectly still until something broke the silence—the boat rubbing against the rock, the croak of a passing raven, a fish jumping somewhere out across the lake—and then the spell was shattered and he'd unpack his sandwich and drink his beer. He'd stare at the wild striations of the sandstone canyon walls and invent lives for the four men he'd killed.

The crew leader's name was Angel. He spoke perfect English. As was usually the case, he'd hired his cousins and brothers to work for him. They did block, concrete flatwork, and stone masonry. Rand had been using Angel's crew for a few years. Always on time and dependable. He'd never found fault with their work. On the news there'd been a story about a contractor in New Jersey who'd gotten fourteen months in jail for hiring illegals to build a Wal-mart. There were sex offenders who got less time than that. If a man wanted to work, let him work.

Official company policy was that he needed a copy of a driver's license from any laborer on his job site. Some of the licenses they came in with looked like they'd been printed off at Kinko's. Rand would laugh and shake his head on the way to the copy machine. The guys would leave the trailer grateful. A man who was appreciative of his job made the best worker. Rand had figured that out a long time ago. And, everyone knew that the Mexicans were the best bricklayers around. Theirs was a country whose history could be sketched out in the transition from stacked stone to adobe brick to rebar-enforced concrete block.

The weather that fall had been unusually bad—a foot of snow on the ground on Halloween day. By Thanksgiving, they were over a week behind schedule. It was a residential job, a huge stone-and-timber ski chalet–style house in the Yellowstone Club

Ski Resort development complex. The owner was some sort of tech genius. He'd made a fortune creating apps. Rand was peripherally aware of what an app was. The guy wanted to be in the house by New Year's, in time for his annual ski vacation. The place had a private lift line running up the mountain from the garage. Rand was pushing, paying out more overtime than he would have liked. Then Thanksgiving hit. The thought of the project being stalled for one whole day at this stage set his teeth on edge. Angel's crew was in the process of building the large stone pillars that offset the main entrance, one of the final touches to be completed on the home's exterior. He was supposed to give the owner's representative a walk-through soon. If they could get the pillars done, Rand thought that the whole endeavor would have a more finished feel, despite the fact that the interior was still a mess of raw walls and floors and wires spewing from the Sheetrock.

On Thursday, none of the other guys were going to be working. If there was one thing Rand had learned in his years on job sites it was that you couldn't fuck with Thanksgiving. There was the holy trinity of football, food, and booze to contend with. The electricians and plumbers and finish carpenters had knocked it off early on Wednesday afternoon. It was bitterly cold and supposed to only get worse. The next day was forecasted to reach zero degrees for a high. Rand sat in the job trailer all afternoon looking out the window at the house, those damn unfinished pillars. Angel and his crew had the stone worked up about halfway but there were at least two more full days of work to be done.

The more Rand sat and looked at the pillars, the more he knew they needed to be completed before the walk-through. He went out to talk to Angel.

———

The masons were gathering their tools. Their big diesel was already running in the parking lot. The sky over the Spanish Peaks was going a washed-out pastel pink. He stood under the scaffolding, hands jammed into his pockets, waiting for Angel to finish what he was doing and climb down.

Mexicans didn't celebrate Thanksgiving anyway. He figured it wouldn't be a big deal—that they'd want to work. They always wanted to work.

As it turned out, they didn't want to work.

"I already told my guys to take the day off," Angel said. "Sorry."

Rand sighed and spit into the snow. "Shit, man. I was really hoping you would be able to make some headway on this thing tomorrow."

Angel shrugged. "Gonna be too cold anyway. We should have heaters as it is. The mud isn't setting up right."

"I'd consider it a big favor if you'd come in tomorrow. I've got a walk-through coming up. These pillars. If they're done the whole thing looks more done, you know what I mean?"

Angel shrugged again, he was gathering an extension cord, wrapping it in loose coils around his arm from hand to elbow. "Sorry, man. The guys already have plans. No one else is working anyway, right?"

"I'll be here."

Angel smiled. He was missing a canine, and Rand could see the pink mollusk of his tongue through the gap. "But, you're the boss," he said. "No days off for the general."

"Okay," Rand said. "Sure." He kicked a little at a chunk of snow. "I understand." He started to walk away and then stopped. He cleared his throat. "Hey," he said. "There's another thing that has recently come to my attention. Now, I just want to say that this is coming from the higher-ups, my boss, you know? I'm getting some pressure to verify that everyone on my job site is legal. I'm not implying anything. I'm just saying it could be an issue. Get me?"

Angel was still smiling. "I was born in San Antonio," he said, squinting a little.

"Sure. I know that." Rand nodded toward Angel's crew, up on the scaffolding gathering their tools. "I don't know about them, though. And, up until this point, it hasn't mattered. I'm just saying that might change."

Angel nodded slowly. "And if we come in to work tomorrow?"

"I don't foresee any problems. Can I count on you?"

Angel's smile tightened. "Heaters," he said.

"I'll get them set up tonight, personally."

Angel shouted up to his men, and Rand headed back to his trailer. He didn't understand what Angel was saying but he could tell his crew was unhappy. There was rapid-fire Spanish, grumbling. One of them threw a shovel down from the scaffolding and it hit an overturned metal mortar trough. There was a hollow boom that echoed once, and then was swallowed up by the cold. It would be dark soon. An inversion cloud was forming over the distant peaks, a pewter sheet turned down over the sky.

When everyone had left, Rand bundled up and pointed his truck so the headlights were on the house. He felt bad about coming at Angel that way, but that was sometimes the way things had to go. Years ago Rand had thought that getting into the building trades would be a simple, straightforward, honorable profession. You made things with your hands, and at the end of the day you had hard physical evidence of your effort. You wouldn't get rich but you slept well—sore muscles and a clear conscience, that sort of thing. That might have been true in the beginning. When he was a journeyman carpenter swinging his hammer for a paycheck things had been much easier. But, as it happened, he'd been good at his work, and he'd advanced.

He hadn't done any serious shovel work or walked joists in years. He wasn't complaining—he owned his own home, he had a fishing boat and his truck was paid for—it was just, now, at the end of a day, he had a harder time determining what it was exactly he'd done.

Managing people. That's what he concerned himself with these days. It was tricky, but he'd discovered he had an aptitude for it. He didn't have a construction management degree like many of the kids the companies hired now. He'd come up through the ranks and he thought the men respected him for this. He knew what it was like to work for an hourly wage, to actually *do* the work. He was familiar with the grind. That was something you couldn't learn in college. Case in point, here he was, after dark—his truck thermometer had read minus seventeen—making a tent around the pillars and scaffolding with lengths of plastic sheeting. The plastic would retain the heat from the forced-air propane blower. The stonemasons would get the pillar done in comfort. The walk-through would go well.

Rand dragged the heater in place, made sure the propane tank was full, gave one final look over his work, and was satisfied. He was halfway home before the pins and needles subsided in his fingers and toes. It really was brutally cold. He'd go home and make a pot of coffee, put some bourbon in it. Crank up the woodstove. Go to bed early to wake up and do it all again, Thanksgiving be damned. Like Angel had said, he was the general. He had never once expected anything out of a worker that he himself was unwilling to do. That was fairness.

Earlier that week, his friend Sam had invited him over for Thanksgiving dinner. He had just gotten married and was irritatingly happy. "We don't acknowledge Thanksgiving, for obvious reasons," Sam had said. "But Stella decided to make a big old turkey dinner on Thursday. Just a coincidence, really. We'd love to have you." Sam was laughing and Rand could hear Stella scolding him playfully in the background. Sam's new wife was from Lodge Grass—a member of the Crow Nation. Her maiden name was Estella Marie Stabs-on-Top. Sam was a short, pale-blond Swede from Minnesota. Stella was a long-limbed black-haired woman of the plains. After their marriage, Sam and Stella had taken each other's names. They were now, officially, unbelievably, Sam and Stella Stabs-on-Top-Gunderson.

"It's for the kids we're eventually going to have," Sam had explained. "It's unfair, not to mention chauvinistic, to expect her to take my name. And, our kids should grow up having a fair representation of their heritage present in *their* name. I mean, Gunderson is only half of the story here."

When he got to the site in the morning, they were already there, their radio blasting mariachi out into the snow-laden pines. It was the kind of brittle temperature that froze the mucus at the corners of your eyes, made your nose hairs prickle, made you cough if you breathed in too deep. Rand got the coffee going in the trailer and did some paperwork. Once, he looked up from his desk to see a string of elk emerging from the edge of the timber.

They looked patchy and miserable, their caution lost to the cold, moving aimlessly for warmth.

At noon Rand bundled up and went out to check on the crew. He brought a case of Miller High Life. A peace offering. Angel nodded at him when he ducked under the tarp. Rand saw that they were making good progress.

"Warm enough in here?" he shouted over the radio.

Angel gave him a thumbs-up.

"I brought you some Thanksgiving beer." Rand set the beer on a bucket.

Angel gave him a double thumbs-up.

"Okay. Good work, guys. I appreciate it, Angel. I'm going to take off. Make sure the propane is unhooked when you leave."

Angel nodded and shouted, "Okay!" His crew had barely looked at Rand. He wasn't sure how much English they understood, although it had always been his experience that they understood more than they let on.

Rand went to dinner at the Stabs-on-Top-Gunderson's and had a good time. He felt a little guilty about leaving work early, but he had been caught up on his progress reports and would have just been sitting there twiddling his thumbs anyway.

When they sat down to eat, Stella said, "For the record, I have no problem with Thanksgiving." She pointed her fork at Sam. "Who could argue with a holiday based on giving thanks for what you have?"

Sam shrugged. "I'm going to eat the hell out of this turkey, but I just want everyone to know that is no way indicative of me endorsing this gluttonous festival of oppression."

They ate and drank too much, and then all pitched in on the

dishes. Rand watched Stella and Sam as they bantered and snapped each other with dishtowels and talked about their unborn children as if they were not so much possibilities as certainties that just hadn't happened yet.

Rand rarely wasted too much time thinking about women. He'd spent enough years on construction jobs to know that this put him in the minority among men. There was a Korean massage parlor in Billings that he visited once a month. The women there were probably closer to fifty than forty, but he didn't mind. They were good-natured, motherly almost. He tipped well and, if they didn't have another customer right away, sometimes he stayed and had a cup of roasted barley *boricha* with them. Occasionally, he fixed things around the place that needed attention. He hadn't had a serious girlfriend in ten years.

After dinner, Rand returned to his empty house. Everything was in its place, and if it wasn't, it was because he was the one who had misplaced it. That was comfort. The woodstove was casting its glow in the living room and he made himself a whiskey and sat in his recliner. He switched on the TV and watched some sports highlights. He didn't think his life lacked for much of anything, at least there were no holes that couldn't be filled by getting a dog. Last spring, his old lab Charlie had gone to chase the big tennis ball in the sky. He thought enough time had passed now and maybe he'd go look at the shelter sometime soon.

The day after Thanksgiving, he got to the job site early. He figured he'd be the first one there and do a walk around to see what was what before any of the crews showed up. He was somewhat surprised to see Angel's truck in the parking lot. It had snowed a bit overnight, just a couple powdery inches, but it was enough to cover the tire tracks in the parking lot. No one had come or gone this morning. He couldn't figure out why Angel's rig was there. It just didn't make sense, really.

There were no tracks to the Porta John, to the lift, to the pallets of stone—no tracks of any kind. A white blanket of snow. Complete quiet, until a jay shrieked in the pines. Rand was out of the truck now, walking fast and then slowing, stopping. There was a dark shape pushing against the semi-opaque plastic around the pillars where Angel's crew had been working. When he got closer, he could see that the shape had a face. Rand wanted to turn, run, get into the truck and drive, but he forced his feet to move, kicking through the snow. He ducked under the plastic. It was cold. The propane tank must have run empty.

They were all there, three men slumped on the scaffolding, and Angel, sitting, back against the stone pillar, eyes closed as if he were taking a nap. Rand knew immediately. It was impossible to mistake it for anything else.

It was carbon monoxide, they told him. Somehow the heater exhaust had been covered by the tarp, filling the area the men were working in with deadly fumes.

Two of the men—Angel's cousins—had been illegal after all.

There was a delay in the construction, while the situation got sorted out. But then, sooner than seemed decent, they were back at it. A new crew came in to finish the stonework. The carpenters and electricians wrapped up the interior. And, not long after the first of the year, Rand's trailer got hauled away and the whole affair was complete.

He never actually met the homeowner. The final inspection

was handled by the app genius's wife. She had their young son with her, happily running and sliding in his stocking feet on the new wood floors.

"Donald can't wait to get away," she said, leaning against the kitchen island, tousling her son's hair. "He is so busy right now working on a product launch. He checks the snow report three times a day. He really loves to ski. I like it okay. I'm not very confident, though. This little guy is going to get lessons this year. Donald is adamant about starting him out young. He says a child has to start before he has a real fear of falling. That's the best way. I didn't start until I met Don, which was too late, really."

Rand was nodding. He'd never skied in his life. "So," he said. "If you don't have any more questions, I'm going to get out of your hair. I'll leave you this refrigerator magnet here, it has the company's contact info and my personal cellphone. If anything, and I mean anything, comes up, please don't hesitate to call me."

When Rand turned to leave, she followed him to the door. She stood on the threshold, one hand on the door, perfectly manicured nails tapping on the knob. She looked back into the house to make sure her son wasn't within earshot.

"There was one thing," she said. "I heard about what happened. Those workers. I've been handling most of the details about this house. I never even told Don because I knew he would worry. But, I just, well, this might be weird, but I have to know. Were they in the house, I mean, actually *inside,* when it happened? It shouldn't matter, it's such a tragedy, but for some reason I'd like to know exactly where, they were, um, discovered."

She had a small, fixed smile on her face. Rand thought that this was a woman who was used to being found ridiculous. Her husband, a tediously practical man, was no doubt in the habit of acquiescing to her desires, but not without first patronizing her.

Rand had a brief urge to lie, to tell her Angel and his men

had been working on the stone fireplace, that he'd found them slumped right there on her living room floor where the kid was slipping around in his socks. He wanted to give credence to her fears somehow but he couldn't, because she had that smile, the fragile kind.

"Outside," he said. "They were working on the entryway. They never even went in the house."

"God, it shouldn't matter," she said hurriedly. "It's just such bad energy, a horrible way to christen a beautiful new chapter in our lives. And after all the work you've done, I mean this place is fabulous, you must be very proud. Something like that is such a *detraction*."

Rand shrugged. "It was unfortunate. An accident. They were good workers. I didn't know them well."

She nodded and crossed her arms under her breasts, hugging herself. She must have been cold in the doorway with no coat. "I'm going to put up a wreath," she said. "Right on the entryway there. It's not much but it will be my own little memorial. I don't think I'm going to tell Don. It's not something he'd deal with well."

Rand shook her hand and got in his truck and never set eyes on the house or its occupants again.

After Rand told him about the accident, Sam was constantly inviting him to do things with him and his new bride. Come over for dinner, Rand; Stella is making spaghetti. Meet us out at Jake's; Stella and I are going to get a drink. Stella and I are going camping; you should come along. Rand managed to wriggle out of most of these invitations. The latest was he wanted Rand to join him in a sweat lodge ceremony.

"This is just what you need, man. It's purifying. I did one

last month and I felt like I'd been wrung out and hung out, you know what I mean? In a good way. I felt light."

Rand had been avoiding Sam, not returning his calls, and then one evening, as Rand was loading up in his truck to head home after work, Sam pulled in, blocking his way. "Hop in," Sam said. "We're going to be late."

"What? I'm going home. I'm tired."

"Nope. We've got sweat lodge tonight. I told everyone I'd be bringing a friend. They're expecting you. Let's go. I brought you a towel."

Sam drove them out of town and then on a series of ever-narrowing roads that wound back into the low hills. The sun was setting behind them as they pulled up in front of a pale-blue trailer house. There were half a dozen other vehicles parked in the drive. Two paint ponies stood motionless in a corral. There was an elk skull and antlers on the trailer house roof, long tapering lodge poles leaning like massive knitting needles against the porch railing.

"This is Stella's grandparents' house," Sam said. "They raised her. They're different from most of the people around here. They brought her up the way they themselves had been raised. Traditional, you know? They still follow the old ways."

"The old ways?"

"Yes. Notice, for example, the fact that they don't have a satellite dish on their roof. Everyone out here has a satellite dish. Stella told me they just got electricity a few years ago. They used to spend the whole summer in a lodge up in the Bighorns. A tipi, Rand. They lived half a year in a tipi gathering berries, fishing, hunting, living. That's why my wife is so beautiful, right? She was running wild out in the hills as a kid, not drinking Pepsi and watching *The Real World* and working at a casino, living shabbily off whatever scraps we toss their way."

"We?"

"Yes. We. Call me crazy but I feel like in small way she and I are doing some sort of small mending in the huge tear that we made in these people's universe."

"I didn't tear anyone's universe. I don't want to do this. I'm going to just sit in the car."

"Nonsense. They've adopted me, Rand. I'm family and you're my guest. It's going to be great, trust me."

Moments later, Rand stood shivering in his underwear in front of a low, canvas-covered dome. There was a fire going outside, rounded river rocks were piled in the blaze. He could hear talking and laughing coming from the lodge. Sam motioned for him to follow and ducked into the low entrance.

A furious wave of wet heat hit Rand upon entering. He coughed and dropped to his knees next to Sam, sweat already pouring from his face and shoulders. It was dim. Faces periodically appeared in the steam. There were half a dozen men seated around a pit filled with rocks. Rand watched a man, his bare torso shiny with sweat, reach out of the lodge with a pair of metal fireplace tongs and bring a rock from the outside fire. The rock was still glowing faintly red in the gloom, and he placed it carefully on the other rocks in the central pit. He did this twice more, and then squirted water from a two-liter soda bottle onto the rocks. There was a great hiss, and huge gouts of white-hot steam filled the air. Then, a noise like a rifle shot in the enclosed area as one of the rocks split. Rand swore and flinched. There was soft laughter from the shadows. The increase in steam made Rand feel as if his skin were being parboiled from his body.

"Relax, man," Sam said. Smiling, his blond hair plastered to his skull with sweat. "Focus on your breathing."

Sam introduced him around. All of them were relatives of Stella. Brothers, cousins, uncles, and the oldest, her grandfather—

long thinning gray hair, small compact potbelly and skinny crossed legs. The old man was staring at him. Rand lowered his head and concentrated on taking shallow breaths.

"Hey," the old man said. "How tall are you?"

Rand looked around. The old man was still staring at him, one eye perfectly black, the other with the scalded-milk skim of cataract.

"Me?"

"Yeah. What, like six-two, six-three, something like that?"

"I'm six-three."

The old man nodded as if this confirmed a suspicion he'd held all along. "So, you're a forward? Maybe a small forward? I'm saying that only because you don't look quick enough to be a shooting guard. No offense."

"I—what?"

The old man raised his arm and pointed across the lodge. "That's Nolan, my grandson. He's going to take us to the championship this year. He's not real tall but he's got a quick release. Quickest release off a screen that I ever saw. A leaper too. Nolan can jump right out of the gym. Only a sophomore this year. And college coaches are coming to watch him play. Gonzaga. That's big time. What do you say, Nolan?"

Nolan scratched his head and wiped the sweat from his face. He looked to be about forty, with a sunken chest and the burst nose of a serious drinker.

"I don't know, grandpa," he said. "I'm going to try."

There was silence in the lodge for a few minutes and then someone on the other side said, "Hey, Sam, you're looking skinny. My sister's cooking not agreeing with you?"

Soft laughter. Then, another voice from the steam, "Eh, it's not the cooking. I got married once. I'm guessing she's keeping him fed just so she can wear him out at night."

"Succubus," Nolan said, pouring water on his face. "All the women in this family. I believe I warned him before they got hitched."

"Suck-what?"

"Shit, my ex-wife? On my birthday, if I was lucky. You young guys have it better."

"MTV. That's what did it. And, all the hormones in the water. Makes women shameless."

"And Bill Clinton. It's not even sex anymore."

Sam was laughing, shaking his head. Rand watched, not saying anything, sweat stinging his eyes. Sam was part of some sort of unlikely brotherhood—a side effect of marriage that Rand had never before considered. It seemed like a good thing, but he didn't let himself get too sentimental. In reality, while the Stabs-on-Top men adopting Sam into the fold meant friendship, sweat lodges, manly companionship, it probably also included the occasional jailhouse call for bail money.

Eventually, the heat overwhelmed Rand and he had to stumble out of the lodge before he fainted. He stood outside in his soaked underwear, steam rising from his shoulders and arms, his neck craned back looking at the stars. Out here, town wasn't even a glow on the horizon. As Rand was trying to find the Big Dipper, there was a soft whistling, a flock of mergansers, up from the river, flying low over his head—dark swimmers, moving in formation upstream against the flow of the Milky Way.

The men were laughing in the lodge, and then he could hear Sam's voice rising up a little above it and then it was quiet. He knew they had been talking about him and he thought it was ridiculous of Sam to bring him here. He decided he wasn't going to go back in. He stood shivering, listening to the horses breathing in the corral.

"The poor old guy's got Alzheimer's," Sam said in the car on the way home. "It's an unfortunate thing. Sometimes he's perfectly clear. Everything is clicking. He tells stories, about his childhood and older ones, you know, legends and stuff, the history of the people. It's really great. And then sometimes he gets on his basketball kick. He used to be a coach. Just ungodly what it does to a person. Anyway, I'm glad you came with me tonight. Stella and I, you know, we worry about you, man."

"I'm fine."

"It was her idea about the sweat lodge. And, she thinks you need a girlfriend."

"I've been thinking about getting a dog."

"Well, there you go. I'll tell her that."

Sam dropped him off back at his truck, and when he drove away Rand walked across the parking lot down to the new job site. They were building a massive ski chalet–style dentist office. They had the floors poured and the walls framed in. The roof was still an empty framework of jutting steel beams. He overturned a bucket and sat with his back to a wall, looking up at the moon coming up a bloody egg-yolk orange. He thought, behind the roof joists like that, it looked like some sort of mottled internal organ, a pulsing lunar heart lodged between the ribs of a giant skeleton.

For some reason he couldn't stop thinking about Nolan. The basketball star. The great leaper with the quick release. The obviously ruined alcoholic. Had he led the Hardin Tigers to the state championship all those years ago? Maybe in the finals game he'd choked, missed the potentially game-winning free throw, and then started his downward slide—no championship banner, no Gonzaga, no longer any reason to stay in shape, the new dedication to drinking, puking in cold frozen fields, pickup games at the dingy rec center gym where that free throw went in every time.

Maybe some people wouldn't think something like that was possible, that such a small event could precipitate so great a fall— everything in a man's life hanging on a hoop, a net, the soft spin of the pebbled leather kissing the fingertips goodbye on the release. Rand was not one of those people.

Summer. From his desk, in the mornings, he could see sandhill cranes stalking the fallow field across the road. Rand watched their stilted movements against the rimrock hills. The dentist's office job was coming to an end. A month or so more of loose ends and then they'd come and haul the trailer away, and Rand would be embarking on a whole new project. He wasn't sure exactly what yet, the company had put an aggressive bid in on a small, high-end, ski chalet–style strip mall in Bozeman. He was having a hard time drumming up enthusiasm for a new job.

The site was in a small wooded area just off the freeway, and Rand took his lunch out into a thicket of pines and immature aspens and ate his sandwich sitting on the ground in the shade. He brought his pup with him most days. He was a small block-headed black lab mix whose existence revolved around food, searching it out, devouring it as quickly as possible, and retrieving sticks. On his lunch break Rand would let the dog out of the trailer to run around cadging treats from the guys.

On the weekends, he ran his boat upriver. He was fishing again. One day he caught his limit of walleye in an hour. The puppy hadn't been fond of the water at first. Eventually Rand caught him by the collar and tossed him off the dock. After a few moments of thrashing, he figured it out.

Mostly things were going okay, and it seemed that the events of the winter would eventually fade—the sharp edges ground away by the simple everyday adherence to routine. He walked the dog in the early-morning dark. Made coffee and went to work. Put in a full day. And then he went home, walked the dog, and made dinner, watched TV—his dog on the floor next to him. He could hang his hand over the edge of the couch and rub the dog's ears.

Occasionally, something would come to him. Sitting out in the thicket on his lunch break maybe, chewing his dry sandwich while the dog sat impatiently waiting for the crusts. He'd remember a simple thing, like the way Angel's crew used to cook their lunch outside. They'd bring an electric skillet and set it up on an overturned bucket. Someone would have a plastic bag of marinating beef and someone would have tortillas, and they'd throw together simple tacos, filling the air with the scent of seared meat.

Once, Angel had called him over and offered him some. Rand had ended up eating three, juice running down his chin, wiping his hands on his jeans like the other guys. They were good tacos.

"Better than a sandwich?" Angel had said. And Rand had nodded, his mouth full, thinking that not all food cultures were created equal, that maybe he should bring a hot plate into the trailer and cook his lunch. He never did, but at the time it seemed like Angel's guys were onto something. They had a knack for enjoyment. All the other workers were sitting in their trucks, eating fast food or choking down the same ham-and-cheese their wife had been making for them for years—and here these men were, cooking in the open air, talking, laughing, eating a real meal.

Remembering this wasn't much, just enough to make his sandwich stick in the back of his throat.

In late August, Sam called to tell Rand that Stella was pregnant, and to invite Sam to another tribal ceremony. This time it was something called Crow Fair, specifically the culminating event—a sun dance.

"This is the real one, man. I really hope you'll come."

"What do you mean, 'the real one'?"

"Yeah, they have a dance that's open to the public—concession stands, moccasins for sale, Winnebagos full of lost South Dakotans looking for the Little Bighorn Battlefield—and then this one, tribal members and close friends only. I'm going to be dancing."

"You? Why?"

"For my unborn child. To show my gratitude. For good luck."

"I didn't know you were a dancer. I mean, how do you know what to do?"

"I will be fasting, meditating. Other things I can't reveal to you. It's a whole weeklong process. The dance is just part of it. Anyway, it's not a goddamn tango competition or something. Everyone dances their own way. Some of the guys who really feel it stick bone skewers through the skin on their chests and lean back against ropes and dance until they rip out. Stella says that if I try to get macho and do that she'll divorce me. So, are you going to come?"

"Jesus. Okay. Sure."

"Great. Really great. And, just so you know, this kid is going to grow up calling you Uncle Rand. You ready for that? I mean, if something happens to me, I like to think of you stepping in and taking care of business."

"I don't really know anything about kids."

"I don't either. That's irrelevant. This is about you taking care of my family if I kick it for some reason. This isn't something you argue about. You just say, 'Right, sure thing, Sam, you can count on me.' I've already talked to Stella about it. She thinks it's a great idea. You're the godfather, man. She said she's always thought you were pretty good-looking and would do a decent job as fill-in husband."

"Wait, what?"

"Yeah. I'm making a will, just in case. I'm going to include a special letter to you. In this letter will be several pointers, suggestions, an instruction manual, basically, that should be useful to you as you undertake the care and fulfillment of my wife. I mean, you're an F-150 driving man. She's a Ferrari. You could get hurt, that's all I'm saying."

"Christ. Are you serious?"

Rand could hear him slapping his desk. "Hell, no. I'm not serious. About Stella, anyway. If I die you better keep your grubby hands off her. But about the kid, I'm dead serious." He stopped laughing. "If you ever have a pregnant wife, you'll understand. You have to promise me you'll take care of them as best as you can. I know if you say you will, you will, not to get lame here but that's the kind of guy you are. You're the only one I can trust with this."

"All right. Fine. If you die, I'll take care of business."

"There, that's what I'm talking about. Okay, then, I'll see you at the dance. Wish me luck."

The afternoon of the ceremony was a hot one, approaching one hundred degrees on the sun-baked field. Grasshoppers clattered away in droves as Rand walked through the dead grass. There were wildfires burning in the western mountains, the air hazy with smoke.

A single cottonwood tree rose in the middle of the empty meadow, and its branches had been adorned. String, strips of colored cloth, feathers, twisting and flapping. Around the tree, the dancers shuffled, their bare feet stirring small clouds of red dust. There was drumming, shrill piping, and chanting. People milled around, and Rand had a hard time discerning who were participants and who were spectators, if such a distinction existed. He tried to pick Sam out of the crowd. He stood near his truck feeling conspicuous, out of place, unwanted. He had made up his mind to leave when he spotted Stella making her way toward him.

"I'm glad you came," she said.

"Maybe I shouldn't be here."

"Nonsense." She grabbed his wrist, and he was relieved, as if being attached to her might lend his existence there some credence. She led him through the throngs of people to a place near the edge of the dance circle. Up close, he spotted Sam immediately, dancing slowly, his pale torso streaked where the sweat had run rivulets through the dust.

Standing next to Stella, he watched her as she watched Sam dance. She was wearing a light-blue sundress and had one hand on her just-beginning-to-swell belly, looking serene and beautiful despite the heat. He was going to be a godfather.

She caught him staring at her, and she smiled and reached out to squeeze his arm.

The dancers—twenty or thirty of them, mostly men—rotated slowly, around the decorated cottonwood tree. The sun beat down, the wildfire smoke turning it an angry red as it neared the horizon line. Rand had no idea how long this thing lasted. Was there a halftime? Was there a finish line? Already several of the older dancers had collapsed or stumbled off. Sam kept going, the circular shuffle, eyes squinting out at some point far above their heads. Then, Rand spotted Nolan. The fallen basketball star was dancing too. His bare feet slapped the dirt, and his calf muscles were like knotted brown rope, his head thrown back, eyes closed against the sun. Most of the other dancers looked as if they were just trying to survive, slow foot stomping, plodding. Nolan, though, was dancing like he wanted to die—quick jerky movements, chest ballooning and caving. It was a hard thing to watch, a man giving birth to something that might kill him.

At a certain point, the sun sank, and still the dance continued. Bonfires were lit on the edges of the circle. The drums had taken up residence in Rand's chest. They were the echo that threatened to overtake his heart. Stella had drifted off. Sam had fallen out of the dance, and she had gone to take care of him. But Nolan still carried on, if anything, his movements had increased their desperate tempo.

Then Nolan danced his way to the center of the circle and took hold of a long rope that had been dangling from the center tree. He resumed his place in the circle and his grandfather emerged from the crowd. He came to Nolan and helped him do something with the rope. Rand couldn't see what. Nolan's back was to him. And then the old man retreated, and Nolan was dancing again. The firelight cast its glow, and Rand could see the purple streaks of blood on Nolan's torso. He was leaning back against the rope, his skin stretched taut at the points where the bone skewers ran through his chest.

As Nolan danced past him—close enough that Rand could

have reached out to touch him—he searched Nolan's face for any sign of pain. He found just ecstatic blankness.

By now, many of the other dancers had filtered off. Two other men were attached to the center tree in the same manner as Nolan. Rand didn't want to be there any longer but he couldn't leave. He was so close, he could smell the sweat of the dancers, see the way their muscles trembled on the verge of collapse.

What was a basketball championship in the face of this? How could anything compare? This was absolution. This man had poured his whole life out on the ground to make room for vodka, and then, in one moment, he'd gotten everything back. Possibly fleeting, but no less real.

What do I have? Rand thought. *What is available to me?* Rand was aware that he was now the only stationary person in the crowd. Painted figures were moving on all sides of him. There was the clicking of beads and bone and jangling bells and shrill whistling, and he knew that dancing himself, or leaving, were the only two easy options. He tried, did one slow, heavy, foot-stomping revolution, and then he stopped, feeling ridiculous. He was an impostor. Maybe someone else could have done it, danced it away, but not him. In the end he just stood, stock-still, looking straight ahead so that the circle of dancers were forced to part around him, their eyes flashing as they went by.

Someone was pointing at him from across the fire, and then there was a hand on his shoulder. They were going to drag him out, he thought, and that was fair. That was their right. But he would make them do just that, drag him. He wasn't going to move an inch on his own. The hand was on his back now, patting it, trying to get his attention. He turned. It was Stella's grandfather, bare chested, his braids swinging like silver ropes over his shoulders.

The old man was dancing, a strange flapping motion, elbows out, rising on his toes, doing something with his hands. Dancing, but not quite. There was a post up, a pump fake, a pivot, and finally, the fade-away jump shot, his wrist crooked in perfect follow-through form, a wide, toothless smile on his face.

OFF THE TRACK

FOR JAMES McMURTRY

The day before Terry had to report to Saginaw to start his sentence, he went fishing with his grandpa. It was late summer and the lake was choked with lily pads, the surface a near-solid mat of rubbery green. Terry rowed, and with each stroke his oars churned and uprooted the plants, the pads slapping the aluminum hull with a sound like a clapping crowd heard from a distance. It was hot and everything was shades of green—the pad-covered lake, the Russian olives and willows that crowded the bank, the flat, manicured carpet of his grandfather's lawn sloping up to his house. Terry tried to get it all in his memory, each degree of green, the pitch and drone of the cicadas, the roughness of the oar grips, the sweat running into his eyes, the fetid smell of the lake. He tried to save it all up for a time not too far distant when he might need it. Terry rowed and he thought about two years, all the ways it could be figured—twenty-four months, seven hundred and thirty days, two trips around the sun, one-eighth of the total time he'd been present on the earth. Terry stared at his bobber and he was scared.

Terry's grandpa had taught him when he was just a kid that the best way to catch bass—truly large bass—was to use a shiner minnow under a bobber. He showed Terry the proper way to rig the minnow, sliding the hook point just under the dorsal fin below the spine.

"Too deep you kill the minnow," he said, "not deep enough and the minnow flies off when you cast. Now, you try it."

Terry could still remember his first minnow-rigging experience, the shiner struggling in his hand, the slight crunch as the hook point scraped through the tiny ribs and passed under the spine. That crunch, something more felt than heard, gritty and uncomfortable, like chewing a piece of eggshell in your omelet.

Terry's grandpa had taught him that when fishing for bass with shiners, you can tell if you are about to get a strike by watching the movements of the bobber. The shiner minnows were big, some of them five inches long, and although they couldn't quite pull the bobber under, their movements would set the bobber bouncing. No movement meant you had a dead shiner; slight bouncing or jiggling meant the shiner was doing its thing, alive and swimming around calmly; violent jerks and dragging from side to side meant a bass had appeared and the minnow was agitated. This was when you had to get ready.

"A bass likes to inspect his meal," Terry's grandpa said. "He'll sit underneath a minnow and just wait. The minnow will be up there going crazy and the bass will be sitting there trying to figure it out. He's used to minnows fleeing. A minnow that stays put and just swims in circles is unfamiliar to him. So he waits and watches until either his predatory impulse overwhelms him or his innate caution sends him swimming off in search of food that acts

the way it should. That's all there is to it, really. You just present
the bass with a choice, and he either takes it or he doesn't."

With fewer than twenty-four hours before his incarceration,
Terry couldn't concentrate on the fishing. The small rowboat was
confining, and he found himself moving constantly, shifting his
weight, repositioning his feet, making the boat lurch from side to
side. They hadn't caught anything. Terry's grandpa said it might
be because it was so hot. The bass, he said, had retreated to the
deepest part of the lake and hunkered down until dusk, when
things would cool off a little. Terry had sweat running down his
back. He had to press down on his knees to make his legs stop
jigging up and down.

"Pretty hot," he said, squinting at his bobber.

His grandpa nodded and reeled in his rig. His minnow had
died. He removed it from the hook and pitched it out to the lake
where it landed on a lily pad with a wet slap.

"Let's call it a day," he said, "it's hotter than two rats fucking in a wool sock out here."

This made Terry laugh, and when he pulled up the anchor
and began rowing back to the house, he felt a little better.

In the kitchen, Terry's grandpa made tomato sandwiches,
the tomatoes heavy and warm, fresh from his garden, liberally
salted between two slices of soft white bread. There was a Tigers
game on the radio. They ate and half-listened to Ernie Harwell's
gravelly play-by-play. When it started to cool down, they went
out on the back porch to watch the nighthawks skim mosquitos
as dusk came down over the lake.

"I didn't mean for it to happen that way," Terry said, eventually. "That counts for something, doesn't it?"

Terry's grandpa sucked in his cheeks as he worked at a piece
of soft bread stuck to a molar.

"Going into a place like that, you are accepting a certain amount of risk. That's how I feel. No one is a complete innocent or complete victim in a place like that. That guy had a wife and a kid. What was he doing there in the first place? It's over and done now, of course, beating a dead horse here, but that bitch judge thought you needed saving, and she was the one to do it. Would have been better if it had been a man."

"I think if my dad was the judge I'd have gotten the chair."

"Fathers are always the harshest judges. That's the way it's always been. But still, there's something in me and you that's not in your dad. Sometimes these things skip generations. And I'm not saying it's a good thing or it's a bad thing, probably life's a whole lot easier without it, whatever it is. But, how do I say this? Your father was a good boy and is a good man, but he could never fathom a situation such as the one you got yourself involved in. Something like that is as foreign to him as breathing underwater. Your dad can't understand what you got yourself into and he can't understand what going inside that place for two years is going to be like for you. I think I got an inkling and I know it ain't going to be a trip to Candyland for damn sure. But you'll do it, and you'll get out, and you'll find that there is a lot of life for you left, and you'll have learned some things at a young age that take many men a hell of a long time to get figured out."

It got dark and Terry's grandpa went inside. Terry stayed out on the porch. He pulled two chairs together and stretched out on his back. Mosquitoes gathered around him in a droning chorus, and when Terry raised his bare arm a half a dozen clung to his forearm in a line, like pigs lining up at a feed trough. He swatted at them, creating a smear of blood, a process he would repeat innumerable times until the sun came up and his grandpa came out to get him for the three-hour drive down to Saginaw.

———

Terry had always been big for his age. That had probably worked against him in court. The judge looked at him and saw the broad shoulders, the large hands, the deep-voiced *yes ma'am*s and *no sir*s, the stubble on the cheeks that Terry had begun shaving when he was barely through middle school. Terry looked like a man, and he would have been judged like a man if it weren't for laws about prosecuting minors. As it was, he got two years in the Saginaw juvenile detention center. Some said that was too much. Some said it wasn't near enough. After all, there was a man who wasn't ever going to return to his family—a woman without a husband and a boy without a father.

According to the police report read during the trial, Terry showed up alone at Hiphuggers Gentleman's Club with a fake ID. He played three games of nine-ball and won all three. He had six shots of Ezra Brooks whiskey and chased each one with a draft beer. Some time before last call there was a scuffle and the patrons of the bar streamed out into the parking lot. The ones slow to get off their stools saw nothing but the aftermath. By the time they made it outside all there was to see was Terry standing— another man, on the ground, bloody, his body racked with seizures.

Denise, Terry's kid sister, cried for two whole days after he went away. She cried, aware for the very first time in her life that something had passed and things would never again be exactly how they were before. That is adulthood and it comes in many forms. For Terry it came in the parking lot of that topless bar, two counties over, where no one knew his name—his breath coming hard, blood leaking into the gravel, a longneck bottle broken and clenched in his fist. Or, if not there, then some time after, in his bunk after lights-out, looking up at the mattress above him, the exposed box springs like the skeleton of honeycomb, the rusted spring coils groaning under the strain of his bunkmate's masturbatory vigor.

While Terry was away, his grandfather died. They found him sprawled in the grass next to his backyard lake, his torso and legs still on the ground, his head and arms and hands trailing out into the stagnant water like pale, moisture-seeking roots.

"I already talked to the people there," Terry's father said when he called. "They're not going to let you come to the funeral. I told them it was your grandpa and that you were close but they said it doesn't matter. No releases of any kind for the first year. It's bullcrap, Terry, I know. But, maybe it doesn't matter. It'll just be a body there, at the service. Your grandpa has passed on to his heavenly reward, and that is something in which we should rejoice. He lived a full life, and that's what we need to remember. Anyway, it's going to be a closed casket. They said he had a stroke and the way he fell, in the water like that, well, it wasn't pretty. There were a lot of turtles in that lake, you know that. Remember you and your sister catching those little baby snappers and trying to get them to race? Anyway, he was in the water for a couple of days like that, and the turtles had been at him a little bit. Your mother took that pretty hard. She was the one who found him. She went over there to trade him some rhubarb from her garden for tomatoes from his. He was overrun with them this year, you know, couldn't give them away fast enough. Anyway, I told her it was just his earthly vessel, and it doesn't matter because his eternal soul is sitting at the right hand of Christ, our Father in heaven. Well, son, I have to go be with your mother now. It seems that God has given us many trials this year. It is important to keep the knowledge of your faith at the forefront of your consciousness. We pray for you every Sunday."

A year ago Terry might have cried at the news of his grandfather's death. But now—holding the phone in the sweat-and-mashed-potato-smelling common area in Saginaw—he did not. He just listened to his father speak, heard his newly discovered God-love dripping from his every word like a self-righteous accent. He hung up and went to his room and lay on his bed and stared at the bunk above him until the box springs swam before his eyes.

Later, when his bunkmate came in, and, predictably, the mattress started to shift and squeak, Terry rose without a word and grabbed him by his neck and leg, pitched him from the bunk onto the concrete floor, and gave him one silent, sharp, vicious kick to the face. He was a skinny kid, about half Terry's size. He had an explosion of zits across his scrawny back, and he was lying facedown, whining, one of his hands still jammed down the waistband of his boxer shorts.

That kick got Terry a new bunkmate and an additional month's time. Sometimes, he had dreams where he was fishing with his grandpa. He would turn to him in the boat and see half the flesh stripped from his face—leaking, gaping chunks missing from his neck.

While Terry was away Denise had her thirteenth birthday. He called her and told her he was sorry that he couldn't get her a present and she said it was okay. Mom and Dad were finally letting her get her ears pierced and she was going to the mall today to get it done.

"They make you get studs, at first," she said. "And you have to wait two weeks before you can change them."

"Why's that?" Terry said.

"It's so the hole doesn't close up. After two weeks, though, it's permanent and the holes will be there forever. Did you know that Grandma never got her ears pierced? She used to wear clip-on earrings. That's what Mom said."

"No, I never knew that."

"Mom said that Grandma always wanted to, but that Grandpa didn't let her. So, she got clip-ons and only wore them when she went to the store and stuff. Anyway, I'm going to get some blue ones with gold studs. I already picked them out. But when the two weeks are up I'm going to get some that have feathers on them."

"Feathers?"

"Yeah, dangly ones. They sell them at the mall. All different types of feathers. From real birds. They come with a little card that tells you what kind of bird the feather is from, and also about the Indian tribe."

"Indian tribe?"

"They're made by Indian women from somewhere out west. They pick the feathers up off the ground and then they attach them with pretty gold and silver wire to earring hooks. My friend Kristy has some made from heron feathers and they are so pretty. They are so light. They just float around her ears, like, well, feathers. I can't wait."

"That sounds great. I can almost picture them. How's school?"

"It's fine."

"Do people talk about me?"

Denise was silent for a moment. Terry could hear the sound of her phone cord hitting the receiver as she twisted and untwisted it absentmindedly.

"A little. Not too much."

"Yeah? Anyone giving you a hard time?"

"No, not really. But, Kristy says that you're hot, and that she would totally make out with you, if you weren't in there. I told her she is a slut."

Denise laughed and then Terry's time was up on the phone.

"You tell Kristy that in about four years I might take her up on that offer, and you, missy, better not be making out with anyone, you hear me?"

"Eww. Gross, Terry."

"I'm serious."

"I don't like any boys. And I'm not going to date or get married until I find one that's exactly like you, you know that."

"Okay. I have to hang up now, Den. Happy Birthday. I miss you."

Terry went back to his bunk, laced his fingers behind his head and searched for a long time but couldn't come up with anything, one single thing or person, idea or possibility, now that his grandpa was dead, that he loved more than his sister.

While Terry was away his mother, Janelle, let the vegetable garden go to weed and decided instead to cultivate a relationship with a woman she met in a bereavement group at the church. Merriam was forty years old, three years younger than Janelle, with no children or husband. She had lost her twin sister to breast cancer, and she told the group it was like she'd had a limb amputated, or a lobe of her brain removed. She was an operating room nurse and sometimes she laughed and referred to her sister as her phantom limb, and then would cry in tight, dry gasps with her hands over her mouth and her eyes clenched shut. Janelle went to the bereavement meetings initially because of Terry. She felt a little out of place at first because, after all, Terry wasn't dead. But, he *had* caused death in another and, to Janelle, this meant that her son had changed in some fundamental way that was not un-like actual death, just more shameful.

After their group met, Janelle and Merriam often went to a diner close to the church. They sat in a booth, coffee going cold in the cups in front of them while they talked. One day, Janelle told Merriam that she would rather Terry had been killed him-self. This was the first time she had admitted this fact aloud and saying it was like letting out her breath after holding it for a very long time.

"If he were simply gone it would be easier for me to live with," she said. "And that makes me a horrible person. What kind of mother am I?"

"Well," said Merriam, handing Janelle a tissue from her purse, "if it makes you feel any better, I had a doctor friend write me a scrip for ten milligrams of Valium—that's the highest dose—because I said I was having a hard time sleeping. I sometimes pour the whole month's supply in my hand and sit there crying, the pills in one hand, a glass of water in the other, and I can't make myself do it, quite, and that makes me feel worse than be-fore."

Surprisingly, this admission did make Janelle feel better—or, maybe, it was Merriam reaching over the table to grasp her hand and the way their hands locked on the table between them. Merriam's strong, capable fingers and blunt-cut nails interlocked with her own, skinny and pale, her nails long and freshly painted before their meeting.

It was a month before they talked about anything other than Merriam's sister or Terry. And then, gradually, Janelle started telling Merriam about how she had decided to put new wallpaper up in Terry's bedroom and how Denise was refusing to help. They agreed that thirteen was a difficult age and that muted beige with a plaid-pattern trim would be a good choice in wallpaper.

"And then when he moves out," Merriam said, "you can still use the room as a guest bedroom and it won't be overwhelmingly masculine."

"That's a good idea," Janelle said. "I'd never thought about it like that."

Janelle and the kids used to attend church every Sunday. It was a Lutheran church, stolid and small, whose pastor had a lisp that always sent Denise and Terry into convulsions of suppressed laughter, especially when he said certain words like *salvation* or *Christ-crucified*. Terry's father, Todd, never went to church. Sundays, for him, were a day spent on the lawnmower with a beer in an insulated cozy and a radio with headphones tuned to the classic rock station. When Terry was ten he asked Janelle why his dad never went to church, and she replied that mowing the lawn was how daddy prayed. The next Sunday, Terry informed her that he thought going fishing with his grandpa was the way he prayed best—and then didn't talk to her for a whole week when Janelle made him go anyway. During the week he didn't talk to his mother, Terry thought long and hard about God and the possibilities of hell. One night, lying in bed in the silent house, his family asleep, he clenched and unclenched his fists, raised his arms above him to fend off the lightning bolt that was sure to strike him down, and then he turned over and pressed his face into the pillow and said it so quietly that no one could possibly have heard it except for a God who could hear everything.

"Fuck you, Jesus," he said.

With the release of words, and the firebolt that didn't come, Terry felt himself relax, felt a lightness come over his body. He turned over and sat up in bed, shadow bars from his window blinds cast across his body. He said it louder.

"Fuck you, Jesus."

He laughed and said it the way Pastor Lundt at church might say it, with feeling, "Jethuth, you cockthucker. Fuck you!"

When Terry informed Janelle that Jesus was make-believe and that he didn't want to go to church anymore, she told him that until he was confirmed, he didn't have any choice in the matter. So, until he was fourteen, Terry went to church. He sat in the pew with his mother and sister and—to Janelle's great embarrassment—refused to stand up and sing hymns with the rest of the congregation. Pastor Lundt would say, "Pleath thtand and join in thong," and everyone would rise and hold their hymnals, except for Terry, who sat staring straight ahead with his arms crossed over his chest. He had always enjoyed the singing before, but now it felt wrong, like singing happy birthday for someone who wasn't even having a birthday.

During this time, Janelle came to the conclusion that Terry's behavior was a direct result of his relationship with his grandfather, and forbade Terry from seeing him. No more fishing. No more weekend sleepovers. No more after-school bus drop-offs. Todd tried to convince Janelle that keeping the boy away from his grandfather was not going to help matters, but she was adamant.

For a month, if Janelle entered a room, Terry left it. If she asked him to do something, he did it without acknowledging that he'd heard her voice. Toward the end of the month Janelle was going out of her way to do things for him, making ribs for dinner twice a week, even letting up on harassing him about his school-work. Terry accepted these new developments in stride, and still refused to interact with her in any meaningful way.

The day Terry won was, fittingly, a Sunday. As usual, Terry took in the service immobile in the pew, clad in a too-small polo shirt (he was forever outgrowing his clothes) and wrinkled khaki pants, with his arms crossed over his chest. In the van on the way home, Janelle suggested they go for ice cream. Terry shrugged noncommittally. Behind the wheel of the van, in the church parking lot, Janelle broke down. At first she tried to restrain herself.

"I know you idolize him, and that's only natural. But your grandfather was—is—not a nice man. Okay? You don't know him, not what he's really like. Maybe it's time you learned some things. I have bit my tongue and bit my tongue, but I won't any longer."

Janelle's voice started to rise, and when Terry turned briefly from looking out the window, he saw her knuckles go white at the wheel.

"Your father grew up in fear of your grandpa. Did you know that? When I first met your father, he wouldn't take me to meet his family until we were engaged to be married. It was because your grandfather is a tyrant. Do you know what that means? It means a very bad man who makes other people do what he wants them to do without thinking about what they might want to do themselves. Do you understand? Your grandfather, who you idolize, wouldn't let your grandmother leave the house without his permission. For twenty years! How would that make you feel?"

Janelle was yelling now. She was crying and wiping at her eyes. In the backseat, Denise started to whimper. Terry didn't say anything. He just kept looking out the window. He thought about the way his grandpa could cast a Jitterbug farther, and with more accuracy, than anyone in the world. The way, with just a flick of his wrist, he could send the lure sailing in a flat arc to land precisely where he wanted—the shadow under a dock, a small gap in the lily pads, right up underneath an overhanging bush. Terry himself couldn't do that, not even close, but if he tried his whole life maybe he could. And that's what he wanted more than anything.

When Janelle finally wound herself down, they sat there for a while in silence and then Terry said he'd rather not get ice cream. And, that if Janelle could just drop him off at his grandpa's house, he could ride his bike home later.

At this, Janelle exhaled through her clenched teeth and rubbed her temples.

"If you're not careful, mister, you are going to end up just like him. I can see it in you, and I don't like it."

While Terry was away, Denise informed Janelle that she would no longer be accompanying her to church, and—although Denise was only thirteen at the time and hadn't been confirmed—Janelle didn't argue. In fact, Janelle herself stopped going to church for a whole month. She gradually quit going to the bereavement group. And, although they continued for a while, she allowed herself to fall out of touch with Merriam. Janelle knew she had hurt her feelings, but their conversations had begun to falter. She wasn't sure why, but it seemed that they'd run out of ways to talk about their grief and sorrow—and, as a result, had found out they had nothing in common. During their last few meetings, neither of them had said much. Merriam would occasionally grasp Janelle's hand and squeeze and look like she was about to speak, and then wouldn't. Both of them drank their coffee and got refills. They spent long silent moments looking out the windows into the dark street.

Eventually, Janelle resumed attending church services, at New Directions Non-denominational Church of Christ. New Directions was a congregation of over a thousand, and instead of a choir, it had a band that played Christian rock music, the lyrics of which flashed across a Jumbotron. There were no hymnals. The pastor was tan and a beautiful sermonizer. He reminded Janelle of a Kennedy. Janelle found herself looking forward to Sundays in a way she never had before. She tried to get Denise to join her. Denise refused. But, surprisingly, one Sunday, Todd neglected the lawn and accompanied her.

While Terry was away his father accepted Christ into his life at New Directions Church, and it was like he had discovered some necessary bodily function that he had somehow been living without. He accepted Christ like eating, like drinking water, like sucking down great draughts of cold, clean air. When Pastor Clint got up on the stage and gave his sermons, Todd felt his words as if they were meant for him and him alone. Todd liked the way that New Directions did away with all the old religious claptrap. There were no robes or candles or ridiculous ceremonies involving dunking people in water. At New Directions, it was just the words of Pastor Clint, a thousand brothers and sisters in Christ pressed around you in support, and some music that really glorified God, with drums and amplifiers, the way music was meant to be played.

Eventually, it was Todd who forced Denise to attend New Directions with them on Sundays. He told her she would come to church and receive the Word of God if he had to drag her there and tie her to a pew.

"Maybe I failed your brother," he said. "Maybe I didn't fulfill my duties as a father in the eyes of the Lord. But I will not make that mistake with you. You will be a Godly young woman and a sister of Christ."

And, on a Sunday when Denise refused to get out of bed and locked the door against him, Todd, sure in the knowledge of the Lord, kicked her bedroom door open and pulled her, sobbing, from her bed. Denise lay sprawled on the floor while he ripped clothing from hangers in her closet and threw them at her. She screamed for her mother. Janelle didn't come. Denise eventually got dressed and slumped in the backseat of the van. For the whole church service, and most after that, she watched her father, his eyes closed while he absorbed Pastor Clint's sermon, and she imagined, she wished, that Terry had killed him instead of that guy at the bar. With Todd gone, two years with Janelle would be bearable until Terry came back and then they could go somewhere else to live. Where didn't matter. What they would do when they got there didn't matter. As long as she and Terry could be together they would be okay.

At first, Terry thought about it constantly. The events of that night on an endless loop reeling through all his waking thoughts, polluting his dreams. And then, halfway through the first year, he didn't think about it much at all. It became something about him, an alteration that was somehow more physical than emotional. Some people have their wisdom teeth out, some people don't. Some people have diabetes, some people don't. Some people live with the knowledge that they caused the death of another human being, some people don't. Whenever certain thoughts reared their heads, Terry breathed deeply while staring at a fixed object and they passed, like car sickness.

For some reason, he was less successful in his attempt to forget the day of his sentencing. The thinly veiled look of revulsion on the judge's face when she addressed him. The way she moved her glasses down low on her nose, and told him she hoped two years was enough to get him back on track. He regularly carried out imaginary conversations with this woman, debates where he pled his case eloquently, expressed his sorrow in a completely honest and believable manner, where he presented, unequivocally, the truth that two years in Saginaw would not, could not, get him—or anyone else—back on track.

Once, he had a dream where he skewered the judge on a giant hook, pushing the point right through her skin, through her ribs and under the spine, and then tossed her in a great blank body of water where she hung suspended under a bobber so big it blotted out the sun.

Over the course of the two years, there had been visits. For the first few months, they made the drive downstate every weekend. They sat in the communal visiting area and listened to the subdued voices of the other families at tables near them. Other families, with other sons, who all seemed to have a lot more to talk about. During the second year, the visits had decreased to just holidays, an arrangement that suited everyone except Denise, who would have camped in the waiting area had they let her.

It was June when they let Terry out, and he hadn't seen his

family since Christmas. Terry's father shook his hand and said, "Welcome back, son. Praise the Lord." Out in the parking lot, in the bright sunlight, Terry thought Todd seemed older, grayer. He wore a gold crucifix and had his shirt tucked into his jeans. Terry's mother hugged him and cried. She seemed to have lost some weight. She had dyed her hair to cover the gray, and her nails were painted tomato red. Denise came to Terry last. She hugged him as well, jumping up to get her arms around his neck, practically clinging to him. He could smell her shampoo.

Terry picked her up and slung her, squealing, over his shoulder, realizing as he did so that she wasn't his gangly, tomboy kid sister anymore.

"Jesus, Den," he said, as he put her down. "I don't see you for a little while and you get full grown on me."

Denise turned red and didn't say anything and when Terry got into the backseat of the van she sat next to him, her head resting on his shoulder. It wasn't until they were almost home that Terry's dad told him about the house.

"Your grandpa left it to you, his truck too—pretty much everything he had. It was a surprise to us, too. Believe me, no one was expecting that. But the lawyer says it's legit and a man's will is a man's will, and there's nothing anyone can do about it if he is proven to be of sound mind and body at the time it was drafted. He got it drawn up pretty soon after you went away. Didn't tell anyone about it. It definitely came as a surprise to us, but, well, I suppose it's God's will. You're a homeowner, son. Eighteen years old and you got a house that's paid for. What do you think of that?"

Terry nodded and said he thought it was fine.

"Could you drop me off there," he said, "on the way by?"

"But I planned to make you dinner," his mother said, turning in her seat to face him, "I've had spare ribs in the Crock-Pot all day."

"I'll come over later. I'll drive the truck over. I just want to look at the place. Have a look at the lake. I guess that's where I'll be living from now on. I guess it's mine."

"I just thought we'd all have dinner together," she said. "It's been so long. I thought a good dinner would sound nice to you." She smiled and her lips moved like she was going to continue but Terry's father put his hand on her arm and she turned back in her seat.

They dropped Terry off at the house. Denise wanted to stay with him but Todd said that Terry might want some time alone. Terry shrugged. "It's fine with me if she wants to stay."

"See? It's fine with him." Denise started to get out of the van but Todd stopped her.

"You're coming with us," he said. "Leave your brother alone."

Denise slouched back in the seat with her arms crossed, and they pulled away—Todd with both hands on the wheel staring straight ahead, Janelle waving out the window and exaggeratedly mouthing something that Terry had a hard time understanding for a moment until it became clear. Spare ribs, she was saying. *Spare. Ribs.*

Terry stood in the driveway and considered his grandpa's house. The house where the school bus used to drop him off, the house where he spent every weekend night until he discovered girls, the old white farmhouse that creaked and groaned and had a root cellar and woodstove, glass-globed lightning rods on the roofline, a slight sag in the porch—and his grandpa's worn overalls in the closet. All of it his now, memories to foundation.

The lawn was a tangle of green. A knee high jungle of weeds

grew where his grandpa's tomato patch should have been. Inside, the house was musty and hot. Terry wanted to open the windows but there were no screens—his grandpa always took them down in the fall and put them back up in the spring and Terry used to help, standing on the ladder, his grandpa handing the screens up to him. Here it was, mid-August and no screens. You couldn't open the windows without mosquitos coming in the house. His grandpa never would have put up with that.

From the kitchen, Terry could see out over the lake. The lily pads were as thick as ever, in bloom, the green mat festooned with spiky white flowers. He went to the porch and sat on the step, looking at the lake, the small rowboat overturned on the bank, the splintered old dock half-submerged and leaning into the lake like a broken-toothed smile.

The turtles were out, lined up on fallen trees on the bank, their heads poking out like periscopes around the open water of the dock—box turtles and painted turtles and even a few huge snappers, their backs mossy and ancient, their necks craned to catch the last rays of sun coming down over the tops of the willows.

Terry sat, hunched on the step with his arms around his knees, and watched the turtles. Then he went back in the house and down to his grandpa's den. Normally, the old rolltop desk was open and cluttered with papers, greasy lawnmower parts, old wooden bass lures, Hula Poppers and Jitterbugs, a cribbage board made from deer antler, spinning reels in all shapes and degrees of brokenness, and always—presiding over this mess like a miniature duke and duchess of chaos—a pair of stuffed fox squirrels that some sophomoric taxidermist had arranged in an eternal act of coitus. Now, the desktop was perfectly empty, not so much as a single piece of paper on its scarred oak surface. It sat in the room like some strange alien craft, sterile and foreign. Terry pulled open drawers until he found keys to the gun cabinet.

Against his parent's wishes, Terry's grandpa taught him how to shoot when he was young. Terry's grandpa shot skeet at the gun club every weekend and liked to wander around out in the fall woods looking for grouse and woodcock. When Terry turned ten he bought him a youth-model twenty-gauge that immediately became Terry's most prized possession. His parents wouldn't let him keep it in the house, so it stayed in his grandpa's gun cabinet, lovingly cleaned and oiled after every use. Terry had outgrown the shotgun in a few short years, and for his sixteenth birthday—three months before he went away—his grandpa bought him a new Benelli twelve-gauge pump-gun. It was a little too much gun for woodcock and grouse, but it was a clay-pigeon-breaking machine. The last time Terry and his grandpa had shot at the gun club he'd gone fifty-five for sixty on skeet, the first time he'd ever beaten his grandpa.

The gun cabinet stood in the corner, and when Terry swung open the door he breathed in the familiar tang of Hoppe's 9 gun oil. There were boxes of shells in the cabinet drawers, and Terry filled his pockets and loaded his gun, racking the pump action as he climbed the stairs. He strode across the lawn to the edge of the lake, and, in the last few moments before the sun went down, he shot as many turtles as he possibly could, hammering the pump so the foregrip was a blur, spent shells smoking and spinning into the grass, the turtles diving frantically, breaking and sinking, the pieces of shattered shell and beaks and claws and tails and blue-black blood, iridescent and slick like motor oil, fouling the lake's surface.

———

There were a few beers left in the fridge, long gone to skunk, but Terry drank them anyway. He ran an oil-soaked rag through the barrel of the twelve-gauge and rubbed a little oil on the stock and grip before putting it back in the cabinet. He got out the screens and put them in the downstairs windows, opening them wide, and then he sat in the easy chair in the living room and watched the curtains blow.

When he knew everyone would be asleep, he got his grandpa's Ford started and drove over to his parent's house, killing the lights down the drive and coasting the last few yards on momentum. The door was unlocked and he kicked his shoes off, padding quietly down the creaky wood floor in the kitchen. The Crock-Pot sat on the counter, still warm, and Terry filled a plate with ribs, eating and wiping his fingers on his jeans as he headed up the stairs. In his old room, Terry shut the door behind him before flipping on the light. He sat on his bed with the plate of ribs and regarded the changes: the new wallpaper, a stack of vintage suitcases, an antique lamp made from an old earthenware jug, a Shaker-style rocking chair. His dresser was still there, presumably his clothes, and his bed, but other than that? Nothing. His *Field & Stream*s and *Gray's Sporting Journal*s—subscriptions his grandpa had started for him years ago. His football trophies. The mangy raccoon mount his grandpa had given him. And, he got up from the bed and lifted the mattress to check, his *Penthouse* collection. All of it gone. Janelle had told him about her wallpaper project. She had neglected to mention the systematic eradication of his presence from his own bedroom. He finished the ribs and wiped his hands and mouth on a brand-new four-hundred-thread-count Egyptian cotton pillowcase. He was lying on his back with his hands laced behind his head—considering the freshly textured beige ceiling—when Denise came in.

"I stayed up 'cause I knew you'd come over eventually."

She had her hair pulled up on her head in a way he'd never seen before and he was struck again by how much older she looked. She had earrings on, each one made from the iridescent bottle-green eye of a peacock feather. The earrings were huge, and rather ridiculous the way they bookended her narrow face. He wanted to say something to tease her but when she sat down on the bed—solemnly tucking her hair behind her ears—he couldn't bring himself to do it. He leaned over and flicked one of the feathers with his fingernail.

"Nice," he said.

"Yeah, thanks. Do you like them? I got them just in time."

"Sure. What do you mean?"

"The store in the mall. Remember I was telling you about the Indian women who gather the feathers and then make them into earrings?"

"I remember."

"Well, they shut the store down. I guess the women weren't just gathering the feathers when they fell, you know what I mean? They were killing all the birds, even the endangered ones, like herons and cranes and stuff. So someone found out and shut them down. I'm pretty lucky I got in there in time. A lot of girls didn't. I had that rich bitch Macey Simons offer me a hundred bucks for mine. Can you believe it?"

"What did you tell her?"

"Come with two hundred and then we'll talk."

This made Terry laugh like he hadn't in a long time. He laughed until he had to push his face into the pillow to muffle the sound.

———

When he left the house he brought the rest of the ribs with him in a plastic bag. Denise came behind him with her backpack on. She got in the truck and Terry sat behind the wheel with the key in his hand looking at their childhood home in front of them, shadowed and silent. He turned to Denise, her earrings catching the faint glow of the yard light, making the side of her face pale green.

"What are you doing?" he said.

Denise had her arms around her backpack resting on her knees. She didn't look at him.

"Get out."

"I'm coming with you."

"You can't."

"Let me."

Denise slid over in the seat and tried to put her head on his shoulder but Terry shrugged hard, his hands still on the wheel.

"I could come with you. Why not?"

Terry reached over to open her door and when she tried to hug him he grabbed both of her thin wrists with one hand and squeezed until she whimpered. He pushed her out of the truck and she landed awkwardly in the gravel, her hair undone and in her eyes, crying. Terry pitched her backpack out beside her and shut the door.

"If you come over tomorrow," he said, "I'll take you out in the boat."

The truck rumbled to life, and Terry backed slowly down the driveway. He didn't turn on the headlights until he hit the main road.

As he drove, he remembered the last time he'd spoken to his grandpa, on the phone, a month before his death. He'd called Terry at Saginaw to tell him he'd caught an eight-pound bass, the biggest one he'd ever gotten out of the lake.

"The thing had a mouth on it that you could have stuck a dinner plate down. Didn't fight worth a damn either, just let me reel her in like a wet dishrag. A big female. Belly on her like a basketball. I think she was full of eggs, it's that time of year."

They were quiet for a moment. Theirs was not a relationship that lent itself well to the measured give-and-take of the telephone. Terry would find himself nodding, forgetting to respond verbally, and his grandfather's speech would often take on a stiff, formal tone that was unfamiliar to him. Often, one of them would rush to fill a silence, his words colliding with the other attempting to do the same thing.

"Well, Terry, that's about it," his grandfather said after a while. "I just wanted to call and tell you about the bass. It was a fish of a lifetime and I thought you should know."

"Are you going to get it mounted," Terry blurted before his grandpa hung up.

"That might be hard to do," he laughed. "She's still swimming around out there I suppose."

"You put it back?"

"I know. I know. Surprised myself too. You know I always said I wanted a real big one to put up in the den. But then when I reeled it in and the damn thing didn't even put up a fight—like she knew she was swimming to her death and decided to do it with some dignity—hell, I don't know. I've killed thousands of bass. I'm not sure what came over me. Maybe I'm finally getting soft in my old age."

"Now no one will believe you. I'd've killed it."

"What? Are you saying I'm a liar, boy?" Terry's grandpa dropped his voice, pretending he was mad.

"No. I believe you. But, you can't believe anything anyone says about fishing or their dick, unless there's proof. That's what you always say."

"Yeah, I know what I always say. But you know what else I say?"

"What?"

"My give-a-damn is broke. I don't care what people think. Anyway, you're the only one I'm going to tell, so it doesn't matter. I just wanted to let you know that I caught it and it's still out there. Maybe you'll get her when you get back home. I thought maybe that might help you out in some small way in there— knowing that a fish like that can be caught out here."

Terry didn't believe in premonitions, not really, but whenever he thought about this conversation he got a sense that his grandpa had known, somehow, that his time was near. He wasn't sure why, but he couldn't help but think that if his grandpa had killed that bass, he might have lived another fifteen years. He felt like his grandpa had known this fact as well, and his decision was something that Terry had a hard time wrapping his mind around.

The yard light was burned out over his grandpa's garage. There was a small sliver of moon and the oaks in the front yard cast their towering shadows across the driveway. The house was dark, and, upon entering, Terry had the disconcerting experience of not being immediately able to locate a light switch. It was strange, after all the time he'd spent there, that he should have to grope around to find the kitchen light. It seemed like something he should have known, some simple piece of knowledge that a mere two years spent away should not be enough to eradicate. But, then again, how many times had he ever entered this house as he did then, alone and in the dark? His grandpa had always led the way, or was already inside, the kitchen lit up, the Tigers play-by-play coming up faint and incoherent from the basement as if the house itself were vocalizing its own garbled interior monologue.

Terry eventually found the switch, tucked in between the doorjamb and the windowsill—and the kitchen flooded with light. After the kitchen, he moved around the rest of the house. He floundered through the living room, bathroom, den, dining room, bedroom, finding the wall switches, the pull chains of the lamps; his arms leading the way through the pitch-black as if he were swimming.

When he had every possible source of illumination in the house glowing, he sat on the couch. He'd left all the windows open and the house had taken on the damp odor of the lake. He could smell it in the upholstery, in the curtains. The musty dankness of it rose from the carpet, and, as if heeding its summons, Terry went out across the backyard and stood on the first splintered board of the dock. The moon threw just enough light that Terry could see out over the surface of the water, the lily flowers closed up into hard white buds against the darkness.

The dented aluminum rowboat was next to where he stood in the grass, and he flipped it over. There was a silhouette on the ground under where the boat had been—a sun-starved outline that glowed a sickly greenish white under the moon, like skin on a broken arm after the cast has been removed. Terry fit the old, warped oars into the locks and slid the boat off the bank. He rowed as slowly and as quietly as he could, the pads whispering against the hull, the oars emitting a barely audible squeak with each stroke. The lake smelled different at night, more subdued. The frogs were silent, everything tucked into itself and no longer broadcasting.

He was out in the open water, as near as he could tell to the middle of the lake, when he stopped rowing. The moon, weak to begin with, had finally succumbed to the clouds, and the sky was a dense inkblot above him. There was no wind and the boat didn't rock or drift. It just hung, as if suspended in a void. Terry found that if he tilted his head back, he could look up into a fathomless universe of blackness, a starless sky so immense that it seemed to pull at his eyes. It was like his pupils were made of small pieces of this same dark matter—broken obsidian shards of it—that he'd been carrying around with him his whole life as if they were his own, only to find out that they were borrowed, and that now their true owner wanted them back.

But then, if he turned around, behind him, the house glowed, an overflow of light spilling from all its windows like a welcoming beacon. And, from this distance, if he squinted his eyes just right, he could make shapes, like shadowy human figures, move across the windows. He could almost convince himself that someone was there, waiting for him to come back inside.

CROW COUNTRY MOSES

I was lost.

Well, more accurately, my father was lost and I was with my father. Does that make me lost by default? I suppose so. Some would say that it is an inherited trait, being lost, like having blue eyes, alcoholism, or a tendency to see the glass half-empty.

In Crow country, there are horses everywhere. Mostly wild patchwork paints with mismatched eyes that give them a crazed feral look. There are horses and the land is always on fire. Not all of it, of course, but some of it always, at least every time I have ever been there. In the early spring, after the snow melt but before green-up, men walk the fields with flamethrowing devices, the fuel canisters strapped to their backs, the flames shooting from long metal tubes. They walk the tangled field edges, the creek bottoms, the orange and blue flames stabbing out like tongues bitten ragged, tasting the air. The alders and hunched Russian olives and tangled brown grasses smoldering black and bursting into flame, as pheasants cluck and run senselessly across the bare fields. An apocalyptic scene set against a backdrop of arthritic, leafless cottonwoods and the flat hills that hide the Bighorn River.

We were lost in eastern Montana, Crow country, looking for the Little Bighorn Battlefield, site of Custer's glorious defeat— my father behind the wheel, piloting our silver compact rental car over red clay roads greasy from the runoff of melted snow. Smoke rose from the charred fields in gauzy patches, filling the car with the faintly narcotic smell of smoldering weeds. Our luggage was in the backseat. My large red pack—the kind supposedly favored by hikers on the Appalachian Trail (a gift from my father)—and my father's wheeled leather suitcases. My father's fly rods in their cylindrical leather cases were there, as well as two of my father's side-by-side twenty-gauge shotguns in their fleece-lined leather cases. One of these very shotguns, incidentally, I had stolen from the unlocked gun case in his den and tried to pawn when I was fifteen years old. This was sixteen years ago during what my father eventually came to call my "rough patch," a hazy span of time nearly a year in duration during which I stole rampantly and masturbated frantically, sometimes five to six times a day. My father was aware of the theft, obviously, of the masturbation I'm not sure, although I wouldn't be surprised, as I stole a copy of Leopold von Sacher-Masoch's *Venus in Furs,* leaving a large, noticeable hole in the volumes on the shelves in his den. I kept the leather-bound volume under clothes in my closet, and abused myself to a pulp daily in that very closet, the wooden folding doors shut behind me, the chain for the overhead light dangling over my head where I knelt with my jeans around my ankles, my favorite passages dog-eared for easy reference.

I stole mostly from my father's house, but occasionally from the houses of my friends—rarely ever from stores or people I didn't know. I stole a Montblanc pen and a fake Rolex watch from the father of a friend of mine who was a federal judge. I stole a set of Wüsthof knives from my father's kitchen, and spent half a day throwing them at trees in the woods behind the house. I stole a necklace from my mother. It had once been my grandmother's, quite possibly it had been her mother's. It was old, medieval looking, the gold tarnished from the multigenerational sweat of the matriarchy. I stole every ashtray from my father's house, and spent half an afternoon throwing them at trees in the woods behind the house. I stole five bamboo fly rods—made by a certain R. L. Winston in Twin Bridges, Montana—from my father's den and spent half an afternoon splintering them magnificently in a vicious sword fight battle with a friend of mine in the woods behind the house. During this time I masturbated, mostly in my closet, but in many other places as well: in the woods behind the house, in all of the various outbuildings on my father's property (the garden shed, the guesthouse, the garage, the other garage), in every room of my father's house including the attic (excluding my father's den), the bathroom at my school and in the bathroom at the Lutheran church we attended once a year on Easter Sunday.

The day I stole the shotgun was much like any other day that year. I attended school five blocks from my house, a distance I walked. I got home from school and masturbated once or twice, ate something that I could microwave easily, and then looked around for something to steal. I sat in my father's den, swiveling in his chair behind the large empty oak desk. I took one of a matched pair of side-by-side twenty gauge shotguns—made by a certain James Purdey & Sons of London, England—and a handful of shells, and I went to the woods behind the house where I spent an hour or two shooting at the tree trunks. When I ran out of shells, I put the shotgun in my backpack with the barrel jutting through the zippered opening and rode my bike six miles to a pawnshop that had a row of ten-speed bikes chained together on the sidewalk and glass with steel mesh embedded in it for windows. The man who owned the store also lived in an apartment above the business with two daughters and a wife who had died of breast cancer when the girls were young. I would lose my virginity to one of the pawnshop man's daughters a year after the shotgun incident. Her name was Sara and she was two years older than me—and for an event that I had anticipated for so long, to this day I don't really remember much about it at all, whether it was awkward or sweet or even whether or not she was pretty.

When I walked into the pawnshop, I was still wearing the backpack, the twin shotgun barrels sticking up over my head. The pawnshop man undoubtedly knew my father or at least knew enough of him to know that he could be found in the phone book under Swank & Howe, Attorneys at Law but instead of calling my father, the pawnshop man in fact called the police. As it turns out, the pawnshop man was enough of a firearms expert to notice that the gun I dropped on his counter—with its fine, blued barrels and elegant scrollwork, the etched scene of a pheasant flushing in front of a pointer (whose tail was so finely rendered it was possible to see the breeze ruffling in the hair)—was probably valued at over $30,000 and most certainly stolen.

That was my childhood. I trafficked in rare antique munitions, and jacked off to first editions. It's not that I was dumb. It's just that I really hadn't the slightest idea what things were worth.

———

This was our first trip together since my mother's death. We mostly drove in silence. We never did find the Little Bighorn Battlefield, but truth be told, neither of us really cared that much about history. We had a few hours before we needed to be at the airport in Billings, and it seemed like the right thing to do. We pulled off the highway at Lodge Grass for gas, my father driving slowly on empty streets. A dog here and there. A burnt shell of a trailer house with smoke still breathing from broken windows. A Catholic mission and health clinic with mostly intact windows, and an IGA with broken windows covered by sheets of corrugated cardboard. We passed a faded sign for Custer's Last (ice cream) Stand. The sign had a cartoon image of Custer, blond hair and cavalry hat, holding a triple-scoop ice-cream cone, his tongue out as if he were licking the ice cream off his drooping blond mustache. There was an arrowhead and fletching protruding from either side of his head as if the shaft had entered one ear and come out the other side. There were people on a front porch that sloped toward the street. Teenagers in dark stocking caps and coats and black baggy jeans, some had sunglasses on.

"I have been here before," my father said, "but it was in Detroit."

We stopped at a 7-Eleven where there was one window broken and one window not, the broken window had been replaced by a sheet of plywood. The 7-Eleven was busy with locals. It was a dry reservation, and apparently this was the watering hole. A trio of dusty diesel trucks pulling horse trailers commanded the parking lot, and furtively I watched their occupants. All of them wore dark-brimmed Stetsons and dark Wranglers tucked into dark leather boots. Some of them had braids and some of them had their hair cropped short above the ears. A few wore belts studded with oval slabs of turquoise and fastened with large silver buckles. The young men were lean and acne ridden and the older men had compact potbellied stomachs straining against the dark, striped work shirts tucked into their pants. The older men had coffee in Styrofoam cups and pocked faces and the young men had plastic bottles of Pepsi and candy bars and legs that curved like empty parentheses.

They swung into their trucks, and diesel fumes filled the parking lot and the crazy-eyed paint horses in the trailers stamped their feet. It was clear that the Indians had become cowboys or that the cowboys had all turned into Indians or that the Indians were all cowboys to begin with just nobody ever noticed. Well, maybe that wasn't clear but what *was* clear was the fact that something wasn't quite right.

I got out to stretch my legs while my father pumped the gas. Our rental car was a small silver pony. The red clay clotting the panels made it look as if our pony had taken an arrow in its forelock and its heaving sides were fouled with sprayed blood and chunks of lung matter. I took my hand, pressed it into the red gumbo, then reached and made a splayed red handprint in the middle our silver pony's chest, right over the engine. We left Lodge Grass in silence.

The fishing hadn't been very good this trip. My father had hired us a guide, a young guy about my age, with shaggy hair, who spent most of the day apologizing. "I don't know," he would say, "usually it's better than this. Fish can be fickle."

"Well, hell," my father said. "At least we have the scenery. There's worse things we could be doing. At least we're not at work." For some reason then, I became acutely aware that the guide, hunched miserably at the oars, was indeed at work. I wondered what he thought of us. At the end of the day my father gave the guide two crumpled one-hundred-dollar bills and told him it was the best day he could remember having for quite some time.

After, in the car driving to our hotel, my father said, "Sorry the fishing was so bad. I'd hoped it would be better. But, that's the problem with having a young guide. When the fishing is good, it's not so bad. The young guide is going to work for it, keep you out late—he's enthusiastic, see? But, when the fishing's off, you're screwed. No amount of enthusiasm is going to make up for lack of experience. I know if we would have had some old crusty salt out there today we would have caught plenty. But, that's how it goes. That's why they call it fishing, not catching."

This was a phrase my father loved. Often he applied it to situations that had nothing to do with fishing. Once, I called him in misery after a longtime girlfriend had left me. After a few consoling words his closing remarks were, "Well, son, that's why they call it fishing, not catching."

I looked over at my father, driving, still in his fishing vest and obnoxious fishing hat, the one with the sweat-stained band and a line of ragged flies stuck in the brim.

"Maybe it's just us," I said. "Maybe we're not that good. I bet the guide is somewhere right now talking about how when the fishing is bad it really sucks to have poor fishermen."

My father laughed at this. "Could be," he said. "I guess there is always the other side of the coin."

I thought about the night they admitted my mother into the hospital in Grand Rapids. I'd come as soon as I could but she was already in the ICU. I sat with my father there, all night. When the doctor came out to talk to us, I remember my father's ill concealed disbelief, his rage. The doctor looked all of twenty-two, a young woman with henna-colored hair and a nose ring, who spoke in clipped British tones.

"Your wife has suffered a powerful stroke," she said. "She is not responding to treatment."

"And who are you, chippy?" my father said. "Just who the fuck do you think you are? Where is the doctor in charge?"

In the waiting room, the TV had been turned to a channel running some sort of classic western marathon. Eastwood. Peckinpah. Bronson. McQueen. Kristofferson. All the dramatic gunfights, the stolen horses, the barroom brawls, the slow pinwheeling deaths. We watched these movies, a seemingly endless loop, blurring together in one continuous meandering storyline, and then, sometime after dawn, the doctor came out again to break the news to us. This time my father had nothing to say to her. I shook her hand. I thanked her. I don't know why.

Eventually, after driving around aimlessly for almost an hour, we got out the map and found our way back to the highway and the airport. But, before we did, we passed through a small town, a blink-and-you'll-miss-it type of place—a post office, a laundromat, a small Baptist church with graffiti sprayed on the brick—the whole place unremarkable except for the mounds of tumbleweed piled up against every standing surface. It was bizarre, like the weeds were some sort of fast-reproducing vermin threatening to overtake the town. We hadn't seen a single sign of inhabitance. The whole place was empty, except, in the parking lot of a run-down motel, there was a pile of tumbleweed burning. The flames towered over a man, wearing fluorescent orange sunglasses, who stood with a hose in his hand to keep the fire from spreading. The man had a dark ponytail, and he held the hose like a six-gun. As we passed, my father did something remarkable, a thing that I will never forget. He pointed at the flaming tumbleweed and the man with the hose. My father's hand was a cocked six-gun.

"Crow country Moses confronts the burning bush," he said, and began humming the theme song to *The Magnificent Seven*.

I joined him. We did this for miles.

At the airport, we sat at the terminal and waited for our flight. My father had a bag of trail mix and was digging through it for the almonds. We could see out past the planes staging on the runway, the flat expanse of just-greening grassland. Antelope were grazing. A plane came in to land, and its shadow moved directly over their backs and they didn't even look up.

"You want some of this?" my father said, shoving the bag of trail mix toward me.

"Did you eat all the almonds?"

"I think so."

"Why don't you just buy a bag of almonds? They had those for sale right next to the trail mix."

"I like searching them out amongst the other stuff I don't want."

"Seems like a waste."

"I'm offering what's left to you."

"I'm not hungry."

"Well, then you're the one that's being wasteful, not me. All I can do is offer." He was still wearing his fishing hat. His stained vest. The sunburn on his nose was starting to peel.

"What are you going to do?"

"I'll just save the bag, maybe someone on the plane will want them."

"That's not what I meant."

"Oh. You mean what am I going to *DO*. I don't know. I'm sixty-two years old. She managed the office for thirty-two years. Can you believe it? Men say stuff like this all the time, but I wouldn't have acquired half of what I've got now if it wasn't for her. I was thinking today, you and I are too much alike. You know that if she was with us there is no way in hell we wouldn't't've found that damn battlefield. She would have had the directions printed up last week. A brief synopsis of important facts regarding the massacre, and the location of a nearby café whose lunch menu featured reasonably priced healthful options with a local flair."

"What's that supposed to mean?"

"If it wasn't for her, I don't know what way my life would have gone. Maybe it sounds pathetic, but she picked me up, put me under her arm and ran with me like I was a football."

"Regrets?"

"Oh no, but at certain moments you can't help but imagine how things would have been different. I didn't come out of the womb wanting to be a tax attorney, you know."

"What would you have done instead?"

"What's past is past. How about now? I've been thinking about moving out here."

"What would you do?"

"Fish. Relax. I think there's some sort of golf course around here somewhere. I'm sure it's no Pebble Beach, but I bet you don't have to call ahead for a tee time. I could get a dog. Chase birds in the fall. I'm not joking. I've always thought that had things been different for me, I'd've ended up out here as a young man." He patted the carry-on bag at his side. "I picked up some real estate literature. I'm going to look at it on the plane. If I sold just the house back home I could buy a whole damn ranch out here. Think about it. Land you couldn't ride across in a day."

"What are you talking about? Ride? You don't ride."

"I might learn."

Two years later, I had to come home to Michigan to handle my father's affairs. As I was cleaning out his desk I found a stack of real estate brochures in the top drawer. BIG SKY COUNTRY REAL ESTATE: OWN A PIECE OF THE LAST BEST PLACE. REAL WEST: EXPERIENCE THE TRADITION. There were glossy photos of middle-aged men holding large trout, middle-aged men smiling in ski gear with their pretty second wives, middle-aged men in Stetsons doing things with horses. My father had suffered a heart attack waiting in line at the DMV to get his driver's license renewed. To me, this seemed like a punch line to a joke, not a legitimate way for a person to die. He'd never moved to Montana, of course. The process of disentangling himself from the practice proved insurmountable. The last time I'd talked to him had been on the phone for my thirtieth birthday. I'd told him I was thinking of going back to school, or going to Alaska to work at a salmon cannery for the summer to save up enough money to go to New Zealand—or possibly signing up to teach English in Korea.

He'd laughed. "Was I hard on you when you were a boy?"

"Not especially, no."

"I didn't think so, either. My dad was hard on me, and it didn't make any damn difference. I think women are the only real source of motivation in the world for men. You know what your problem is?"

"What?"

"I can say this because I recognize my symptoms in you. You and I, we have a capacity for work, dedication, all that. It's just that we suffer from the diffusion of desire."

"I have a lot of things I want to do."

"I understand. And we should do something before you move to Alaska or New Zealand or Korea. We should go to Montana, do a little fishing. Maybe we'll take a day and look at some land."

After the brochures, the rest of the papers in my father's desk were inscrutably impersonal. He had a whole drawer full of receipts for gas, lunches, and travel expenses. He had another drawer full of warranty statements for every appliance in the house dating back to the first microwave he and my mother ever purchased in 1979.

I ended up just throwing everything away, brochures and all, and sitting in his chair with my feet on his desk. I thought about how you could tell a house was empty, even a big house like this one, just by how it feels when you're quiet. A house can give a sense of emptiness that moves beyond mere silence. It's a hollowness. You can be more alone in an empty house than anywhere on earth. And now, the house was mine—all the stuff and all the absence, the empty dark matter between the stuff. I realized for the first time what it must have been like for my father here, and this, too, was something I'd inherited—a newfound awareness that nothing amplifies the emptiness of a place like ownership.

I got up from the desk and went to the gun cabinet, opening the door on the neatly aligned regiment of English and Italian shotguns. I ran my fingers over the blued barrels, the glossy hardwood stocks. The Purdey was there, the one I'd tried to pawn all those years ago. I took it out and swung it like I was following a low-incoming grouse. I sighted down the barrel at the Tiffany lamp on my father's desk. I broke the gun open, and smelled the tang of Hoppe's 9 oil. I snapped it shut and the barrel reseated with a satisfying click. I stuffed some shells in my pocket, and headed out to the woods behind the house.

IN HINDSIGHT

I

1.

Lauren followed the drag mark for a mile down the gravel road and then another half a mile down her dusty driveway—and then parked her truck and cried. The bastard had shot one of her steers—of which she had six, red Texas longhorns—and dragged it down the road by its neck and deposited it here for her to find, practically on her front step.

She'd gotten her taxes done that day at the free tax preparation kiosk in the County Market. Lauren hadn't filed a tax return since Manuel died, two years before. She wouldn't have this year either, but she was in the store and had just gotten her mail and she had the W-2 forms in her pocket, and thought, what the hell? It was free. As it turned out, she had almost one thousand dollars coming to her as a refund. Manuel's death had put her in some sort of different tax bracket.

She'd left with her groceries and was feeling pretty good all the way home. And then, the drag marks. None of the cattle were to be seen except for the dead one. Its tongue hung from its mouth. Its eyes were open and skimmed with white. Its neck was twisted strangely and one of its horn points was buried in the dirt. That was what had made the groove all the way down her road. The poor animal's beautiful, ivory-colored horn scraping through the dirt as he dragged it to her doorstep.

Lauren wiped at her eyes with her shirtsleeve and got out of her truck and sat on the animal's massive flank and cried some more. And then she wiped her eyes on the other sleeve of her shirt, opened the back door to let her dogs out, and went to track down the rest of her cattle.

There was a section of fence down, and she followed the tracks leading through the gap—and there they were, just over the first rise, on the vacant lot next to hers where there was a small creek and the grass was tall and green. They watched her approach, and she talked to them like she always did. She didn't have names for them. She called them all Red.

"Hey there, Red. You goddamn Reds. Let's go now." She was behind them, waving her arms and hazing them back toward the fence. With some reluctance, they left the creek bottom and trudged in single file to their own rocky pasture. Lauren twisted the wire fence-ends back together. It had already broken once, and her mend had failed—and so she pulled the wire a little tighter to overlap the ends and then twisted. Fixing the fix. The definition of insanity was continuing to fix the fix.

Her dogs sat and watched her work, two small brown mutts of indeterminate breed. They'd shown up together a few years back and decided they would stay. They were two neutered males and they seemed to be good friends, old traveling companions.

She'd named them as a unit, not separately, because they were never apart. Elton John. That was their name.

With the cattle back in the pasture, she stood and looked some more at the dead steer. She pulled on one side of its horns to get its head straightened so its neck wasn't in such a gruesome position. It was getting close to dark, and she thought about driving down to Jason's house. He had a big German shepherd that he let roam and it was pure black and didn't ever bark, just growled, a wet rumbling deep in its chest. She didn't like that dog and she didn't like Jason and Jason didn't like her and she knew damn well it was him who'd shot and dragged her steer. She didn't want to go down there because it was dark. She didn't want to go down there at all, really. But, she was going to make herself go down there, because a dead steer was not just something a person could turn a blind eye to. She wasn't going to go down there now, though. She'd wait until morning and then she would do it.

She called in Elton John and fed them and put out two bowls for the cats. She heated up soup for herself and crushed half a bag of saltines into it and ate standing over the kitchen sink looking out the window into the dark, thinking alternately about her dead steer and her one-thousand-dollar tax refund. That's how it had always gone for her, her whole life, one fortuitous turn of events followed by equal or greater amounts of heartache and tragedy. Her life was one of those electronic poker machines, rigged for the house. Feed you enough sugar to keep your hopes alive and then crush-crush-crush; a little more sugar, and then, crush some more. Elton John sat and looked at her expectantly. She put her soup bowl down and they licked it, each on separate sides, noses nearly touching. Now she wished she had just gone right down to Jason's and confronted him first off. She would think about it all night long and wouldn't sleep at all.

She and Manuel had been married for only two years. They hadn't been particularly good years. But, during that time, her life had been occupied by another person. There was something to be said for that, even if that other person was just Manny, wheelchair bound toward the end—and mean, even at the beginning. Since Manny's passing, she'd filled her life with the animals. She had the cattle, a miniature pony, three hogs, three Nubian goats, two peacocks, Elton John, two alpacas, several cats who existed as cats tend to do, on the periphery, and an ever-changing number of chickens.

She cared greatly for the animals, but sometimes she missed a weight on the mattress next to her at night. There were times when the sound of her cattle muttering in the yard and the snoring of Elton John wasn't enough to make her fall asleep.

She did her chores in the early morning gray. It was the weekend, and she didn't have to go to work. She was a custodian at the high school in town, a job she neither liked nor hated. It was just what she did for a set number of hours a week to feed her animals.

She tried to avoid the red mound of the steer on her front lawn but she had to scatter feed for the chickens, and as she walked by the dead animal she saw that something, a magpie probably, had pecked out an eye. The hole yawned at her. She went back inside and climbed into her bed and pulled the covers over her head.

Lauren had ten acres of land upon which grew not a single tree. At some distant time, it had been a riverbed, and her pasture was cobbled river rock sparsely covered with grass. When the wind blew, great swirling clouds of dust rose and sifted into her house forming deltas of grit under the doorways. There wasn't enough forage for the cattle, so even in the summer she had to buy hay.

The land and the small house that sat upon it had been left to her by Manuel. It was half of a twenty-acre plot, the other ten acres belonged to Jason, Manuel's son from his first marriage. Jason worked at the Stillwater mine and was gone for long periods of time. He had a trailer house on his section and a jeep up on blocks. When Lauren hadn't seen any sign of his presence for a while, her hopes would rise slightly and she would think fondly about explosions, tunnel collapses, equipment failures, and then when eventually he returned and she saw his truck parked and that evil-looking shepherd dog stalking around in the burdock, she'd feel vaguely ill, as if he were the returning symptom of some chronic disease.

Jason begrudged her the land Manny had left to her. He and Manny, the way it often is with father and sons, had hated each other every day of their adult lives and toward the end didn't speak for months. That much hate takes almost as much work as love and, in the end, the two might be nearly indistinguishable. With that in mind, she tried not to hate Jason. She just wished he didn't exist.

She lay in bed until nearly noon when Elton John's whining at the door forced her to move. She let the dogs out and watched them sniff around the dead steer. After a while, still in her flannel pajamas, she put on her boots and went to the shed. She rummaged around and found a length of chain and a flat nylon tow strap. There was a large greasy rag on the workbench and she grabbed that as well. She pulled on her gloves and with the rag covering the steer's head—its gaping, vacant eye-socket—she looped the chain around its neck, snugging it up behind the horns. After hooking the tow strap to the chain, she secured the other end around the hitch on her truck. She opened the door for Elton John and they jumped in and sat next to her on the bench seat.

She drove slowly, looking behind her once, to make sure the steer was hooked up tight, but not looking again because she hated the way the steer's neck stretched under the chain and the way its legs crossed all akimbo and its tongue lolled in the dirt like a huge pink mollusk pulled from its shell.

A half a mile down the road, she turned off and drove to the edge of a coulee that ran through a section of fallow pasture. She didn't know who owned the land but there was a real estate sign at the corner of the property. She'd heard that the piece had been subdivided but as far as she knew not a single plot had sold. She drove parallel to the coulee, as close as she dared, until the steer swung in behind. She stopped and let Elton John out. They stayed close, raising their legs occasionally on clumps of sage-brush. She'd brought a piece of two-by-four, and, with a rock as a fulcrum, set to work levering the huge animal off the edge of the coulee. The wind was up, as usual, and she had grit in her teeth. The animal was as obstinate in death as it had been in life. She was grudgingly appreciative of this quality. When it went, it went slowly as a sinking ship, hindquarters first. It landed in the sand, some six feet below, with a wet thud she could feel through the soles of her boots.

It was early evening now. Spring, according to the calendar, but the wind still carried with it an edge of snow, and she was headed down to have it out with Jason right then and there. Still in her damn pajamas with her barn coat over them.

As she drove by her place and saw the drifts of wind-driven dust rising from the pasture, she had an idea. She pulled her truck around and sat visualizing the way it would look. Trees. Her tax return. A whole line of them planted close together, some kind of hardy pine. A shelterbelt. She grew excited and went inside and spent an hour making drawings on yellow legal pads. She drew her house, and then a series of different tree placement configurations. She found a number for a nursery. By that time it was dark and she had to do her evening chores.

She stood on her porch just after dawn and watched six turkey vultures spiral through a thermal, their wings motionless. The crows and ravens had shown up as well. She could hear them, a dark flock rising and settling in the coulee, black as dumped coffee grounds against the backdrop of dried grass. She thought maybe she should have shoveled some dirt over the carcass, but then again, maybe this was better. A Buddhist funeral. She'd heard this was how the Tibetans did it.

Yesterday, the sight of the birds feeding on her steer would have debilitated her, but today things seemed better. A project was all a person really needed in the world to keep her going. A task, a goal, a pursuit, an objective: these had always been truer husbands to her than Manny or even her animals. And who was to say, maybe Manny and her menagerie were just variations on the same theme. Do a job, and lose yourself in the doing of it. Animals were guarantors of perpetual tasks. A man like Manny, even more so.

She did her morning chores and thought about trees. Elton John followed her around as they always did, respectfully sniffing the chickens, steering clear of the cattle, engaging in mock stand-offs with the cats.

When the pigs had been slopped and eggs gathered and feed tossed to the chickens, Lauren walked her property boundary. The wind came predominately from the east, and she stood leaning on a shovel imagining the way it would look. A border of trees, close planted so their branches intermingled into a net that would catch the wind and bring it to the ground. She could hear how it would sound, the wind screaming into the trees, the branches fringed with soft needles opening like welcoming arms, smothering, softening, subduing so she could stand on the lee-ward side, her hair barely tousled. She wanted the trees now. She wanted them ten years ago. To plant a tree one had to be fairly certain that one was going to be around long enough to eventu-ally enjoy it. Otherwise, planting a tree was—what? A symbolic ritual? A gift to a future generation, one that probably wouldn't give a damn about you in the first place? To hell with that. If Lauren was going to plant a tree, she was going to reap the ben-efits. After she was gone, the world could do what it wanted. She needed trees that grew fast.

The cattle got out again. Lauren was making herself and Elton John lunch and she saw a red rump walk by her kitchen window. She put down her sandwich and went out to scream and plead the cattle back into their enclosure. They'd broken through the fence, a different spot this time. One of her mismatched poles had just been pushed over. Probably, the animal had been scratch-ing itself and unwittingly knocked it down. Still, she was worried about this. Two escapes in one week. The fence was flimsy, that was true, but it wasn't the physical fence that kept the cattle in anyway, it was the idea of the fence. She had to wonder if maybe the cattle had come to believe less and less in the magic of the wire. She reseated the toppled post and stacked rocks around its base. The cattle watched her balefully. She tried to read their blank eyes for signs of insurgence.

She didn't go speak to Jason. She was in a good mood and figured that they were hard enough to come by so she shouldn't ruin it. That night, she heard coyotes howling down in the coulee. Elton John whined to go out early. It was still dark. She rose and opened the door for them. They filed out like normal and set to their routine sniffing of the yard. She went back to bed. When she woke several hours later to start her chores, Elton John weren't at the door. They weren't in the yard either. She never saw them again.

She blamed herself. She never should have let them out with coyotes around that close to the house. She blamed Jason, for shooting the steer that brought the damn coyotes in the first place. She blamed Manny for dying and leaving her alone. She called in sick for work and spent a morning driving all the back roads calling their name.

It was a full moon, fat as a tick stuck to midnight's flank. The coyotes worshipped it faithfully. They made their home in the coulee for a week and she could hear the snapping and popping of their teeth. If she had owned a gun, she would have left the coulee littered with their corpses. If she had a gun, she would have gone down and shot Jason and his black dog. If she had a gun, maybe she would have sat down on her couch and never gotten up from it again.

Her refund check came. She ordered her trees, two dozen blue spruces, and spent a weekend with a pick and shovel digging holes. Two dozen pits, neatly spaced, with the piles of dirt and rock next to them, like little graves awaiting occupants. At night, she had long conversations with Jason during which she showed him the error of his ways in a multitude of devastatingly articulated reproaches. She didn't go down there and actually face him though, and each day that passed it seemed less likely that she would.

The trees came. Much of her excitement was gone but she planted them carefully, tamping the loose dirt around the roots, sinking them deep so the wind wouldn't blow them over. She spent a whole afternoon watering each one of them in turn, standing with the hose, looking out over the backs of her cattle, to the mountains that hunched white and silent over the valley. The trees were small. She had no idea they would be so expensive. To get the number she wanted she had to settle on spruces that were only slightly larger than seedlings. When planted, her shelterbelt, her brilliant idea, only came to just above her knees. The trees themselves seemed fragile. She wondered if she should have used her money in some other more responsible way. That one thousand dollars would have bought a lot of feed. She watched the trees pitch and blow with the wind, the strong gusts nearly laying them flat.

It was early summer now. Lauren watered the trees every morning before she left for work. She watered them again in the evening. They all seemed to have taken root just fine. She sometimes
plucked a green needle from a tree and chewed it as she did her
chores. She liked the taste of pine. It was astringent and clean. It
seemed like she'd had a bad taste in her mouth for as long as she
could remember.

It was just past dark when Lauren drove home from work.
It was summer school now, which meant shorter hours. Fewer
students meant fewer trash cans to empty, fewer toilet paper
spools to refill. The night was warm and she had the windows
down so she could smell the river and the cut hay in the fields.
She was nearing her driveway when a huge, red-brown form filled
her headlights. She braked and cursed, and the steer stood with
its massive horns lowered, its eyes like rolling white marbles in
the glare.

She honked her horn and shouted, waving one arm out the
window, and the animal turned and ambled slowly down the road
toward home. Lauren followed and saw other shadowed forms
moving in the ditches. She could hear the cattle's hoofs striking
rocks and their occasional groans.

In her driveway, she turned her high beams on, the twin
shafts of light stabbing out at the cattle milling around in the
yard. When Lauren got out of the truck to assess the damage to
the fence, she saw what had happened. Her trees. They lay in
trampled wreckage, limbs splintered, thin trunks snapped off
near ground level, the whole line of them violently trod to pieces
under the churning hoofs of the escaped cattle. Lauren sat down,
right there in the dust and manure of the cattle enclosure. She sat

with her legs out in front of her and then even this was too much. The earth wanted her flat. She lay back with her arms spread, the headlights running parallel above her, white moths and dust motes swirling through them. She tried, very earnestly, with only a hint of self-pity, to remember the last time someone had said that they loved her.

2.

At age twenty, Lauren was fairly certain she would never be considered pretty. However, she had been told she was *shapely,* and she thought this was better than nothing. She liked to walk. Once she set out from the small apartment she rented in town and hiked along the frontage road and then up the trailhead to Livingston Peak and then up to the peak itself, scrambling the last hundred yards over loose, sliding scree as the sun set behind her. It was a one-way journey of some twenty miles. She'd brought a sleeping bag and a few granola bars. She found a declivity in the rocks out of the wind and looked out over the range stretching down and away to the south, dark and silent under the wash of stars. She hiked back home the next day after watching the sunrise.

She had boyfriends. She liked to dance. She could two-step and jitterbug and waltz a little. On Friday nights she'd go to the Longbranch and sit at the bar and drink soda water and twirl on the floor with anyone who would ask her until her feet hurt in her boots and the small of her back was damp from the hands of her partners.

She went to school. For three semesters, she'd been a college girl. She worried about finals. She worked part-time at the Western Café serving breakfast. She lived in the dorms. Once she'd had sex with a boy she'd met only that night and never saw much again after. She still marveled about this sometimes; not the act itself, just her ability to perform it. It seemed like something someone else had done.

She had the idea that she might want to be a nurse. It wasn't something she'd put a lot of thought into, but she had a vague idea that nurses were generally optimistic and competent and rarely lacked for employment opportunities. That is what she told people when they asked her what she was studying. "I'm *pursuing* my nursing degree," she'd say, liking the way it sounded, as if the degree were something she had to chase down. She pictured the diploma—the piece of paper itself, the little embossed seal and looping signature of the dean—wind-borne, fluttering out across the empty field behind her house. Herself in pursuit.

Three days a week she opened the café at six in the morning. The early crowd was mostly old men who wore jeans and pearl-snap shirts and Stetsons that they would put beside them on the bar top when they ate. These were men whose wives had finally gone on to rest after a lifetime of ranch work and whose children hadn't yet gotten up the courage to suggest a retirement home.

She liked the job well enough. She poured endless cups of coffee and laughed and rolled her eyes when one of the old buzzards made a feeble pass at her.

And then, a regular she knew by first name only, Edward, had a stroke in the bathroom and she simultaneously learned two things. First, that she wouldn't be able to continue working at the Western and second, that she might not have what it took to be a nurse.

The realities of the old men's prostates coupled with severe coffee consumption meant that the single-stall restroom at the Western was in near-constant use every morning. When a line four-deep had formed at the closed door, and the occupant wasn't responding to knocks, she was forced to do something. Still holding her coffee pot, she rapped sharply on the door and there was silence. Everyone in the restaurant was watching now, and she didn't know what to do. She cleared her throat.

"I'm going to come in, Edward," she said, surprised to hear her own voice. It was her do-you-want-another-refill voice. There was no reply and she handed the coffee pot to the nearest man and put her shoulder to the thin door. It splintered at the lock, too easily, and she stumbled in under her own force and almost landed in Edward's lap. He was slumped on the toilet, pants around his ankles, his legs spread, with a long line of spittle trailing out from his crooked lips. She remembered clearly that his eyes were open and that they watched her, dully. He was still alive, but he had cow eyes.

She tried to stick it out for a while longer but no matter what was cooking on the hot line, the Western smelled like the bathroom had smelled that day—the rankness of Edward's loosened bowels spiked with the chemical odor of the air freshener. It made her nauseous. What troubled her more, though, was what this incident seemed to reveal about her own lack of backbone. A nurse would have taken control, would have felt an innate sense of compassion and made the best out of a horrible situation. Lauren had, as it turned out, a weak stomach. She'd backed out of the room with her hands over her mouth, Edward's bovine glare following her every move. The old men had to do everything. She'd even been unable to make her fingers work to dial for the ambulance.

At school, she felt like an impostor. She knew that it would only get worse. She would have to attend to people in pain. Wipe excrement from people's bodies. Go home and wash blood and worse from her scrubs. It all seemed too much. She looked for signs among her classmates. Did anyone else sitting on either side of her in the lecture hall have this inner recoiling when confronted with the sight and smells of humanity most basic? If they did, she saw no sign. These women seemed staunch and solid. The type who could look unblinking into fevered faces, smooth the brows of children with incurable ailments, not panic when confronted with the unnatural sight of limbs mangled in a car accident. Her classmates were people who could be unperturbed by ill health. She had been tested and found wanting. Simple as that.

She stopped attending classes. She moved out of the dorms and back in with her mother until she could find her own place. She got a job.

3.

By age thirty-two, Lauren had been sole caretaker for her mother for three years. Her mother had given birth to her when she was forty-one years old. An accident, with a man she had no intentions of marrying. She'd been divorced once already, and said that she wanted no part of that song and dance. "I met him at the rodeo on Fourth of July and we watched the fireworks," she said. "I think he was maybe twenty-two years old. I mean, come on. We had fun for the weekend, and he left when the rodeo pulled out. Don't think of him as your daddy. Think of him as a sperm donor working pro bono. He was good-looking and smart, for a cowboy."

Lauren always had the vague idea that at some point she would track down her father, just to meet him. Maybe an awkward conversation over coffee so she could have a face to attach to the word, and then that would be that. She didn't want a relationship with the guy, but it did seem that she almost owed him the knowledge of her existence. In her time at college, Lauren had taken a biology course where the professor had tried to show them that the one constant for life in the universe, the purpose of life, if you will, was procreation. When it came right down to it, the goal of life in nature is simply to create more life. This had always stuck with her and she didn't like the idea that maybe the sperm-supplying half of her biological makeup might be a broken-down old cowboy who didn't know that he had a daughter to show for his years on earth.

When Lauren was young, her mother always maintained that she didn't know how to get in touch with him. But Lauren was pretty sure she could have if she'd wanted to. She was just protecting her from disappointment. Lauren figured that at some point she and her mother would get a little drunk on wine and the whole thing would come out, and she'd get his name and last known address and at some point would track him down for that awkward conversation over coffee. As it turned out, her mother, entering her late sixties, began to experience periods of slippage. She'd stop in mid-conversation and hold her finger to her nose the way she always did when she was thinking hard. "Now," she'd say. "What? What were we talking about just then? Jesus, I must be tired."

A year later, she'd been in two car accidents and had her license taken away. A year after that, Lauren found herself moving back home once more. This time to take care of her mother, who, the doctors said, in another year's time might not remember how to feed herself.

This was a typical dinnertime conversation:

"What is this, chicken? I don't want chicken."

"You love chicken, Mom."

"I don't like it. Do we have any cookies? I'd like a peanut butter cookie."

"You can't have a cookie for dinner."

"And who hired you to tell me what to do? Did Lauren put you up to this?"

"Mom."

"Don't call me Mom."

"Eat your chicken."

"Am I a prisoner in my own home? Lauren wouldn't be happy if she knew the way you treated me."

"Mom. I am Lauren. Eat your chicken. I cut it up for you."

"What? I know you're Lauren. I'm not an idiot. Shouldn't you be doing your homework?"

"I don't have homework anymore."

"Well, why the hell not? You think you can just coast through school without doing your homework? Young lady, you're going to be in for a real surprise when you hit high school."

"Okay, Mom. Eat your chicken."

"I hate chicken. Do we have any cookies? I'd like a peanut butter cookie. With milk. Lauren would let me if she was here. Where is she? I'd like to call her now."

Lauren had been worried about her ability to care for others. She thought herself prone to wilting under the smelly reality of human corporality. It was almost laughable now. Lauren washed food stains and worse from her mother's clothing, struggled to get her spongy body into the shower, kept the knives in a locked drawer, endured horrible looping conversations that weren't conversations as much as they were brutal endurance events. Demonic anger followed by tearful bouts of recognition and apology. Her mother had cataracts coming on, and when Lauren looked into her eyes it was like watching a star die back there in some far distant galaxy behind the white veil of the Milky Way.

4.

At age thirty-nine, Lauren fell in love for the first time. She was working at the veterinary clinic in town as an assistant. She'd clean cages, fill food bowls, calm skittish cats, and help lift large dogs onto the table for surgery. She was living alone. Still renting the house she'd grown up in.

She'd had her mother cremated and she hiked up to Livingston Peak with the tin urn of ashes in her pack. She waited for the wind to gust, and tossed the ashes up and they were borne away, a small matriarchal cloud, scudding across the sun. At the top of the mountain there was a USGS survey plaque bolted to the rock and a small cairn of stones. On the top of other mountains Lauren had climbed there was often a container with a logbook or just loose notes scribbled by other hikers on whatever paper they had handy. She liked to read these little glimpses into the lives of other walkers. Most were simple. Some were flippant. Some were beautiful. She'd brought a small spiral-bound notebook and a pen and she sat on the rock cairn and tried to think of what to write. She wrote the date. She sat and thought and then wrote: *My mom and I made the hike this morning. It was nice and sunny. My mom is staying for a while. I'm heading down now.* She signed her name, and put the notebook and pen in the plastic bag and pushed the bag down into the tin, pressing the lid down tightly. She wedged the urn in between some rocks and left it there, hoping the mountain goats would leave it alone so others could do as she had.

———

Lauren put the knives back in the drawers, threw away the packages of moist wipes and the weekly pill dividers and adult diapers. She had long silent meals with a magazine open on the table and a glass of wine in her hand. She'd felt mostly relief at her mother's passing, and was fairly certain this made her a bad person. She worked as much as possible at the clinic, picking up extra shifts whenever she could. She occasionally thought about returning to school, but it had been so long. She couldn't imagine sitting in a classroom. Coming home from work to memorize anatomy terms.

She got up early. Made coffee and drank it while she walked the two miles to the clinic. Work was work, but with the arrival of the new veterinarian, Dr. Genther, it had become something more. Sandra Genther, DVM, was short and compact. Wide hips, strong legs, thick black hair that she kept in a braid twisted up in a severe bun. She'd come to work at the clinic in Lauren's third year of employment there and surprised her by asking her name and remembering it, using it even, in conjunction with a smile, every morning when she walked through the door. The previous in-house vet had retired. Leif Gustafson was a taciturn old Swede who'd ignored the assistants as much as possible outside of the occasional barked order. In the three years she'd worked with him, Lauren couldn't recall Gustafson once using her name. They had worked well together. But, this new doctor—Dr. Genther. Dr. Sandra. *Dr. Just-call-me-Sandy, honey*—she was something altogether different. She came from some deep southern state— Louisiana, or Alabama—one of those places. Dr. Sandy could calm a high-strung bird dog with a touch and a few murmured words. She was gentle, but she was strong too. Lauren had seen her single-handedly hoist a sedated ninety-five-pound Chesapeake Bay retriever from floor to operating table. She worked with a smile, and was a hearty clutcher of arms and rubber of backs and giver of enthusiastic high-fives.

She was a few years older than Lauren and had small parentheses-like creases that formed at the corners of her mouth when she smiled or was concentrating, but otherwise her face was smooth and unwrinkled. Sometimes the nature of their work would put the two of them in close physical proximity and from these instances Lauren learned that Dr. Sandy smelled like GOJO citrus soap and that she had a few strands of gray hair interspersed within the black.

Dr. Sandy was gentle and she was strong and she had lived her whole life in other places. She started giving Lauren hugs in the parking lot sometimes before they went their separate ways. Nothing much. Just a quick tight squeeze and a *good job today; see you tomorrow.* Lauren was still walking to and from the clinic then, and she'd wave as Dr. Sandy pulled out and drove by in her Subaru wagon.

And then, on one rather blustery cold evening in late fall, already nearly dark at five-thirty, Sandy slowed and pulled over next to Lauren who was striding toward home on the sidewalk. She reached over and opened the passenger door.

"Get yourself in this car, honey."

"I don't mind walking. I prefer it, actually."

"Oh, come on, it's colder than a well digger's ass out there."

Lauren laughed. Her nose was running, and she sniffed and wiped it with her glove. She looked up and down the street. The wind coming through the power lines sounded like a Saturday morning cartoon ghost. Dr. Sandy patted the passenger seat and smiled. Lauren got in.

"That was always my dad's line, by the way. About the well

digger and his ass. I use it whenever I can, and I think of him. He's been gone for a good while now."

"My mom always said it's hotter than the hinges of hell."

"Don't get me started on hot, girl. I'm from Lafayette. I know a few things about hot. It's hotter than a tick on a dog's balls, hotter than a half-bred fox in a forest fire, hotter than a two-dollar pistol on the Fourth of July—it's so hot I want to take off my skin and sit in my bones."

They were both laughing now, and Dr. Sandy was slapping her own thigh and Lauren's alternately. She drove Lauren home and they sat in her car, talking, for a long time. They picked up the next night right where they left off. And the night after that. And before long they were taking turns cooking each other dinner and sometimes, at work, Lauren would be standing at the sink washing her hands, and Dr. Sandy would come up behind her and rest her hand right on her hip. She'd reach around Lauren with her other arm and pull paper towels from the dispenser and give them to her with a smile, close, practically in an embrace, their faces almost touching.

Years removed, Lauren would realize that if this had happened to her—if Dr. Sandra Genther, DVM, had happened to her—when she was younger or older, her life might have taken a surprising and beautiful turn. It was strange to think about, but the young and the old seem to be uniquely positioned to take advantage of the opportunities that life affords. It's that middle time that's a bitch. That time when you first realize without a doubt you can't do everything you wanted to do, or be everything you wanted to be, but you still cling to the hope that if you just *make the right choices,* it will all work out in the end. Of course, as a result, you are paralyzed by indecision.

For Lauren—age thirty-nine, unmarried, not a homeowner,

underemployed, mother a drifting cloud of ash—every choice made carried such *weight*. How ridiculous. Never in her life had she been so unencumbered. If only she'd known it at the time.

One night, Dr. Sandy put her wineglass down in mid-conversation, leaned over the dinner table, and kissed Lauren full on the lips, one hand wandering and getting tangled in Lauren's hair.

Kisses have a way of gathering mass unto themselves—first there is a snowflake, then a snowball, then an avalanche. Dinners became sleepovers, and Lauren walked around feeling like overnight she somehow sprouted a strange new appendage, or woke up to find that an unexplored room had appeared in her old house. It was disconcerting, but not unpleasant. Definitely not unpleasant.

The Montana winters were hard on Sandy, sweet blooming flower of the South. She had arthritis in her knee from a riding accident she'd suffered as a girl, and when cold fronts blew down from the Canadian Rockies, she'd hobble and swear. Lauren bought her an electric blanket and made a point of coming by to shovel her out on the mornings when they'd gotten new snow. They made frequent trips down the valley to Chico Hot Springs to soak in the mineral water. Sandy said it helped her knee, and Lauren loved the way the thick white steam hung in the cold air, blanketing the pool, and how they could sit there, arms around each other, and no one could see a thing.

In the early spring, Sandy's mother fell and broke her pelvis and Sandy took two weeks to go be with her. During this separation, Lauren spent a good deal of time trying to figure out just what in the hell she was doing. She was thirty-nine. She could still have kids or a kid, at least, if she wanted to. She could get married and all the rest. She didn't have to resign herself to anything. But, she missed Sandy. It was an almost visceral truth. Had she ever wanted kids anyway, or was that just something she thought she *should* want? From what mixture of head and heart and womb do these thoughts arise?

Sandy came back and things continued as they had for a while. It was summer, maybe the best summer of Lauren's life. They hiked up to the lakes above Pine Creek and had a picnic. They stripped and jumped in, shouting and cursing at the shock of the frigid water, then they dried off, lying side by side, shivering on the sun-warmed rock.

Fall came, days when you could taste the coming snow, the bloody-copper tang of it on the wind. People in town burning leaves under gray skies. Great flocks of geese making their way south, the ragged lines of them like stitched wounds in the bellies of the clouds.

Sandy's mother was not doing well. She was going to need full-time care soon. Lauren could see what was coming. She wasn't surprised when Sandy, after dinner one night, grasped her hand and said, "I've got an idea." She had a smile on her face, hopeful, but scared too, she was putting her heart in her hands and offering it to Lauren. "What if you came with me down to Lafayette? You'd like my mother. She's an old southern belle but smart and tough and I can see you two sitting on her porch drinking sweet tea and talking and that thought makes me happier than anything else I can think of. It's warm there. There's pecan trees and the people are so nice."

Lauren thought about it. She really did. She got up and ran

water in the sink and put the dinner dishes in to soak. She came back and sat at the table.

"What would I do," she said. "In Lafayette, what could I possibly do, other than drink tea with your mother?"

Sandy was holding her hand again. She had both of hers around one of Lauren's. Lauren was briefly aware of how alike the two of them were, their hands almost indistinguishable from one another. Blunt nails, dry cracked skin on the knuckles from frequent vigorous washing.

"You'd just help with my mother. I'd work—my old practice would be glad to have me back—and you'd make sure mom was okay. It wouldn't be too demanding, and mostly you could do whatever you wanted. It would be perfect. I'd feel better having my mother looked after by someone I love and trust, and you wouldn't have to find a crummy job someplace." Sandy kept talking, her words speeding up and colliding with one another. Lauren had mostly stopped listening. She leaned back in her chair, pulling her hand from between Sandy's.

Sometimes an action you think is born of conviction, staunchness, taking a stand, is actually a simple product of fear of the unknown. At the time she was indignant. How dare Sandy even ask that of her, after everything Lauren had told her about her own mother? Did Sandy really think she would be content to be some combination of housewife and caretaker? How would it look, their happy little family? Lauren stuck in the house with a querulous old woman in the Louisiana heat while Sandy went out and made a living for them both? Absolutely not.

Lauren's self-righteous anger carried her through that fall. Work became awkward, and she slowly became aware of a growing suspicion that she'd been wrong, and cruel, and an idiot on top of that. But, she'd lived her entire life in one place. It was too late for her to reimagine herself as someone who could just pick up and leave. Louisiana wasn't real to her. It was a swamp.

Dr. Sandy was gone before the snow hit. On her last day at the clinic, they had a going away party. They hugged and Lauren said something, choked on tears. "We'll stay in touch. I'll call you. Maybe I can visit?" They were in the middle of a crowded room and Dr. Sandy kissed her full on the lips and shook her head. "That's not how it works with me," she said. "I don't do half-ways."

Then someone came and wished Dr. Sandy well and they were separated. Lauren watched her for a while. She was talking, laughing, even, holding a paper plate with a piece of cake on it. Dr. Sandy would be fine. It was written all over her. She was a woman who would make a good life for herself wherever she ended up. Lauren had the peculiar feeling that it was she who'd had her affections spurned, not the other way around. She never spoke to Dr. Sandy again.

No one had ever told Lauren that you could be in love and not know it until after the fact. It seemed like love, the very state of it, should be self-evident. That this wasn't always the case rendered the whole enterprise suspect. If you were in love and didn't know it, were you in love? If love didn't clearly reveal itself to all parties involved, did it even exist on this planet? Was love a thing or an idea or just a hope? Does love have gradations? Levels? Volumes? Variations in force or intensity? Or, is love, as it seemed like it should be, a perfect natural phenomenon like the homing instinct of salmon or the supreme vision of an osprey or the incredible tensile strength of spider's silk? Is love the human animal's one ceaseless, oft-neglected gift from the universe?

5.

If you live long enough, eventually there is a doubling back. In old age, there is a regression to childhood, of course. But before that, even, late middle age can become more like young adulthood than would seem possible. At age forty-eight, Lauren was again in the habit of going to the Longbranch on Friday nights. It actually wasn't called the Longbranch anymore but its new name never registered with Lauren, as she was now part of the demographic that mainly knew things by what they used to be, rather than what they actually were.

She drank whiskey and ginger ale, and sat with her back to the bar watching the dance floor. Occasionally, drunks would ask her to dance, and she'd shake them off silently. Sometimes, more rarely, nondrunks would ask her to dance and she'd turn them down as well. She met Manny there one night. The bar was full, and he came stumbling through the crowd, cane in one hand, sloshing drink in the other. As he was making his way past, the stool next to her became vacant, and, simple as that, he lurched himself onto it and into her life. Something was obviously wrong with his legs, and he had a hard time getting up on the stool. His cane whacked her shins. He nearly spilled his drink on her, and he was cursing. When he got settled, he turned to her, hanging his cane by the crook from the bar top.

"No," he said. "Don't even ask. I will not dance with you." Then he turned away from her and began drinking. She had to laugh, despite herself.

Many drinks later, they did dance, slowly. He was without his cane, so she had to hold him upright, although by then she was none too steady herself.

That night, he'd told her he had nerve damage from taking shrapnel in Vietnam. A few months later, after they'd gone to the courthouse and signed the papers, he admitted he'd never even been to Vietnam. His number never got picked. What he had was multiple sclerosis. He could look forward to the continued degeneration of his body on a timeline and severity scale known only to the disease itself. He might remain more or less as he was for years, or, over the course of a few months, devolve into a complete invalid.

Lauren quit the veterinary clinic and took the night custodian position at the high school. The pay was similar but the health benefits were much better. She missed the animals and the normal hours. Getting to work as the sun was going down was disorienting, but it did mean that she could sleep most of the day when Manny was awake, which turned out to be good. She'd moved in with him, his modular home on the windswept bench on the west side of the river. He'd gotten the cattle a few months before his MS diagnosis. It had been getting increasing hard for him to take care of their feed and water, and he had been on the verge of selling them before he met Lauren. Now that he had her, he decided to keep them.

Manny clung to the cane for as long as possible before succumbing to the wheelchair, and, when this transition finally came, it was not pleasant. Lauren lay a sheet of plywood down on the front steps for a ramp so he could come in and out on his own. When it was warm, he'd roll outside to drink in the front yard. When it was cold, he'd stay inside and drink with the TV on mute while Lauren slept. During the week things between them were bearable. They saw each other for one or two hours at best. On weekends, though, it was different. He'd yell for her to bring him more ice for his drink or change the radio station or to adjust the volume of the TV. In nice weather, he'd be outside rolling around, drinking Lauder's scotch from a travel mug, shouting out things that needed her attention.

"Come out and look at the steer with the white on its face. Is there something wrong with his hoof? Come here and look at the corner of the foundation here. Is that a crack? The mailbox post is tipping a little to the left. The next big wind, and the thing is going to fall right over. You need to get out here and shore it up or our mail is going to get scattered all over the damn countryside. Goddamnit, Lauren, I need you to keep this place from crumbling into the dust. I'm counting on you here."

Occasionally, when Manny was especially far gone, and she was helping him into the bath or onto the couch or bed, he'd become enraged and lash out at her. Once, he'd connected, a hard, closed fist to her eye, and she'd seen an explosion of white sparks and then she'd dropped him, and left him, on the floor of the bathroom. She went and sat in the kitchen with a bag of frozen peas on her swelling eye, trying to ignore him as his angry screams turned to sobs, the first of their kind she'd ever heard.

In the summer months, Lauren began taking small road trips on the weekends. She'd load up the truck with a cooler and an inflatable mattress and a tarp and head out. She went to the Bighorn Canyon and then over to the Little Bighorn Battlefield monument. She went to the Lewis & Clark Caverns and took a candlelit tour, the hanging mineral formations breaking and sending the flickering candles' glow in a million different directions.

Manny didn't like her to be gone, but there was nothing he could do to stop her. And even he realized that when she left for the weekend she was generally in good spirits for the rest of the week when she got back.

On one of the last nice weekends in October, Lauren packed up and headed to Butte. She wanted to see the Berkeley Pit and walk around the old town to see the crumbling copper-king mansions. It was a beautiful weekend. She camped one night and then, on the second night, sprung for a room at the Finlan Hotel with its ornate, high-ceilinged lobby, the chandeliers and wall accents made of pure, polished copper. The room was pretty and had a clawfoot tub, and she soaked until the water began to cool, and then she drained and refilled the tub and soaked some more. She had a steak at the Cavalier Lounge and drank a dirty martini. She walked around town some more at night so she could see the neon bar lights, and, way up on the hillside, the white glow of the ninety-foot-tall Our Lady of the Rockies statue.

Sunday morning, she woke up late and took her time getting back. She stopped more than she needed to—for coffee, for water, for the bathroom, for gum. Despite all this, she still made it home before dark. She pulled into the driveway as the sun was getting ready to set. The cattle had come to the edge of the fence and were looking at her as she sat in the truck, taking deep breaths, trying to retain, for a little while longer, that good, carefree, weekend-away feeling. She got her bag and went inside. Usually when she returned she found the kitchen a disaster area of dirty dishes and empty soup cans and beer bottles and puddles from dropped ice cubes. Upon hearing her open the door, Manny would begin shouting about something that needed her attention and she would set her bag down, square her shoulders, and get started cleaning things up. Today, however, the house was quiet, the TV off. There was only one empty soup can in the sink and Manny was nowhere to be seen. She went to the back porch to see if he was outside smoking, but he wasn't there either.

Eventually she spotted him, and she knew immediately. He'd wheeled himself out to the far corner of the pasture and his back was to the house. There was a turkey vulture resting on his shoulder like some hideous overgrown parrot. From a distance, it looked like the bird was whispering a secret into his ear. When she came closer she saw that the blast from the shotgun in his lap had removed the part of his head where his ear would have been and the bird was doing something there altogether different.

With Manny gone, once again her life resumed its simple course, dinner with wine, magazines on the table. She stopped the weekend trips.

She decided to sell the steers. She'd made a call and set up a time for a livestock truck to come and take them away. The day before its arrival, she'd come home to find that they'd broken out. It was early morning, and she was tired after a long day. She saw the fence was down and the cattle were gone and she decided to go inside and sleep for a few hours until it was light enough to see, and then she would go out and round them up.

She lay down with her clothes on, and was awakened a short time later by pounding on the door. It was just past dawn, the mountains still black, the pasture streaked with gray light. Manny's son, Jason, was at the door, his long hair tangled, eyes shot with red, looking like he hadn't slept in a long time. His black shepherd dog sat on the steps staring at her more directly than any natural-born dog would dare. She hadn't seen him since Manny's funeral. He'd spent the whole service eyeing her murderously.

Jason was holding a long section of vinyl house siding in his hand. When she opened the door he waved it in her face.

"See? Look at this. You see this? I'm watching TV and I come out to see your goddamn loose animals tearing up my lawn, rubbing themselves against my house. This is Timber Tek siding. The best they make. It's made to look like wood. You see that? That's simulated wood grain right there. You don't get that unless you pay extra. I paid extra for the wood grain, and now you are going to pay to get everything put back just the way it was."

He kept ranting. She was having a hard time following. Something about court-appointed attorneys and the invalidation of wills composed while incompetent. His words were running together, and he repeatedly wiped at his mouth with the back of his hand. And then, he flung the piece of siding at her and retreated a few steps. He had one hand raised in the air, his index finger up and pointing at the sky.

"Get your house in order," he screamed. "Or, so help me god, one more of those shitting animals steps on my property and I'll shoot it dead and drag it to your doorstep." He turned and stomped off the porch, the shepherd dog at his heels.

The livestock truck was scheduled to show up the next day, and right then she decided that she was going to call and cancel. Lauren put on her boots and set out across the pasture to retrieve her cattle. An hour later, she had them back in the enclosure and she mended the break in the fence. Splicing the wire together in the first of what would be many fixes. While she worked, she thought of each person she'd known in this world who had died or left and she tried to put them on a scale against the people she still knew who were still alive and in her life. Never had finding a balance seemed more desperate.

The Reds stood, flies blowing around their flanks, seemingly as happy to be fenced in as they were to be roaming free. "That's enough of that," she said to them. "I don't expect anymore of that out of you lot."

II

1.

Wind and loneliness, interminable fatigue, and broken trees. Also, animals that needed to be fed. The same world that wanted to steamroll you also contained goats bleating their hunger, eggs that would go to waste if they weren't gathered, cattle that would run wild if they weren't contained. Lauren watered. She milked. She grained. She gathered. She collected all the splintered pieces of her trees and doused them with kerosene in her burn barrel. She tossed in a match, and there was a concussive whump as the pines caught fire, and she didn't even stand there for one second to watch them burn.

Winter came creeping down from the north, frosting the hill pines, taking up residence in her hands. She swallowed four ibuprofen every morning. In the long evenings, she sat at the kitchen table, soaking her stiff fingers in a bowl of hot water. Sometimes, before night fell, she could see Jason's shepherd dog padding across the snow-blown field between their houses.

The wind picked pieces of her house and sent them spinning out into the drifts. A shingle here, a section of trim there, a blue sliver of siding, piercing a backdrop of pure white.

There was a storm that lasted for three days. Her road was drifted shut and all night she lay awake, listening to the house shift and creak under the weight of the snow.

When the storm broke she emerged, a brilliant sunny morning, the light frantic with nowhere to settle. The cattle sensed her coming. They shifted, sleep-eyed, red coats made piebald with matted ice and snow. The goats sprang from their shelter, kicking through the fluff—in disgust or delight, she couldn't tell. A cat appeared from behind a hay bale. It slunk, weightless, toward her, and sat still, allowing her to rub its ears clumsily with her gloved hands. One of her roosters let loose, softly at first, as if clearing his throat, checking his tone, then louder, a raucous crowing that seemed as clear and timeless an affirmation as one might ever expect to hear. The storm was over, a clear dawn. Lauren had to laugh. Roosters, like males of other species, seemed to have a knack for stating the obvious.

Lauren quit her job at the school. She was sick of working nights. It had been fine when she'd needed to avoid Manny, but now it felt like she was starting to exist on some strange dark planet, conjoined maybe but ever separate from the rest of the daytime world. She wanted to sleep at night like a normal animal.

She got a job at the Frontier assisted-living facility and was somewhat surprised to find out that she loved it. The residents could be cranky, but most of the time they were happy and wanted to talk to whomever they could, even if it was just her, the janitor, emptying the trash cans in their rooms or shaking out their rugs. She had one old gentleman who liked her to sit for a few moments and listen to music with him. He had a record player and the scratchy songs were ones she vaguely remembered her mother listening to on the AM radio in the kitchen.

"If I was a little bit more spry, I'd ask you to dance, young lady," he'd say. "You wouldn't be able to chase me off with a stick." He was in a wheelchair, his legs atrophied to pipe cleaners. "Well," Lauren said. "Probably for the best. I'm not much of a dancer, anyway. I just like to listen."

"We make quite a pair then," he said giving a phlegmy laugh. "The last of the great listeners."

Sometimes Lauren had to clean rooms whose former occupants would never be returning. Often no one would come to claim the resident's belongings, and she would be charged with bagging up clothes for donation. She sometimes thought working at Frontier was the best thing she'd ever done, but this, the handling of remains, she didn't like. She didn't like the idea that someone would have to come along and sift through the pieces of her life and decide what could be donated and what was trash. Maybe this is part of why people had kids, so, in the end, at least it wouldn't be strangers rifling through their belongings. She wanted everything she owned to precede her into death. She wanted to pass out of this world with nothing much more than a pair of comfortable wool socks, broken-in jeans, a thick flannel shirt. Maybe it was hard to arrange the particulars of your dying, but all things being equal, she'd like to go on to her eternal rest in her work clothes, all her faculties intact until the very end. She thought maybe she should start throwing things away.

2.

At some point Lauren decided that she wasn't going to cut her hair ever again. It had been white for a long time now. Although occasionally she discovered a dark one in there, and it came as a surprise. She remembered finding her first white hair somewhere near her thirtieth birthday and it had sent her on a tailspin for half a day. It's starting, she'd thought then. The follicle that produced that hair is dying. I've reached the tipping point and from now on it's nothing but slow decline.

Now, she regarded the random brown strand as offensive. A vital hair on the head of a seventy-year-old woman was like the kind of optimist that no one can stand. The person who will sit there on parade day under torrential skies and say *I think it's going to clear any minute now.* The kind of person who will cheerfully fight to the death for a crumbling government, lacking the good sense to surrender. Lauren supposed that, on a cellular level, we never surrender. That was part of the problem. These days, when she saw a brown hair, she pulled it out immediately.

It was hard to believe, but, somehow, in old age, she'd gotten vain. She loved her hair. It was long, pure white. She kept it in a thick braid, tucked into the back of her overalls when she was out doing her chores, so it didn't get in her way. She brushed it out every night. She only washed it once a week because she'd read in her magazines that too much shampoo could destroy the natural oils that make hair healthy. A seventy-year-old woman reading *Cosmopolitan.* That was something that would probably give some folks pause.

As it was, people didn't quite know how to take an old woman with long hair. In town, she got looks. She'd be pushing her cart through the County Market and kids, shopping with their mother, would stare. She wore her overalls and muck boots most days and her braid hung down near to her waist. She figured that some of these folks in town, newcomers most of them, thought she was some kind of crazy witch, living way out where she did with all the animals. Her old truck pieced together with baling wire, still running forty-some years after it rolled off an assembly line in Detroit.

She had aches and pains. Sometimes on winter days, her

hands just didn't want to work, and she went about her chores like she had flippers on the ends of her arms. Her finger joints were gnarled and swollen and she took fish oil and glucosamine and vitamin C daily without too much noticeable improvement. She chewed ibuprofen like candy, and worked off the rest of the pain petting her dogs.

Since retiring, she'd volunteered at the animal shelter three days a week. She'd adopted dogs, of course, one or two a year, and she currently had nine, mostly mutts, except one purebred Dalmatian that showcased all of the magnificent idiocy inherent in its pedigree. He was a car chaser. Any vehicle that came down her road, he'd be after it, eyes rolled back in ecstasy, barking, slobber flying, trying to bite the tires. He was going to get his empty head crushed. She kept him inside with her most of the time, and he sat on the back of the couch, looking out the picture window to the road, eyeing each passing car wistfully.

She still had goats. She had chickens. She had one Red left. It stood solitary out in the pasture, and sometimes, while tossing hay, she thought she saw something in its eyes, a mean stubbornness. "You're not going to outlast me," she'd say. "Keep looking at me that way, and see where it gets you. I'll take care of you once and for all. I'll have you parceled up in my freezer, wrapped in butcher paper. And I swear to god I won't go to the grave until I've eaten every last piece of your scrawny ass."

Lauren was seventy-three years old, older now than her mother ever had been. It seemed impossible. Probably the only people who aren't surprised to find themselves arriving suddenly at old age are the ones who didn't make it that far.

3.

Jason's trailer had been empty now for years, five or six, she couldn't remember. He'd been there with his dog, same as always, and then one night his truck hadn't returned. It stayed gone. The trailer had a broken window, and she'd seen pigeons flying in and out. Sometimes, she sat on her back porch in the evening and devoted a few moments of her pondering to imagining fates for him. Occasionally, she was feeling generous and she let him win the lottery and move to California. Most of the time he got killed in a drunk-driving accident or addicted to methamphetamine and shot in a drug deal gone bad.

One Saturday, after she was returning from a morning of walking dogs at the shelter, she came down her road and there was a silver minivan in the driveway of Jason's trailer. It had a flat tire and it somehow seemed exhausted, as if it had pushed itself to the limit to get its owner to this point, and now, upon arrival it was giving up the ghost, a trusty steed used up in service.

Lauren slowed. There was a girl standing on the sagging porch. She had a blond ponytail and wore pink shorts. She waved at Lauren and then Jason emerged from inside. He'd gained weight. Lauren noticed immediately. Even from a distance, he looked heavy. He was leaning on crutches, his foot encased in a dirty white bandage. He saw Lauren and made no sign of recognition. He motioned for the girl to get inside and they both went in and shut the door behind them.

It was a beautiful day in mid-June—the sky a smear of bright blue, the sun warming the grass. Lauren could only guess what the inside of that trailer looked like, pigeons and all. She'd had pigeons set up a nest in the rafters of her storage shed once. At first, she'd let them be, out of respect for their eggs. They'd turned her whole workbench white with their shit in a matter of days. Eventually, she had to knock the nest down with a broom and she felt bad about it. The eggs splattered on the concrete and one of them broke open and she could see the alien shape of a hatchling in there.

She had her binoculars, and she often stood at the kitchen window with them trained on Jason's trailer. She felt slightly bad for spying, but so what? She was an old woman with little to do and she hadn't done anything worth apologizing over in a long time.

Jason rarely came outside. But the girl was often in the yard. Doing what, Lauren could not always tell. She walked around the trailer with a stick, hitting the walls randomly until Jason came out and Lauren could see his mouth open wide as he yelled at her to stop. When Jason went back inside, the girl hunkered down in the weeds and her back was to Lauren so she couldn't tell what she was doing, until she saw a thin trickle of smoke rising over her head. Was she smoking? No. She'd started a fire. She squatted next to it, pink shorts and tank top, holding her hands out as if she were warming them. Lauren's porch thermometer read seventy-three degrees, not a breath of wind or a cloud in the sky. Where in god's name was this child's mother? Why was she not in school? The van hadn't moved since they'd arrived. The tire still flat all the way down to the rim, resting on the gravel. What were they eating? Were they living in there with pigeon shit and feathers and who knows what all else? Jason had at least taped a piece of cardboard over the broken window. Through the binoculars, Lauren had observed the birds returning, flying around the roof in vain, their distress seemingly visible in their erratic passes. Maybe they had eggs in there. A nest in the cheap glass chandelier over the dining room table. The young ones chirping hungrily. The adults unable to reach them. An old woman's meandering. Of course, if there had been a nest, Jason would have cleared it out first thing, like she had the one in her shed. There was nothing else to do. If one was sentimental enough to see tragedy in the plight of pigeons, even the happiest human life would be unbearably sad.

She continued to keep her eye out for the mother. Maybe she was inside. There had to be a woman—Jason's wife, or girl-friend, or something. There was no way a girl would be living with him for any other reason. Occasionally, Jason would come out on the porch, always on the crutches. He'd smoke a cigarette, look-ing off at the mountains. Sometimes he would piss simultaneously and Lauren would be able to see the yellow arc of it, glistening in the sun. When he'd finished, he would flick the butt of his ciga-rette into the weeds, zip up, and go back inside, the thin walls of the trailer rattling as the door slammed behind him.

Lauren had never been much of a cook. There was no magic to it though, she knew that. Some people wanted to make out that being a good cook was some sort of artistry and maybe at some level it was, but mostly all it entailed was a basic ability to follow directions. She'd cooked for her mother, whose brain had prob-ably been too scrambled to taste the difference between carrots and chocolate cake. She'd cooked for Manny. He'd never said much either way about it. He never had an appetite for anything other than Lauder's scotch whiskey. She'd cooked for Sandy— well, they had often cooked together, and that was a different thing entirely. Less about the actual food and more about the act of preparation, the whole meal like one big flirt.

These days, Lauren scrambled a couple eggs in the morning and spooned them on buttered toast. She often skipped lunch completely, sometimes had just an apple and a wedge of cheese. For dinner she ate a bowl of canned soup with a handful of saltine crackers crushed up in it. Her doctor told her she needed to watch her sodium levels, so she had been getting the Healthy Choice soup lately. It cost twice as much and tasted half as good.

Lauren thawed some chicken breasts she'd had in the freezer. She dug out one of her good, seldom-used Pyrex baking dishes. She put the breasts in there on top of a bed of instant rice and poured over a couple cans of chicken mushroom soup. She scattered some croutons on the top and put it in the oven. Her Dalmatian—named Rocks, after the contents of his head— watched her move about the kitchen, the expression on his face, if possible, more quizzical than usual. Usually, he got to lick out a soup bowl at some point during kitchen operations, but thus far none had been offered, and he was obviously concerned. He whined.

"Oh, shut up," Lauren said. "This isn't for us. You have nothing to complain about. Be happy you're in here and not outside with all your siblings. Be happy you found the one place where it is to your advantage to be too stupid to remain at large with the general population."

She worked at the shelter the next day and on her way past Jason's trailer she put the chicken and rice on the porch railing. She'd written *Just heat and serve!* on a blue Post-it note and stuck it to the top of the foil.

———

She worked a full six-hour shift at the shelter. She walked fifteen different dogs, one at a time, in a complete loop around the property. She figured that, over the course of the day, she'd done at least five miles and she felt pretty good. Although her hands were arthritic, her knees and ankles were fine. She was still a damn good walker. Lately she'd been thinking about making one last trip up to Livingston Peak. She hadn't done it in years. While she was strong enough to do five mostly flat miles, she wasn't sure if she was capable of a steep scramble at high altitude. She could fairly easily imagine falling and breaking her hip. Crawling around in agony, waiting for the magpies to peck her eyes out while she was still breathing. There was still snow up that high right now anyway. She had all summer to decide if she was up for it. Maybe in the meantime she would pick up the pace. She'd take the dogs for two loops around, they'd love that. The girls who worked at the shelter would no doubt notice and make remarks. I'm in training, she'd say. They already thought she was crazy, the way she walked, fast, head down, sometimes practically dragging dawdling spaniels behind her. Tara, the sweet, chubby little thing at the front desk, was always complaining about being tired. "I wish I had your energy," she said to Lauren. "I don't know about that," Lauren replied. "I'm just worried that if I stop I might not get started again."

That evening, the chicken and rice dish was gone from the porch railing. There was no sign of life and she watched for a long time after dinner, drinking tea with her binoculars by her side, but no one came out.

A few days later she pulled out one of her remaining baking dishes and put together a tuna casserole. Rocks watched her work and she talked to him. "That's the way it goes," she said. "You cook for other people, better than what you make for yourself.

That's some human foolishness right there. A dog wouldn't understand. Church ladies are always doing stuff like this. Any crisis or sad turn in a person's life and they're right there with a nice casserole. Their husband is at home, eating a microwave dinner, smelling all day what they got cooking in the Crock-Pot. *It's not for us, Harold. It's for the Johnsons. Mrs. Johnson's nerves are acting up again and I'm going to bring them this nice roast.* Harold is grumbling, eating his slop, wishing that *her* nerves would act up occasionally so someone would make *him* a roast.

"Why do they do it, Rocks?" The dog, recognizing his name, tilted his head and thumped his tail on the floor. "Are all these casseroles delivered out of pure Christian compassion? Or, is it just an excuse for them to weasel themselves into the situation? A chance for them to stand on the doorstep and hand over some food, say a few condolences, all the while scanning the inside of the house, noting the state of the things so that they might have some juicy details to throw around when they get on the phone to the other old biddies on the church directory.

"I'm telling you, Thelma, it's complete chaos over there. That poor Mr. Johnson. There were dishes piled up in the sink. I mean, a tower of dirty dishes. I hear they've got her over at Pine Rest. A whole handful of sleeping pills is what I heard. I made him a nice roast. I could see how happy he was to have it. I think I might make him some Swedish meatballs this weekend. Maybe you could make him a Jell-O salad and we could go over there together.

"Rocks, I'm telling you, all the charity in the world, I'm suspicious of it. And yet, here I am, a church lady that never got around to going to church."

4.

Early summer days, maybe the finest time of the year. Mountains still capped with snow, the river on the rise, the hillsides electric green with new grass. Lauren walked her dogs at the shelter. She puttered her way through her chores. She had plenty of time left to stand at the kitchen window with her binoculars. The girl came out occasionally, always underdressed in the same pair of shorts and T-shirt. She wandered around the yard hitting things with sticks. She sometimes set out walking down the road toward the highway. She never went very far before she turned around and came back. Frequently she'd squat in the yard with a book of matches. Striking them, letting them burn down to her fingers, one at a time, over and over again. Obviously the child was bored out of her mind at best, some kind of pyromaniac at worst.

Jason emerged less frequently. Once he came out and hobbled over to the van and made some efforts to change the flat tire. He was still on crutches, and he leaned them against the side of the van as he knelt with the jack. He removed the flat tire and was going around to the back to get the spare. He was hopping along, steadying himself with a hand on the van. He'd really gotten fat. His stomach bulged over his jeans and his face was pale and doughy. He tripped over something and went down, and she kept the binoculars on him for a long time but he didn't move. He had a hand over his face so she couldn't see what was there but eventually he hauled himself up, retrieved the crutches, and went inside. The van was still on the jack. That had been a week ago.

Lauren had made them macaroni and cheese with chunks of ham. Now she was out of baking dishes and she was pissed off. Funny to think that, after everything, what finally drove her to his doorstep was the fact that she wanted her good Pyrex cookware back.

She stood on the dilapidated front porch and knocked. He opened the door, and, up close, he looked even worse—lank hair, bloodshot eyes, a gaping hole where a tooth should have been. If he was surprised to see her he didn't show it.

"You shouldn't have shot my steer," Lauren said. It wasn't what she'd planned on saying but that's what came out.

He looked down. Shook his head. Lauren tried to see behind him into the trailer but his bulk blocked the door. There was a musty, fetid, shut-in smell. "It was just a dumb animal and it never did enough harm to you that you had to shoot it."

Jason shrugged. His face might have been slightly red but it was hard to tell. He pointed to his foot, encased in a dingy white bandage. "I got diabetes," he said. "They took off three of my toes."

"I'm sorry to hear that," Lauren said.

"I've been on disability for four years. Hardly enough to get by on. And now I got a dependent." He sighed, and grimaced as if in pain. His missing tooth was like a black portal into the cave of his mouth. "Admit it, you married my dad just because you saw an opportunity to get yourself a place because you knew he wasn't long for the world and you knew you could take it from him. There was no other reason for a woman like you to marry a man like him."

Jason was looking at her now, his nostrils flared slightly, and Lauren had imagined this conversation many times but now that it was happening, she realized it was nothing like what she had expected. Jason looked halfhearted, pathetic. She was old. It was a conversation that had no bearing, had no real reason for taking place. Any emotion attached was a faded shell of what had once been real hatred, fear, anger. They were going through the motions, and both of them knew it.

"Your dad was a miserable asshole, most of the time. You yourself hated him, probably for good reason. I married him because I'd loved someone and made a mess of it, and I wanted something to take my mind off it. To punish myself for being stupid. Maybe I needed to be needed. I don't know. It was a long time ago and things get muddled. I never wanted his shitty land. Is the girl your daughter?"

Jason was going to say something but a voice piped up from inside the trailer. She had obviously been close and listening. "He's not my dad," she said.

"Mind your own business, Jo. I'm talking to this lady."

"My dad's in the army. He's overseas."

"Maybe he is, maybe he ain't. Go watch TV."

"He's a sniper."

"If you say so."

"First thing he's going to do when he comes back is shoot you."

"Hey. That's about enough from you. Go watch your show." There was grumbling, and then the sound of the TV being turned up loud, some sort of violent cartoon. Animated shrieks and laughs and car tires screeching.

"I was in Florida," Jason said. "I was with that girl's mother and then she left to see her sister in Tampa and never came back. I looked for two weeks but her sister don't even exist in Tampa as far as I can tell. I thought about just taking off, but I didn't. I could have, but I didn't." He raised his chin and widened his eyes, as if this were still a surprise—the discovery of a small nobleness existent within him. "And now, I'm here. They took three of my toes and I got a half-wild girl child that's not even my own. All of that, and I'm on disability."

And then, Lauren, surprising herself, started laughing. She felt it coming up from deep within her, a release of something pent up for a long time. She laughed until she coughed. "Those damn red cattle," she said. "Truth be told, there's been times over the years when I would have paid someone to come out and do for all of them what you did for that one. They could be the most frustrating animals I ever had."

She started to turn away and then she remembered. "If you want me to keep making you dinners you're going to have to give me my damn dishes back," she said.

"Hey, I didn't ask you for anything," he said, raising his hands as if to ward her off. "I got your dishes right here." He retreated into the trailer and Lauren tried to look in, but he'd partially shut the door behind him. He came back, balancing her dishes on one arm, crutch under the other. They hadn't been washed. The corner of one pan had something stuck to it, furred with gray mold.

"I'm out of dish soap," Jason said. "Otherwise I'd have got these clean."

"That's okay," Lauren said. Then she thought of something. "What happened to your dog?"

"Huh?"

"That big black shepherd you had."

"Got dysplasia, and I had to put it down. Years ago. Got so it couldn't walk, and it turned mean. Understandable, I guess. I was trying to feed it one day and it bit me and that was that."

"Well, that's too bad."

"Was just a dog."

"I've always liked dogs. That's why I asked. I remember watching that one walk across the field in the snow. A beautiful animal."

"The day you get a dog is the day you sign up to bury it. It's a package deal. No sense getting too attached."

"You could say that about anything. Everything in your life—either you bury it or it buries you. Doesn't mean you shouldn't get attached."

Jason scratched his head and nodded, obviously unconvinced. He pointed at the dishes she was holding. "I got a freezer full of burritos," he said. "But it's been nice to have some variety."

The girl's voice came from inside. "I hate tuna!"

"You'll eat it, and you'll be happy to have it," Jason shouted. He looked at Lauren and raised his eyebrows as if to say, See what I'm dealing with. He cleared his throat. "We appreciate it," he said.

She'd planned on putting it off until later in the summer, but then she knew she'd have to contend with the storms that tended to come up suddenly that time of year, violent, with lightning and strong wind. And, she felt good, *now*. Who knew what the coming months held? When she'd worked at the assisted-living facility one of the residents—a funny old guy who dressed in a ratty coat and tie for dinner every evening—used to say, "When you get to my age, dear, you'll think twice about buying green bananas at the grocery store." Lauren always laughed then; now she knew what he meant.

She drove to the trailhead at dawn. She had a small backpack with a few granola bars and water and a light jacket in case of rain. She had a walking stick with a loop of leather that she could put around her wrist. She brought Rocks, too. If she left him alone for long in the house, he had a tendency to upend the garbage or go into the bathroom and shred the toilet paper roll.

It was a cool morning, and as she started up the trail, the peak above her was obscured by skeins of fog. She'd done this hike many times, and she didn't allow herself to frame this one in terms of finality. She wanted to enjoy it for what it was, not some sad, elegiac trek up the mountain of her own mortality. Rocks was running ahead of her like a thing possessed. Sprinting down the trail, stopping suddenly, ears cocked, then turning to run back toward her, crashing into her legs with enthusiasm. "Go on in front and keep an eye out for moose," she said. "I once saw three different moose on this trail. A big old cow moose would stomp the vacuum right out of your skull so fast, and then I'd finally be rid of you."

The sun had come out, and as she started to gain elevation, the fog burned away. She stopped frequently to rest. Rocks chased the little red pine squirrels, growling and yipping in frustration.

She reached the top in early afternoon. The valley was splayed out below her, green, with the river winding silver down its middle. From where she stood, she could look down on a pair of ravens coasting along on a thermal. Anytime you were up high enough to see the back of a raven in flight, you knew you'd done a good bit of climbing.

She shared a granola bar with Rocks, and then she searched around until she'd found the tin that she'd left all those years ago. The notebook was still in there, swelled a bit with moisture but otherwise in good shape. It was over halfway filled with notes now. Hikers of all kinds had written their messages, and she spent a long time reading them, all the way back to the first one, the one she'd written on the day she'd scattered her mother out over the precipice.

She hadn't thought about it much until right that minute and it came to her now as a slight embarrassment—her mother had never climbed this, or any other mountain in her life. She liked working in her garden. She liked walking by the river. Hiking her ashes up here and tossing them over the edge hadn't been for her mother at all, that had been Lauren all the way. But maybe that's how it should have been. The treatment of ashes and bodies and remnants of all kinds was the duty of the living. The dead have no say, and it was silly to think they'd care either way. That was the rational line of thought. However, it was still something to consider. It was true that in her life Lauren had loved mountaintops. But if you wanted her to be comfortable in eternity, work her in with the cow manure, scatter her ashes for the chickens to dust in, dump her in the slop bucket for the pigs.

The sun was just starting to set by the time she made it down. She was dead tired. She'd twisted her knee on a loose rock and had to hobble to her truck, leaning heavily on her walking stick. On the drive home, Rocks slept on the seat next to her, instead of standing and smudging the window with his nose like he usually did.

She was too exhausted to even heat her soup, though she was ravenous. She opened a can and ate it cold, not bothering to pour it into a bowl. Tomorrow she'd wake up early and do her chores. She'd take a long hot bath, and after that she'd cook them something, maybe a pasta bake. That was easy enough.

Some sausage, some pasta, spaghetti sauce, and cheese. She had all of the ingredients, and wouldn't even have to go to the store. It was a satisfying feeling to have a day figured out like that. One of the few benefits of getting old, an enjoyable economy, short-term planning started to look a lot like long-term planning too.

She rinsed her soup can and spoon and drank a glass of water standing at the kitchen sink looking out the window. It was all but dark now and she could see down to Jason's trailer. The lights were on, the blue glow of the TV faintly visible. Maybe it was none of her concern, but that girl should be in school. She'd tell him that tomorrow. It was obvious the TV was turning her brain to mush. She needed some decent clothes. Maybe she'd like to come over and feed the goats. Growing up in a place like Florida, she'd probably never been exposed to anything like that before. At the very least it would give her something to do besides setting fires. The wrong gust of wind in a couple of weeks when the grass got dry and things could go south in a hurry. She'd have to talk to Jason about that too.

She went to the back door and let Rocks out. He did a quick disdainful bout of nose- and rear-sniffing with the low-caste outside dogs. They came to her, all eight of them, mutts in varying shapes and sizes, all wagging their tails, snuffling at her hands, the more excitable ones among them jumping and trying to stick their snouts in her coat pocket. She made them all sit, a furred mass of anticipatory canine. She tossed them their biscuits one by one, and the air was soon full of the sound of happy crunching. She sat on her porch chair and she rubbed ears and tugged tails and scratched under chins. She'd always thought that petting a dog was the greatest activity in the world a person could engage in while thinking about other things.

Off to the other side of the field she could see her Red. The lone steer standing there, a silhouette, made small by the dark shapes of the mountains rising up behind it. While she petted her dogs she watched it, waiting for it to move—dip its head to graze, or lower itself to the ground, for sleep or something else—but it didn't. It remained poised until the light was gone.

ACKNOWLEDGMENTS

First and foremost, I'd like to thank my family—my parents especially—for encouraging me, a naturally lazy kid, to keep my nose in a book. A home devoid of television, and frequent trips to the library, set me on my current path, for better or worse, and for that I'm extremely grateful.

A big thanks to Greg Keeler, at Montana State University, one of the first people to encourage me in my writing at a point where otherwise I think I might have easily given it up.

Much appreciation to all the folks at the University of Wyoming M.F.A. program, a talented pool of writers and readers from whom I learned a great deal. Special thanks to Brad Watson— the fact that this book exists is due in large part to your generosity and insight. You really did change my life. Also, to Rattawut Lapscharoensap: Without your always brilliant criticism, many of these stories would be pale shadows of their current selves. And to Alyson Hagy, for your enthusiasm and advice. Your work ethic and overall approach to the writing life is something to which I aspire.

Kali Fajardo-Anstine, you've never once been boring. Thanks for calling me on my bullshit and semi-regularly telling me my writing sucks.

Peter Steinberg, you took a chance on a fishing guide in Montana. Thanks, and all the best to you.

Luling Osofsky, kindred spirit and wild animal, you're a good friend and creator of so many things. Thank you for all the letters, lunches, and support.

To the Morley crew, especially Ben and Toby: Old friends are the best friends.

There are many folks in the windy city of Livingston, Montana, who have directly and indirectly influenced my life and writing. To all the fishing guides, here's to another season on the river—keep living the dream. If this book sells any copies, drinks at the Murray are on me. Seriously. Don't hold your breath.

Dan Lahren—world-class fisherman, chef, woodsman, repository of lore of all kinds, sacred and profane, and above all, always a true individual—thank you so much for all the stories, fishing, and meals. I look forward to many more.

Jim Harrison, thanks for the days on the river and for showing me that being a writer means, more than anything else, getting your work done.

Cole Thorne, let's dance.

A number of editors at various magazines have done great work on many of these stories. Many, many thanks to Cressida Leyshon at *The New Yorker*. Your championing of my stories has much to do with this book's becoming a reality. Also, thanks to Deborah Treisman at *The New Yorker*, and to Laura Barber at *Granta*.

I've been lucky enough to spend time at several great residencies while working on various stages of this book. Thanks so much to Willapa Bay AiR, the Brush Creek Arts Foundation, Madroño Ranch, and the Vermont Studio Center.

To Chris Parris-Lamb, a stellar agent, thanks for taking me on. And, finally, thank you, Noah Eaker, my tireless editor at the Dial Press, for your patience, enthusiasm, and keen eye—I'm exceedingly grateful.

ABOUT THE AUTHOR

CALLAN WINK was born in Michigan in 1984. He lives in Livingston, Montana, where he is a fly-fishing guide on the Yellowstone River. He is the recipient of an NEA Creative Writing Fellowship and a Stegner Fellowship at Stanford University. His work has been published in *The New Yorker, Granta, Men's Journal,* and *The Best American Short Stories.*

ABOUT THE TYPE

This book was set in Galliard, a typeface designed in 1978 by Matthew Carter (b. 1937) for the Mergenthaler Linotype Company. Galliard is based on the sixteenth-century typefaces of Robert Granjon (1513–89).